F   8804021
OCO
                                18.95
O'Connor, Philip F.
  Defending civilization

F   8804021
OCO
                              18.95
O'Connor, Philip F.
  Defending civilization
  7/26/93
                                RW

THE BRUMBACK LIBRARY
OF VAN WERT COUNTY
VAN WERT, OHIO

D1161783

DEFENDING CIVILIZATION

Defending Civilization

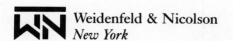 *A NOVEL*

Philip F. O'Connor

Weidenfeld & Nicolson
New York

F
O cc

JM

This novel is a work of fiction. Names, characters, places, and incidents are either the product of the author's imagination or are used fictitiously. Any resemblance to actual events or locales or persons, living or dead, is entirely coincidental.

Published by Weidenfeld & Nicolson, New York
A Division of Wheatland Corporation
10 East 53rd Street
New York, NY 10022

Published in Canada by General Publishing Company, Ltd.

Library of Congress Cataloging-in-Publication Data

O'Connor, Philip F.
    Defending civilization : a novel / by Philip F. O'Connor.—1st ed.
      p.   cm.
    ISBN 1-555-84124-4
    I. Title.
PS3565. C64D4 1988
813'.54—dc 19   87-34038

Manufactured in the United States of America

Designed by Irving Perkins Associates, Inc.

First Edition

10 9 8 7 6 5 4 3 2 1

For Virginia Leland
and
Ralph Wolfe

Thus not only does democracy make every man forget his ancestors, but it hides his descendants and separates his contemporaries from him; it throws him back forever upon himself alone and threatens in the end to confine him entirely within the solitude of his own heart.

—ALEXIS DE TOCQUEVILLE

"I wouldn't pull that handle if I were you, Ollie."

"Don't tell me which handle to pull and which handle not to pull. Now stand back and watch this. Tut, tut and tut. . . . Ohhhhhhhhh!"

—STAN LAUREL AND OLIVER HARDY

Part One

One

~~~~~~~~

From where I stood he seemed enormous, a great Viking warrior, ruddy and intense, his pale blue eyes scanning a wilderness for Celts or maybe wild boars. Lowering his phone, he threw his head back as if for a sneeze, but it came forward in a barrage of laughter that seemed to rattle the window through which I was looking. He kept laughing until his eyes, finding me, collapsed to a frown.

I ducked away, walked around the building, found the entrance I'd been looking for, went in and moved from door to door until I reached one that was open. On it was a scarlet sign with yellow lettering:

> FRANCIS P. SHEA, MAJOR, USAR
> COMMANDING OFFICER
> 46th AAA BN
> RAF BASE, GREENHAM COMMON

"That's pretty good, colonel," he was saying into the phone, "but not as good as the one about the Russian, the piano tuner and the ladybug. . . . That's right, that's right." Again came the laughter, a sound thunder might be measured against.

I felt awkward standing in the doorway staring at him and turned my attention to the crossed cannons and "U.S." insignia on my jacket lapel. The driver who'd picked me up at the pier in Southampton earlier that afternoon had said, "The CO's hell on brass, lieutenant. Hell on everything, but especially dirty brass." He also told me Shea was the only major among U.S. forces in England commanding a battalion, the others being lieutenant colonels, and that the 46th had rapidly become the brigade's best all-around unit. "We're the first one to get a new staff car," he'd boasted, "a '55 Chevy. I wanted to take it to the dock today, but he don't let anyone but his driver drive it."

The major shifted his querying eyes to mine.

I gave him a quick, nervous smile, which he didn't acknowledge.

"We'll come through at the range, sir. Count on it." After saying uh-huh a few times, he hung up, looked across and said, "What do *you* want?"

I saluted and responded in the way I'd been taught: "Second Lieutenant Thomas V. Hanlon reporting for duty as ordered, sir." He didn't return the salute, which meant I had to hold it as he moved around his desk, stopped in front of me and lowered his head toward one of my lapels. I could see little streaks of white flesh between the matted lumps of his reddish curly hair. His eyes rose and punched mine. "Drink?"

"Sir?"

"You *drink*?"

I'd noticed a metal pitcher on his desk. I now saw an empty glass with a broken piece of Spanish olive at the bottom. Drinking on duty was against regulations. I worried that he was trying to trap me. "No, sir, I have drunk, but I don't . . . as a rule."

"That so?" he said, unimpressed. He returned to his desk, half filled his glass from the pitcher, and, watching me, took a sip, then raised his free hand in a kind of wave. I dropped my arm. "Sit down." After I'd lowered myself to the chair in front of his desk, he leaned toward me and said, "See the guns out there?"

"Yes, sir." I'd noticed them as we rode up from Newbury, their long dark muzzles extending to the pink afternoon sky like the necks of preening dinosaurs. It wasn't until the jeep crossed the base that I made out parts of their squat bulky bodies, crouching at great distances from each other behind semicircles of sandbags. In their separate solitudes they seemed even larger and more menacing than they had at Fort Bliss.

"How'd they look?"

"Look? They looked . . . combat-ready, I guess."

"Combat-ready my ass." He took another swallow of whatever was in his glass. "What did they teach you about the seventy-five during the officers' basic course?"

"We were given only a week's training, sir."

"That figures."

Officially nicknamed the Skysweeper, the weapon had been referred to as the last of the Army's antiaircraft guns. "After these will come missiles," said our instructor. "Warfare is being taken away from men and put in the hands of thinking machines." He told us the seventy-five was supposed to be a firing station all by itself. There was a compact radar set on one side of the gun tube and a boxlike computer on the other. "The thing is full of tubes and wires and all sorts of junk like a Rube Goldberg contraption. If they made you learn how all these parts worked, you'd be here until your hair fell out. Lucky for you, they've got an ordnance officer and civilian technicians stationed with all the operational units." What we had to know and know well were the principles of operation: the radar locates the target plane's azimuth and elevation, feeds the information to the computer, which then, "if everything goes right," points the gun tube ahead of the attacking plane and destroys it.

"They ever bring you to the firing range with those things?" the major asked.

"Yes, sir." We'd started to fire at plane-towed targets, but the firing ended abruptly when the radar crept along the metal tow cable, causing a round to nick the stabilizer of the tow plane.

"Then you know it can't hit shit," he went on, twirling his glass in front of him. "Unless maybe a closely bunched group of fat-assed infantrymen. Or a truck. Something like that." He finished the drink in a loud gulp, then glanced across at me. "You keep looking at this booze like you want some. Do you or not?"

I hesitated, then nodded.

He removed another glass from his desk drawer, and a jar of Spanish olives. He scooped two olives out with his fingers, placed one in each glass and poured the drinks. After handing me my glass, he sat, plopped his feet on the desk and pushed himself and the swivel chair against the wall. Except for his soft protruding belly, he was solid-looking. He drank again and said, "We've become the prize outfit in the brigade. Any idea why?"

"I'll bet it's not the guns?" I said confidently.

"What would it be if not the guns?" he replied softly.

"I don't know."

"Well, believe me, it *is* the guns."

"But . . . "

"What are we here for?"

"I . . . I guess your primary mission is . . . the defense of the base."

"Against?"

"Against low- and medium-altitude enemy aircraft?"

"So what would make up a top battalion?"

"Would it be . . . the guns?"

"That sounded like a question, not an answer."

"The guns."

"Of course."

I'd taken a few sips of the drink. It was very strong and was now spilling on my gray uniform trousers. I straightened the glass as I watched him steadily empty the last of what was in his pitcher into his own.

On one side of his desk lay some books and a newspaper partly folded over. I leaned down and read the titles printed on the books' spines. The bottom one, an Army technical manual, was the Skysweeper bible, *75MM Gun, T831*. Resting on top of it was Herman Wouk's *The Caine Mutiny*. One top of that was William F. Buckley's *McCarthy and His Enemies*. The newspaper was *Stars & Stripes*.

"What are you, a detective?"

I glanced up, startled. "No, sir."

He gazed at me for a few moments, his look suspicious. "Things aren't always what they appear to be, lieutenant."

Was he speaking about the books and newspaper? Himself? Me? I didn't know. I nodded and shrugged at the same time.

"As for not knowing the guns, you're not any different from the other second lieutenants who come here. After I get you, I spend weeks trying to unlearn what they teach you at Bliss. Rarely can. Who are we at war with, kid?"

"Uh . . . no one."

"Good. And who are we going to shoot those damn guns at?"

"No one, I guess . . . unless a war starts."

"Maybe you're not as dumb as you sound. And when do we have to fire them, short of war, Christ forbid?"

"I'm not sure."

"When we go to the firing range, as we'll be doing in a couple of days. That's when we have to shoot."

My mother and her sister, Gertrude, had driven me to San Francisco Airport for the first leg of my trip to England. After I'd kissed them both and turned to walk to the waiting TWA Constellation, Mother pinched my sleeve, pulled me back and said, "Thomas, don't ask questions." It was a variation of the same plea for ignorance I'd heard since my father died ten years earlier. She'd been spurred by more than a few calls from nuns and, later, Jesuits. ("I try to teach a class and he wants to debate.") She then ticked off some reminders: the Army knew what it was doing and I should let things happen the way they were going to anyway and God would take care of what my superiors couldn't and . . . I stopped her by giving her a second kiss and telling her to have a good time in Santa Barbara, where she and Gertrude were going for a vacation, her first in several years.

"Understand?" said the major.

To honor Mother I strangled an honest question—"What do you mean, the guns are no good yet are the reason you have the best battalion?"—and just sat there nodding hypocritically.

"And there's another thing." His voice, which had ranged from soothing to angry, was softening again. I knew that if the pattern remained true, he'd be snapping at me in a moment. "You know what the other reason is?"

"No, sir."

He reached across the desk and took back my glass, empty except for the olive, which he fingered out and stuffed into his mouth. "I'll give you a little hint," he said, pointing to my lapel. "One of those gold U.S.'s has a spot on it."

I should have guessed. I looked down but couldn't clearly see the insignia.

"I've had a look at your record, Hanlon. You did well in your course work, not so well in inspections. Why is that?"

"I guess I took the course work more seriously, sir."

"Take it *all* seriously."

"Yes, sir."

"That spot better not be there tomorrow." He stood and looked down at me. "Any questions?"

I stood, less steadily than he had. "No, sir."

"Captain Ball is your battery commander. He should be waiting for you at the officers' club. I'll see you during inspection tomorrow, you and that brass of yours." As he spoke, he put on his field coat and cap. He straightened, looking immaculate, and sober.

I backed toward the door and gave a feeble salute, which he didn't return.

Two

***

ousin Larry was a hero. He grew up in the Bronx and during World War II went to the Pacific with the Statue of Liberty Division. Once when his unit was making a landing, enemy troops surrounded his squad, and he rushed ahead and machine-gunned a dozen of them. He himself was wounded. They gave him medals: the Soldier's Medal and the Purple Heart. I never met him.

Before my father died he used to talk about Larry. I remember him saying, "You wouldn't figure Larry for a thing like that. Lil used to push him around all the time. Larry just smiled. Never knew him to raise his hand to a fly."

My mother and I still received a photo Christmas card from Larry and his family every year. In the photo Larry didn't look at all like a hero. I used to gaze at the photos, trying to see the hero in him. I remember one card. Larry, with a globe of a belly, was smack in the middle of a sagging sofa, one arm around two little girls and the other around his wife, who held a small, frightened-looking boy on her lap. The message said:

> The girls wanted Larry to put his uniform on for the picture. If you look close you'll see he can't get the buttons closed. Oh well, he's still our Larry.

How old is Thomas now? He must be getting very big. Hope to see you someday soon. Merry Xmas.

> Love from all,
> Mary
> Willie
> Louise
> Lil and Larry

I wanted Larry to visit us or us him. When would I be able to get a close look at those medals? (I presumed he carried them around all the time, since they were on his jacket in the photograph.) When would I get to ask the questions I was saving—Do the bullet holes still hurt? What did the Japs look like when you shot them? Did you bring back one of their caps?

San Francisco was a long way from New York, and Larry never arrived. The closest I would get to him was the photo. I held it to my eyes and saw how the ribbons had gotten wrinkled. Still they looked pretty, and after a while Larry began to look brave.

At about the time Larry became a hero, I wanted nothing more than to be old enough to fly around in one of the P-38's that used to have practice dogfights over our town. I would take my plane and roar into battles like those I read about in my father's magazines: North Africa, Battle of the Coral Sea, Guadalcanal. I would get medals like Larry. I began buying comic books: *Wings* and *Combat*. The comics were based on true war stories. I saw how to chase Messerschmitts and strafe trains. I expected a younger, tougher Larry to appear grimacing at me from a frame in one of the infantry stories in *Combat*.

I found other heroes, in the comic books but also at the movies: Alan Ladd and William Bendix. Alan Ladd came out of the sky only long enough to slap Veronica Lake around three or four times per film. William Bendix stayed in his foxhole shooting his rifle until they got him, six, seven, eight times. Afterward Jap bodies surrounded him like a wreath and seemed awestruck, like me. I didn't walk home from Saturday-afternoon movie matinees. I crawled, ran, leaped, going into trees, under cars, around old ladies, my imaginary pistol (the only thing I'd taken with me when I bailed out of my plane) at the ready. The theater was only a few blocks from home, but it took me a long time to make the trip. If supper wasn't ready I went to my room and got out my comic books. Alan Ladd and William Bendix and Larry were in there someplace. So was I.

Before Boy Scout meetings we played games. We got to the schoolyard just after dark, and for an hour or so there was Capture the Flag, Ambush, and Prisoners. We were always stalking, shooting, hiding. By the time the scoutmaster and his assistant arrived to open the auditorium we were sweaty and out of breath, ready to plop down on one of the folding chairs and listen to him mumble about tying knots or building fires. No telling what might come in handy when Uncle Sam called and you put on a real uniform that meant something. We listened.

The games were a lot of fun, but it occurred to me that to do anything noble, like helping win a war, you had to do a lot of other things first. Like get through high school. And if you really wanted to do important things, like fly a plane, you had to take a few more steps, maybe go to college, then flight school. I daydreamed about getting my wings pinned on at Randolph Field in Texas, where they trained pilots in the movies I'd seen. It meant a lot of work, but if I was lucky, another war would come along and then I'd be ready. Lieutenant Hanlon. Captain Hanlon. Major Hanlon. Medals. Cousins to gaze at me. And maybe, someplace, a Veronica Lake.

The Korean War began when I was in high school. You could join the Marines at age seventeen. I was about sixteen when it started. Another year and I might try. I mailed away for booklets on Marine flight training. At first my biggest worry was that the war might end before I reached seventeen. I waited, reading about the battles: Pusan, Inchon, Hill Three-Five-Seven. Dreary, muddy, slow. This wasn't much like that glorious war. This was a lousy foot-soldier war, not nearly as easy to get enthused about. Where were the planes? Where was Alan Ladd?

Not here. And if he was, he wasn't doing an awful lot. At least our side was winning.

I saw a movie called *Grainger's Foxhole*. The main character, Grainger, was a very tough sergeant. For all the action there was also a lot of psychology. The sergeant kept believing in the war, and when he wasn't doing that, he was trying to hold together a corporal who seemed about to crack up. I hadn't noticed corporals like that in the World War II comics or movies. The only crack-ups in those happened when you got shot bad and knew you wouldn't last out the battle. You didn't crack up out of fear for yourself. You cracked up because you weren't going to be around when the slimy little yellow rats were crushed for the last time. And the others would talk about you, recall your sacrifice, at least for a few seconds before the final scene faded from the screen. (Alan told nurse Veronica, "Baby, don't think I'd be here without the help of Medwick and Feldman and Murphy, those mud-loving so-and-sos who built the airstrip." She'd lean into him and they'd look back from the stern of their ship toward the captured island, appreciating.)

What was happening now? The papers said American prisoners were squealing on their fellows. "Brainwashing," it was called. How could they wash things out of your brain when you were a true believer? Wasn't that what we'd learned when the big kids twisted our arms under the elm tree at the end of the schoolyard?

"Where's Marty hiding?"

"I ain't telling."

"C'mon. Where is he?"

"You can break it off but I ain't telling."

Twist twist.

"Ouch . . . uff . . . goo . . . ahead . . . but I ain't . . . telling."

"I'm gonna step on your stomach if you don't tell!"

"I ain't telling."

He stepped on my stomach and I yelled.

But I didn't tell.

The big kids appreciated you then. You heard them saying to their friends afterwards: "That little Tom is tough, you know? Couldn't get a word out of him." It helped to have a reputation when they were choosing up sides for football later in the week. It also helped get you ready for the next war. I was doing just that.

Until Korea, hardly a day passed when I wasn't getting ready. Somebody had slipped a bad card into the war deck. When the Chinese came sneaking across the Yalu, you knew something had gone wrong. What kind of rules were they playing by, anyway? Next thing you know we'd be losing.

"Losing? Are you kidding?" An older friend, Charlie Watson, had just come back from basic training at Fort Ord. "You should see the weapons we've got. Those Chicoms use World War I stuff. How can we be losing?"

I showed him an article in one of the city papers describing how the Chinese were now attacking in waves of bodies, thousands coming as fast as the GIs could shoot them. The supply was endless. Finally the U.S. forces retreated, were retreating.

"They didn't tell us about that," he said, worried. "They probably will when we have our briefing on the ship."

Maybe they told him and maybe they didn't. He left. I worried about him, wondering if he'd be killed. He wasn't, but six weeks after leaving San Francisco he was badly wounded. He wasn't wounded in combat. One of his buddy's grenades accidentally exploded, killing the buddy and wounding several.

I wasn't stupid. I decided to delay my military career by going to college and signing up for ROTC classes.

At the University of San Francisco we increasingly heard reports that some of our St. Ignatius High School classmates had been wounded in Korea. The conflict which President Truman had called a police action began more and more to resemble a war. During my sophomore year I learned that Eddie Boyle, who'd been shortstop on the high school team for which I'd been catcher, had been killed after stepping on a land mine near the thirty-eighth parallel. Soldiers in newsreels and in newspaper photos no longer seemed to be strangers, for I was coloring in the faces of friends.

Some college classmates shared my rising guilt, but most found ways to compensate. ("We may go to a bigger war than Korea, maybe in Germany, Turkey or the Congo. You never know.") Some felt no guilt at all. ("I came to college because I want to live and someday take over my old man's business. I'm not taking ROTC or joining up.")

Slow-talking sergeants taught the military science classes for freshmen and sophomores. You waited through the class hour for one of them to say something amusing. Eventually he did. Usually it wasn't intended. That made it even funnier. A bald-headed master sergeant who admitted to us he'd never gone beyond the fourth grade drew on the blackboard the symbol for a platoon. Someone asked him what the oval-shaped sign was called. He frowned at the blackboard and rubbed his hand over the top of his head: "You don't need to know that. Just remember what it looks like." A student said, "I want to write the name in my notes." The sergeant stared at the board. He shrugged, frowned, twisted up his nose. "A long circle," he said. We all laughed. We were in college, smarter than he. The lit teacher wasn't nearly as entertaining. The early courses were easy: small arms and first aid, the manual of arms, multiple choice and true or false. Easy. Fun. Nothing to it.

Only when I was away from the classes, reading still about the war and feeling vaguely that I was cheating someone—Eddie Boyle or President Eisenhower or maybe myself—did I wonder if I'd done right. I sought out my less guilty friends. They read the papers too, knew the war wouldn't last long. The Panmunjom peace talks had already begun. Even if the talks dragged on a bit, we'd probably beat it. We'd be safe, maybe end up in Germany or Japan and have a ball.

By the time I'd reached Greenham the war had ended and I'd worked off a lot of guilt at Bliss. I'd eagerly serve my country for the year and three-quarters left in my two-year term. I wasn't looking for a war but had persuaded myself that if one came about, I'd be willing to risk injury or death. If there was no war, I'd develop skills so that I'd be ready to fight and lead if and when one came along later.

Solid resolution began to soften after my interview with Shea. He was a little like those tough nameless colonels who ordered Alan and Veronica to flee the threatened island, then coldly left a stoic company CO—slim and resolute Robert Ryan—to lead Bendix and the others in holding off the Japs as long as possible. Ryan would die along with the others, but he would have shown his kindness and brotherhood to his men before using the last of his energy to raise his .45 and plug a screaming Jap entering his headquarters hut. Shea was no Ryan, but maybe my battery commander would be.

Three

.·✓·✓·✓·✓·✓·✓·

I crossed the huge empty ballroom of the officers' club, a multigabled manor house about a quarter of a mile from the base's back gate, and entered a bar filled with officers. I told one in an Army uniform that I was looking for a Captain Ball. He pointed to a small, pensive-looking man sitting hunched at the far end of the bar itself. I made my way to him and tapped him on the shoulder.

His head came up and around slowly. The small dark pinched-together eyes pleaded up at me with the agonies of history. The mouth fell at the sides. "What now?" he said in a croaking tormented voice.

I felt like pulling him to me and patting his back. "Good afternoon, sir," I said gently. "My name is Thomas Hanlon, and I'm your new officer."

He looked me over, groped for and found his beer, pulled it to himself, then closed his eyes and mumbled, "Mttmmm?"

"Sir?"

"The boss," he said impatiently. "Did? You? Meet? Him?"

"Oh . . . yes, sir. About twenty minutes ago I reported and . . ."

"Enough!" His hand came up in a jujitsu movement. "Tell me just what I want to know," he said. "Nothing more. Understand that right now. Understand?"

I didn't, but fearing that anything short of agreement would upset him, I nodded.

He signaled the bartender, who was serving a laughing group of Air Force officers at the opposite end, then pointed a trembling finger at the space in front of me. "This man *must* have a beer." He turned. "The CO puts me against the wall every time there's an inspection or exercise of any sort. Why else would he stick me with you the night before this inspection? Answer."

"I surely don't know."

"That's not good enough. You must learn to know. You'll have to because you're one of us now and we'll try to—Crawford will—teach you to be part of our team. But, then, look at me and tell me, what am I supposed to do with you during the inspection?"

"I don't . . ."

"Never mind. I'll ask Crawford when I get to . . . Where *is* Crawford? I know. Out with the guns, getting them ready. That had *better* be where." He turned away and soon his head began to sink, lower, then lower, until the sharp tip of his nose was entering his glass like a straw. I watched, fascinated, but it didn't quite get in, for the head shot suddenly up like that of a bird alerted by a sound in a thicket. "Here's what." He turned. "You keep out of sight tomorrow. When he's at place X, you go to place Y. When he gets to Y, you go to X or Z. Become invisible. He won't find you. We won't *let* him find you. And . . ." His finger came up at me. ". . . don't *you* let him find you."

"Sir, these places, X, Y and Z . . ."

"Don't ask about places!" He picked up his field cap and slapped it onto his head. "Ask about . . . fuck it." He gave me a little push with his elbow as he popped off his stool. "Tomorrow," he said, angling his way toward the ballroom.

A glassy-eyed chief warrant officer, balder and older-looking than the others, came up, introduced himself as Gilley and took the captain's stool. "He's a card, ain't he?"

"Pardon?"

"Ball. Nervous little guy." The chief was shorter than Ball.

The bartender started to reach for the captain's half-full glass, but Gilley pulled it toward himself. "We're all jumpy the day before Shea inspects. Took off early myself. To have a few beers. Keeps me from shaking."

"You all look overworked."

"Shea rides everyone's ass. Some more than others. Especially Ball's." He'd finished his own beer and now drank from the glass the captain had left. "Hup!" He waited for the air his hiccup had captured to come rumbling out of him: "Barroup! I had this dog once. Named Shivers. Half Lab and half a lot of other things. Put it in a cage when my buddies came over to play cards because people got it excited. It wiggled and jumped all over the place. Sometimes it pissed on the floor. Even in the cage it hopped and banged around and whimpered if any of us came close or even looked at it. Around Shea, Ball's like that dog."

"That doesn't comfort me, he being my battery commander."

"Everyone goes into a panic around the old man to one degree or another. I must have had a dozen COs since I joined up, but none like him. He don't give a damn about who thinks what about him. Stays to himself all the time, except when he's pulling an inspection or taking one of his surprise tours around the gun sites."

"What's his background?"

"No one knows much. A captain named Duke Kendall was operations until Shea, after he was here only a couple of weeks, had him transferred to Germany. He said he'd been through an artillery course with Shea at Bliss, right after Korea, and learned that he grew up in Montana and his father had been a chicken dealer who had trouble with his partners and ended up being murdered. Right in front of the major when he was a kid. Some say he don't trust anyone because of that. Who the hell knows? Perkins—he's personnel—went through his records after he got here and found out that when he was a first lieutenant, he took over his company after his captain was killed and led it out of a gook massacre in one of those passes, Kanu-ri I think. For that he got the Silver Star. You'd never know. He doesn't wear medals. I work in the same building, but he hardly talks to me. That's just fine. I feel like a jackass when he does." He finished Ball's beer. "Hup! We figure the major was sent here to get rid of as many of us as don't meet up to his standards. He's gotten rid of some already. Barroup! I don't think there's even one he likes. Maybe you'll be an exception."

I remembered my meeting with Shea, especially his remarks about my record. "I doubt it," I said. "The major said I'm supposed to be out there tomorrow. But then the captain said I should become invisible."

Gilley shook his head. "The captain's brain rattles at times like this. You're going to have to learn how to take over when that happens. The way Crawford does. You kind of go along with him but then don't. Know what I mean?"

"No, but then I don't know what most of what I've heard or seen so far means. I guess I'll just have to learn to do whatever, at the right time, wherever I'm supposed to."

"Sounds right to me."

"But what about that inspection?"

"Be there, all shined up. Shea likes to put the new ones on the spot. I won't tell you what else he eventually does with new ones. But tomorrow he'll be throwing questions at you. To see if you think like him, I guess. No one does. Have another beer."

The first had warmed me. I hoped the second would help me stop worrying about the inspection. This time it was I who signaled the bartender.

When the beers came, Gilley took a deep swallow and propped his elbow on the bar. "See these flaming pisspots?" He pointed to his lapel insignia.

"Ordnance?"

"I'm supposed to be the gun expert. Been here seventeen months, and I still can't get the damned things to work right. They're nothing like the forties and nineties and one-twenties. These things have brains and bad temperaments."

After the seventy-five at Bliss had knocked off part of the tow plane's stabilizer, the unhappy captain in charge said, "I'm not taking any more chances. I'll give you guys a dry run." He called off the firing, stepped onto the pedestal of one of the disarmed weapons, checked the saucer-shaped antenna, which was tilted forward like the bowed head of a giant, then walked around the gun, ducking under the long dark muzzle, which was pointed toward a distant hill. He glanced at the steel box containing the computer. "Guess it's okay," he said without conviction. He gave the class an embarrassed little smile. "Just wanted to make sure. Never can tell about these babies." He leaned forward gingerly and pressed the power button. The antenna suddenly spun wildly in little half circles, and the computer started making ominous whirring sounds. He leaped back, waving his wooden pointer. "Move away!" He spread his arms and pushed against the standing group of second lieutenants. The muzzle shot up and down, slowly at first, then faster and faster. It began to quiver, then jerk from side to side. "Back! Back!" He pushed against us. Growling, the immense carriage on which the gun, radar, and computer rested stirred and slowly began to turn all by itself. The radar was spinning freely, crazily, the computer screamed, and the muzzle began to perform a kind of helpless flagellation. The frightened instructor waved his pointer at a nearby building. "Someone go get a technician. Hurry!" After several violent lurches, the carriage began to revolve toward us. It came to rest with the muzzle pointed toward a cluster of houses in nearby El Paso. The automatic loading mechanism then began to feed invisible shells into the chamber: clickity-click, clickity-click, clickity-click. Before the technician arrived, the gun had "fired" at several nearby buildings, finally coming to a stop with the muzzle pointing at a distant water tower. The civilian leaped onto the pedestal and switched off the power. The anguished sounds subsided.

I watched Gilley, who was signaling for two more beers. "Can't the technicians here get them to work?"

"No one can get them to work, except the old man."

"What is he? An electronics expert or something?"

"Oh, hell, no."

"How does he do it?"

"Got me." He frowned. "He's got a way with everything. We'll be going up to the North Sea day after tomorrow. Maybe you can figure it out."

"Must be a genius."

"Beats the hell out of me. Him and that gun. Two of the most baffling creatures I ever ran across. And the two of 'em get along like . . . hup! . . . man and mistress." He scratched his head as the air rumbled out of him.

When Ball returned from checking his guns he exchanged pats on the shoulder with the others behind us, mostly captains:

"Good luck, Wally."

"Need it. Need it. Same t'you."

"Mark." Pat pat.

"Stan." Pat pat.

They were like mourners exchanging condolences at graveside. Gilley looked at them and shook his head. "Twenty years in this man's Army and I never met one like him. Him or that damn gun."

After the seventy-five had gone crazy during the Fort Bliss demonstration, the student officers were allowed to examine several weapons whose power supplies had been turned off, and then ask questions. The old sergeant in charge of the weapon I was looking over said, "If they give you a choice, don't get stuck in an outfit full of these things." By then I'd seen enough and didn't really need the advice. When it was time to request assignments I was given five choices. I put forty-millimeter first, ninety second, one-twenty third, "other" fourth and (with what seemed to me flawless logic) seventy-five last.

Yet here I was.

Four

‎‎‎‎‎

*A*t 0830 the following morning, Captain Ball, unhappy with the results of his own early-morning inspection of Battery A's gun sites, barracks and headquarters, paced fretfully from one end of the orderly room to the other. A sergeant pushed open the door. "Where do you want these, sir?" He held up a fire extinguisher.

"What . . . wha . . . under th' beds. I don't care. Where're they supposed to be?"

"On the walls, sir. But we have the squad tents there for inspection." The sergeant's tone, unlike the captain's, was calm. "Why not in the supply room, sir?"

"The supply room. The supply room? Yes, the supply room, for God's sake." He turned to me. "Now, Hanlon, you . . . Grey!" He turned to the first sergeant, a black Buddha who'd been regarding the captain sleepily from behind his desk at the center of the room. "Gas masks. Go check the gas masks. In all the barracks. Should be at foot of bed. Next to socks." The first sergeant nodded, got up and glided slowly out of the room. "Now Hanlon, I want you to get rid of yourself over at . . . Damn! Where's the morning report?"

The battery clerk looked up from the typewriter. "Just about got it typed, sir," he said.

"Hurry, damn it. I can't be signing that when the major comes. Now Hanlon . . . oh Christ, Crawford, you tell him!"

First Lieutenant Mike Crawford, the captain's executive officer, had been asleep at his desk a couple of hours earlier when I, after hitching a ride from the club, arrived late. "You must be the new one," he said, delivering me one open eye. His long legs were stretched over the top of the desk. Grey had gotten up and shaken one of his feet to wake him. "Coffee's on the table in the corner, and this desk behind me"—he raised his hand to his shoulder, thumb out like a hitchhiker's—"is yours." After I went over and poured my coffee, he said he'd heard I'd met the captain and added, "You'll get used to him." By the time I'd put in sugar and cream, stirred it and turned around, he'd fallen asleep again. He didn't wake up until, several minutes later, the frantic voice of Ball sounded in the hallway.

He now explained that I was to eat breakfast while the major inspected the orderly room and barracks areas. I would then go to one of the battery's gun sites in time to check it over before the major arrived. I was to leave the gun site and return to the orderly room after Shea finished inspecting here. "If you have questions, be sure to ask me, not the captain."

Our training officer at Fort Bliss, Lieutenant Roger Brand, had given us friendly little talks about getting settled in our new units. Once he talked about our battery commander: "He's going to be like a father. He's been around. He knows the ups and downs and ins and outs. You confide in him, and he'll take care of you." Ball didn't fit the description. In fact, the Army Brand had described didn't seem to be the one I was serving in.

When I arrived at the gun site, the enlisted men, though they wore dress uniforms, were doing last-minute janitorial tasks: removing empty oil cans, old newspapers and other rubbish. The gun sergeant was sweeping the concrete walk that led from the runway to the Quonset hut which was the crew's sleeping area and tool shed. Near the hut the big gun loomed darkly against the morning sunlight. The sergeant assured me that the area was ready for inspection. He led me through the hut and then to the gun. I was beginning to feel confident, and I removed my jacket to give my brass a last-minute check.

"Look!" someone called out as I was putting the jacket on.

I turned and saw Captain Ball waving from the driver's seat of an approaching jeep. Almost before the vehicle stopped at the edge of the concrete walk, he leaped out and raced toward the sergeant and me. "First thing's important, right now, is—listen to me—stay calm. Have you got that?" Who was he speaking to? I grunted. The sergeant grunted. A couple of enlisted men behind us grunted. "Oh, God, he's clever!" The major, I assumed. "Toilet. You see"—his hands were chopping air—"he's one-upped us. He's looking at toilets in the Quonset huts." Bellowing, he repeated, *"In the Quonset huts!"* The hands fell to his sides. "What in Jesus's name do you think of that?" His eyes begged me, of all people, for an answer.

It seemed essential that I give one. "It's awful," I said.

"It's *not* awful! It's . . . realistic. Can't you see that?"

"Yes, sir."

"I'll get someone in the Quonset right now," the sergeant said.

"Oh, no, you won't. That's just what he wants. Now . . . Hanlon." Though he'd been speaking to me, he looked at me as if for the first time. "What are you doing here?"

"Crawford told me to . . ."

"I want you to vanish." He turned to the sergeant, then back to me. "Check that." He turned to the sergeant again. "You can't get your men dirty. I'll do the toilet myself, then skedaddle out of here. Hanlon, you help get the men lined up. Then I'll take you with me." He started toward the Quonset. "Where's the Bon Ami?"

The sergeant called after him as he entered the hut, "Under the farthest locker!"

The captain's plan seemed clever enough until, a few minutes later, when the sergeant and I were lining up the crew for inspection, I noticed a shiny new olive-drab sedan approaching from the runway. I nudged the sergeant and pointed.

He looked and shook his head. "He reads the captain's mind, I swear." He turned toward the crew. "Ten-hut!" he shouted. "Hope the captain heard that," he whispered.

Ahead of schedule, the major's sedan pulled in behind the captain's jeep. The major stepped out of his car, glanced at the gun, then at the crew, moved directly and alone to the Quonset hut, where he pushed open the door.

The sergeant and I stayed back. Through the open door came the captain's surprised voice: "Oh, my God!" There were a couple of heavy thumps, then growling sounds I took to be the major's voice.

A couple of minutes later, the major emerged and came toward us. I saw a line of water drops across the front of his coat.

"I've been on God's green earth for thirty-seven years," Shea said softly, "but this really does take the goddam cake." He didn't seem to be talking to the sergeant or me. Finally he turned to me, with a pained expression. "Let's go check the guns."

Nervously I followed. On the way he stopped to examine the uniforms of the crew members.

Ball made his way to his jeep, got in, started it and left with his head tilted forlornly to one side.

Shea gave several of the men demerits, then led me to the gun. He gently raised the canvas cover, which had been rolled back and folded over the loading mechanism. "Grease on canvas." He moved around the gun. "Dust on computer dials. String on periscope eyepiece cover not fastened." When he finished finding a large number of deficiencies on the weapon itself, he moved to the five-ton truck that towed it when it was moved from place to place. He removed a small air gauge from his trouser pocket and checked a tire. "Twenty-four pounds instead of twenty-eight." He looked up at me. "You see, Hanlon, it's four pounds short." His tone was benign.

"Yes, sir."

"That's important, isn't it?"

"Yes, sir."

"And so are the other things. Right? The little spot of grease on the canvas, that loose shoestring, the dust."

"Yes, sir."

"Why?"

I remembered something from a field manual: " 'To insure proper efficiency of men and equipment.' "

He bent down to check another tire and said softly, "Bullshit."

"Sir?"

"That's not why at all." He leaned toward me and tapped one of my brass buttons with the tire gauge. I could smell the sweet acrid alcohol his lungs had redistilled. "You're a bright young man, Hanlon. Think about it."

A B-47 was taking off nearby. As he waited for the roar of its engines to subside, he bent down to check another tire. When he rose, he scowled at the plane, which was quickly becoming a speck on the horizon, then moved resolutely toward the sedan.

Before getting in, he looked at me and said, "There's something sly about you, Hanlon. That's an instinct I have. I trust my instincts." His eyes shifted away from mine for a moment, came back. "You give 'book' answers. You observe and comment without committing anything of yourself. That bothers me. You're here and not here. Got any idea what I mean?"

"No, sir," I said, my voice shaky.

"I'll bet. Ever play team sports?"

"Yes, sir."

"Like them?"

I'd been talked into high school football. My history teacher, who was also the football coach, said that with my muscular build, height and weight, I ought to give it a try. I did. I ended up playing right end and linebacker. My satisfactions came mainly as a result of the several good plays I made, not the team's few victories. And I felt no great regret when we lost. "Sometimes," I told Shea.

"A nice evasive answer." He shook his head in a way that told me he hated evasive answers. "There are no separate drums around here," he went on. "It's the team or nothing."

"Yes, sir."

" 'Yes, sir,' " he repeated mockingly. He opened the car door and turned. "Standing here, I count six demerits. I suppose if I looked at your shoes and the rest of you I'd find half a dozen more. I'm not going to look or record them. Never mind why. I'll come back at you on that and a lot of other things soon enough." He got into the car, started the engine and flicked away my salute with a flap of his hand.

He'd identified qualities akin to those I feared in myself: uncertainty, indecisiveness, a lack of real commitment to any single ideal or set of ideals. I wanted to deny the recognition, but my reaction seemed to prove it. Also there was fear and anger and maybe even a touch of hatred. He was, or seemed to be, a tyrant. Yet there were also feelings of attraction for which my experience with priests and professors, coaches, friends, my mother and, a good deal earlier, my father hadn't prepared me. He had a way of cutting through to what mattered to him. I liked that. I'd discovered during my senior year in college the poetry of Wallace Stevens and now saw a resemblance between Shea and the poet's celebrated jar on a hill in Tennessee. ("It took dominion everywhere.") Like the jar, the major seemed to bring order and direction to the chaos around him, even in conversations that took place when he was nowhere near. This, I supposed, was real power.

A couple of hours later I saw a vivid demonstration during the post-inspection meeting of officers in the conference room down the hall from his office. After raging about the deficiencies he'd found, he branched off into personalities. Ball was the most heavily scored. Apparently immobilized by the Quonset-hut experience, he sat forlornly at the room's back corner, apart from the others. Shea's description of him—"the one among you I found playing in a commode"—caused titters among the other captains whose vilifications were being minimized at the expense of his: "I never again want to see an officer doing a job that only a yardbird ought to do."

He also discussed the firing. "You battery commanders get

your miserable weapons set up as quickly as possible." He turned to Gilley. "Is there any chance we can have the radars and computers in operation by firing time?"

"Only one, or two at the most, major."

He rolled his eyes. "One or two out of twelve. Isn't that wonderful? Don't overwork those civilians, Gill. Wouldn't want to do that."

"The electronic tubes have been going out, sir. I keep replacing them, but the new ones don't work either. We don't have enough replacement tubes."

"Why not? Did a submarine sink the ship that was delivering them?"

"No, sir."

"Of course not. What would happen if there really *were* a war? Don't answer me, Gill." He turned to the captains. "You should have ordered new parts months ago."

They stared and said nothing.

"I'm going to be writing some bad efficiency reports if you do as poorly at the range tomorrow as you did in the inspection today."

I heard shoes sliding about uneasily.

"I'm sick of pulling your asses out of the fire."

A couple of captains nodded, as if to say they were sick of having their asses pulled out.

"But that's probably what I'll have to do, isn't it?"

No one admitted a thing.

"Dismissed," he said.

Five

I spent most of the slow convoy ride to the North Sea firing range dozing in the backseat of Battery A's jeep. Ball sat in front and frequently awakened me—"Hanlon, get on the radio and find out from Crawford if we're distancing properly." Crawford rode in the jeep at the rear of the battery. Battery A was leading the entire battalion—"He's punishing me for the inspection," Ball said. The captain was worried that we might get everyone lost. "Hanlon, look at this map and tell me if the road we're on looks like the one that's there."

I took the map from him, put it on my lap, waited until we passed a sign with the highway number on it, then checked the sign against the highway marked on the map. "Seems right to me."

He sighed lengthily, said, "Good, good," snatched the map away and turned to the driver. "Do you hear a ticking noise?"

The driver assured him it was the sound of our oversized tires against the highway surface.

"That's what I thought, but I wasn't sure."

Since I had no firing experience with the battalion, I was assigned to the tower as the major's assistant. After helping supervise the emplacement of Battery A's guns, I climbed the steps of the wooden structure. Inside I scanned the length of the rocky beach, where the gun batteries were testing equipment.

The technicians and crewmen worked frantically over the radars and computers. The major hadn't yet arrived when Gilley entered the tower.

"He'll blow from here to Norway," he said. "None of the radars are working." He sat down, sighing, and lit a cigarette. "Don't know how we can hit anything unless he uses the periscope, which is only supposed to be for ground action." He glanced at a nearby knoll, where a cluster of senior officers had formed. "All the brigade brass here today too." He stood and looked toward the beach. There sat the bulky stubborn weapons, impatiently waiting for injections of power from the nearby generators. Would they surge into whatever angry meaningless arcs they pleased? With the tips of his fingers Gilley pushed back his field cap, and above the relentless metallic drone of the generators and above the whirring, grinding, chugging sounds the guns were beginning to make, there came the protesting "shhht, shhht, shhht" of his fingers on the upper fringe of his balding hair. He put his hands on his hips and looked out at the churning frost-capped sea. "I should've been a sailor."

When he left I picked up the binoculars the major had asked me to bring to the tower, saw that Shea was on the knoll gesturing to the other officers, mostly colonels, as they all looked down at the guns. He finally worked his way over to a fierce-looking man I took to be the brigade commander, Colonel Ernest Stark, because he was the only one, besides Shea, who was wearing the green patches of commander on his epaulets. Shea's jaw was moving steadily. The colonel nodded but seemed unimpressed with whatever the major was saying. Finally Shea turned and walked to the tower, soon thumped up the stairs, opened the door and shot past me to the desk next to the big window overlooking the beach. He picked up one of several field telephones on the desk and cranked the little handle on the case. "South? . . . This is Shea. Can you come up to the tower early? . . . Good." He snapped the phone into its receiver and turned, seeming for the first time to notice me. "Hanlon, go down there and find out how long it's going to take each crew to be ready to fire."

Captain South commanded the radio-controlled-target-plane detachment stationed at a little camp near the range. A weary-looking man with a pallid complexion, tiny eyes, and an unbelievably thin mustache, he had greeted the major on arrival at the range that morning with a profuse smile and had stood nodding to most of what our CO said. Gilley told me as we stood watching that South had been a battery commander in our battalion. He called him an old drinking buddy of Shea's whose loyalty to his commander had been rewarded by Shea's recommendation of him as target-plane-detachment commander. "The softest job in the entire brigade," said Gilley. "And the kind bootlickers often get from Shea."

I was soon on the beach.

The crew chiefs were frantic. Panels had been removed from the guns' computers and radars. Crews observed anxiously as two technicians rushed from one weapon to another, parts in hand, themselves looking as bewildered as the sergeants. I stopped behind Sergeant Bird's weapon and watched one of his artillerymen turn on the power switch. The gun tube began to hop like a bull at a rodeo. Bird himself jumped onto the gun platform and turned off the power switch. He hurried to where I was standing. He was perspiring, and there were red patches on his face that matched his orangish hair. "Sir, please go ask the major if we can delay the firing. I can't get this one even to point out toward the water. I need at least an hour." Sergeant Rivera, chief of the gun beside Bird's, had joined us in time to hear Bird's request. "Same goes for me," he said. "My gun points toward the water but sometimes won't go any lower than forty-five degrees." I said I'd deliver the messages.

I headed toward the tower, saw Shea inside, his back to me, gesturing to Captain South. I moved quickly up the stairs and was about to open the door when I heard him say, "We'll get nothing if you don't, Davey. Now, goddammit, that's all there is to it!" I didn't want to interrupt. I took a step down.

"It's awful damned risky," I heard another voice reply. "Not like last year. Everyone and his brother here today."

"Don't blow 'em up as soon as they take off. Let 'em pass over the water a couple of times. Wait until some of our rounds start coming close."

"You're going to have to make near-hits."

"Jesus, among twelve guns, won't we have some near-hits?"

"I can't do it unless they're real close."

"We'll have close ones. No question."

"I shouldn't be here this long," South said uneasily. "I'm supposed to visit the tower only to coordinate times of flight with your firing."

"So that's what you're doing."

"Right."

"This is important. Can you do it?"

South didn't reply for a few seconds, then said, "All right. I'll do it, Frank."

At Bliss we had learned how to fly the radio-controlled target planes. They were like huge model airplanes. On the hand controls was a button to destroy the craft, for use only if the officer handling it lost control of its flight. Developed by an officer at the Artillery School, it was a safety device. What Shea and South were planning had nothing to do with safety. Since the planes would crash into the sea, there'd be no evidence that they'd been destroyed by an explosive from within.

Shocked by what I'd heard, not knowing how to deal with it, I backed down the tower stairs and kept out of sight until South descended and scurried toward his control shack.

I went up and reported the sergeants' requests.

Shea nodded indifferently, then picked up a microphone, pressed the on button and made an announcement over the loudspeakers: "The firing will take place at eleven hundred hours, as scheduled."

Through the tower's open window I heard cries of disappointment.

Shea ignored them. "Now you'll see something, Hanlon," he said, turning.

Before the firing the major had announced that he'd present a case of Jack Daniel's sour-mash whiskey, a favorite in the battalion, to the gun crew which scored the highest number of hits.

He raised the microphone again, checked his watch, then spoke: "All right. Prepare your weapons."

The firing soon began.

During the first few passes, only a couple of the guns were pointing toward the target planes. Only they were fired. Their rounds didn't explode near the targets, however.

"Let's get with it down there!" Shea shouted over the loudspeaker.

I watched the targets closely.

Soon rounds from several guns were exploding near targets. I saw no direct hits. Finally one of the target planes blew up and fell. A few minutes later another burst into flames after a round exploded no closer than fifty feet from it.

"That's better!"

The guns, and therefore the crews, had been numbered. Each time a plane burst and twisted in a trail of black smoke into the sea, the major would say something like "Who're you inviting to the party, number two?" It was clear to me that Captain South, in his shack at the end of the beach, was deftly using the hidden button. This didn't keep Shea from playing his game with the gun crews, however. He followed each plane to the end of its course and watched it turn, shouting over the loudspeaker, "Get that thing!" He watched the plane dart across the course again, saying, "Number six! If you can't hit it this time, you may as well kiss old Jack goodbye!" The mention of the whiskey worked magically. The gun crews bent over their weapons, waiting to press the firing switches, firing, throwing up their hands whenever a plane fell toward the sea.

As it became apparent that the guns were, or rather seemed to be, scoring a high number of hits, even the battery officers began to cheer. In his devious way, the major was arousing an *esprit* that seemed to infect everyone. Soon the colonels on the knoll began to nudge each other and point in admiration each time a hit was scored.

Before the firing ended, nine target planes had been brought down.

Afterward I stood near the major at the base of the tower. He graciously accepted the congratulations of the brigade colonels. "A helluva job, Shea." The brigade commander said, "You've shown you can make them work, which means the other battalions can too."

"As our battalion motto reads, colonel," said the major, without the slightest betrayal movement of eyes or lips, " 'Hit 'em hard and sure!' "

The battery officers came up the hill after the colonels departed. Captain Ball swayed proudly from foot to foot, a childlike smile on his closed lips. It was his battery that had scored highest.

"Well, Ball," said the major, "you came through after all."

The captain wagged his head, clearly believing he'd been responsible for his battery's success. The other battery commanders congratulated Ball and each other. The major announced that he was going to throw a party that night at the officers' club.

When the captains left to supervise movement of their weapons, the major stood alone, looking vaguely out at the sea. His grayish-red beard now showed clearly. He seemed exhausted, older. As I moved down the hill to Gilley's side, I glanced back and saw that his uniform was wrinkled and that he was a little stooped from his hours of crouching over the telephone in the tower.

"What do you think?" I asked the chief.

Gilley scratched his head and looked down at the guns. "Beats the hell out of me."

On the way back to the base I rode again with Captain Ball, who giggled and laughed and several times punched his driver.

"We showed 'em today, hey?" The driver nodded to every comment.

Finally the captain turned around. "You certainly don't seem enthusiastic, Hanlon. Don't you know what a relief this is?"

"Well, in a way."

"In a way?" He looked at the driver, puzzled, then back at me. "It was beautiful," he said. "Beautiful!"

"Yes, sir."

He turned to the front again. In a few minutes he went back to punching the driver and recalling some of his battery's best shots. Before we reached the base he even sang a couple of Army marching songs, stridently and off-key. The driver's head bobbed as though it were a perfect music.

I pretended to sleep, did so for the rest of the trip. I tried to escape the horrible sinking feeling I was having. What Shea had done was somehow getting beyond this day and that beach. It began to enclose others, like officers who'd taught military science classes and those who'd instructed me at Bliss. The feeling became an expanding envelope, and all my recent experiences, not only military, were falling into it. I recalled the warm parting words of a close female friend and told myself, She says she'll miss you, but she may not mean it. Before we reached the base my fear or cynicism or whatever it was covered years. Just how much of what my father had taught me before he died was actually reliable? You're not being rational, I warned myself. But the feeling grew, forward as well as backward. What matter upcoming inspections, maintenance, promotions? I took deep breaths, counted the hedgerows we passed, tried a guess at the next song Ball was going to sing or hum. Wait until you're calm enough to think it through, I told myself. What kept me from despair was the belief, oddly constant through this letdown, that there was, after all, a credible explanation. Finally I did doze.

About an hour after we reached the base I sat alone at the bar and began thinking in what at least felt like a rational way about, of all things, philosophy.

It was a minor required of students at the University of San

Francisco. Each semester we took one course—Logic, Epistemology, Cosmology, Ontology, Ethics—in which the teacher, usually a Jesuit, spent a lot of time summarizing the ideas of Aristotle and Thomas Aquinas. The syllogisms of Thomistic philosophy were clean, closed and abstract, reminded me of mathematics rather than, say, poetry:

Human beings are capable of morally evil acts.
John is a human being.
Therefore John is capable of morally evil acts.

Proofs and arguments were of course required. All questions about God and the universe could be resolved syllogistically.

Fascinated by Thomism, I soon began to require more of philosophy than it, or at least the Jesuits, was requiring of me. I took electives. In one I became acquainted with Descartes, Hume, Locke and Berkeley; in another with Marx, James, Sartre and Camus; in yet a third, Spinoza, Nietzsche and Spengler. I played all of the other philosophers off against Thomas, perhaps because he'd come first, perhaps because I was best acquainted with him, perhaps because my instructors, even in elective courses, regarded him as the measuring stick for the others. His positions were fixed and clear. In Thomas's works, for example, good was always good, evil always evil. Moral actions weren't matters for individual interpretation. When one found that one was participating in an evil act, one was obligated not only to bring his or her participation to an end but to correct the evil, insofar as possible.

I was in the middle of such thoughts when officers and their wives began to show up at the manor house for the party. I hurried to the snack bar at the back of the club, purchased a sandwich and a small carton of milk, then went up the back stairs to my room.

I sat by the window, looking out at the dark pond in the garden below. I tried to ignore the laughter and music that began to rise through the ancient floor. When I finished eating, I lay down on my bed, hoping to sleep. I couldn't.

I tried to reject Thomas's position on ethics—my own position—and to ally myself with more generous philosophers. I wanted urgently to believe in an adaptable moral view, the sort that I'd found up to then unacceptable: *One is responsible for his or her acts only.* That would have been perfect. What Shea had done could be left as his business, not mine. I couldn't believe in it, however. I wrestled with and eventually fought off other moral positions, some remembered, some newly conceived. My thoughts were constantly interrupted by memories of what had happened at the firing range. In the end, whether by way of Aquinas or myself or the others or a combination, I couldn't separate myself from that.

Very early in the morning I awakened, shivering. I got up and went into the hallway to find the club dark and silent, except for a distant window that rattled against the wind. I had a feeling that somewhere nearby Shea was lurking, observing me. I returned to my bed, curled up under the blankets and watched the morning light invade my room.

Again I recalled the major's conversation with South. What worried me now wasn't the rightness or wrongness of his act but the possibility that he'd figured out I'd overheard him. I didn't know and, not knowing, was unable to get back to sleep. When I heard the footsteps of the other bachelor officers in the surrounding rooms, I got up, put on a fresh pair of fatigues and sat on my bed until it was time to leave for the battery.

Six

~~~~~~~~~~

"*H*anlon!"

I looked across the orderly room, saw the captain's finger wiggling at me from the office doorway. I'd just arrived from the officers' club and was about to sit down at my desk. Instead I turned and headed toward the beckoning finger.

Ball, looking green and tired, pointed at the chair in front of his desk, then went around the desk and sank with a wheeze into his own chair. He wasn't the happy man I'd accompanied back from the firing range. He looked at me under sagging brows, blinked and, when I was seated, said, "This isn't an easy battalion, Hanlon."

"I didn't think it was, sir."

"It's not." he paused. "How old am I?"

"Sir?"

"My age? What would you say?"

I hadn't given a thought to his age. I wasn't good at guessing ages anyway. Besides, he had an unusual face. It was hard to tell. I tried anyway: "Forty-five?"

"There you are." He gave me a masterful nod. "Forty-five." He pinned his small brown eyes on mine. "I'm thirty-nine. What do you think of that?"

"I don't know what to think of it, sir."

"I do." He plucked a long unfiltered cigarette out of the container on his desk, began tapping one end of it on the desk. "I didn't look forty-five when I got here last year. No, sir. I looked thirty-eight, thirty-nine at the very most. My wife used to say, 'Wally, you keep your years well.' She was right. I used to look in the mirror when I was shaving and say, 'The Army's been good to you, mister.' I can't say that anymore. I *do* look forty-five, maybe older."

"I'm not good at guessing ages, sir."

"The battalion, Hanlon. As you may have guessed, life here has been pure hell. That's what's put the wrinkles in my face. That's what's did in Williston and the others."

Who was Williston?

"And it's *him*. He may be a great officer—certainly is—but he's . . ." He looked to his window, then the doorway, and whispered, ". . . a bastard." He'd been patting his breast pockets in search of a lighter or match but now leaned forward, his fists closing, one of them over his cigarette. He pounded his fists lightly on the desk several times. "It's a terrible thing to say, but it's true." He patted his pockets again, at the same time frowning at the wall behind me. "Listen," he said softly. "He's been especially hard on me." He leaned to one side and searched one pants pocket, then eased to the other side and searched the other. "I could tell you stories. But I won't." He scanned the top of his desk. "Not now." He looked at me. "Do you have a match?"

I didn't smoke, didn't have one. "Sorry," I said.

"Then please get one from the first sergeant," he said petulantly.

I got up and returned to the orderly room, where Grey was sitting behind his desk. In one hand he was holding a duty roster. He must have heard the captain, for with the other he was holding up a book of matches. I took them, thanked him and returned to the captain's office. The cigarette, bent, was in Ball's mouth. I struck a match, reached across and lit it.

As he spoke, I'd been making connections. If Ball and others in the battalion looked on Shea as a bastard, they might not be surprised to learn what had really happened at the firing range. I might be able to tell at least one of them. I glanced back at Ball. My immediate commander, he was indeed the one I ought to tell.

Smoke was coming out at two or three places along his cigarette. He didn't seem to notice. He took a few puffs and lowered it. "Yesterday it changed," he said. "Yesterday at the firing he loosened his grip on me." For the first time he smiled. "Not only at the firing. But at the party last night too, at least for a while. You know what he did?"

I shook my head.

"We sat for a long time, the two of us, and exchanged stories about the Korean War. Very pleasant. Very, very pleasant. But then you weren't there, were you, Hanlon, so you wouldn't know."

"I was exhausted," I said. "I went to bed early."

"We were *all* exhausted, lieutenant. Each and every one of us. But we were there, except you."

"Yes, sir."

"Missing one of Shea's parties is nearly as bad as going AWOL. I'd say that without fear of exaggeration." His tone was full of warning. "Much like last night. I didn't care, Hanlon. To tell the truth, I didn't even miss you. For me it wasn't a big thing. A tiny kink in an otherwise aluminum-smooth day. That's all."

"What do you mean, as far as *you're* concerned?"

"The major wasn't happy about it at all. That's one reason I called you into the office this morning."

"It is?"

"When the party was about half over he said, 'Ball, where's your new officer?' I told him I didn't know." The captain paused and raised his eyes painfully. "Oh, Hanlon," he said, "it was pleasant up to then. We'd just been speaking about the firing. He told me he'd been having his doubts about my battery, but after what we did at the range he was beginning to lose them. Then he asked about you. I'd forgotten all about you. He said, 'Ball, you've lost an officer.'" The captain closed his eyes. "He sputtered and he fumed. I said, 'I'll go find him, sir.' He said, 'Don't bother.' I thought he'd be on my butt for the rest of the night, but he wasn't. It's your butt he's interested in, Hanlon." He sucked at his cigarette, expelled little smoke. "Still, you're my officer. What you do reflects on me. Do you understand that?"

"Yes, sir, I do, and I'm sorry. What else did he . . ."

"Before the party broke up he called me over and said, 'What did Hanlon think of the firing?'"

"He did?"

"Yes, he did, Hanlon. And you know something? I couldn't tell him. I could only tell him you didn't seem very enthusiastic when we where returning from the range. And it's true. You didn't."

I felt my legs go tight. "Did he say anything else?"

"No, he didn't. But I warn you, Hanlon. That man has a temper. Before the party ended, he said, 'You tell Hanlon I'm not going to forget this.' "

"What does *that* mean?"

"Oh, Hanlon," he said, standing, picking his injured cigarette out of the ashtray, turning it. "Who can answer such a question?"

I'd hoped he could.

"The point is, you have to keep your nose clean. That's the thing. For some reason he's watching you, and the minute your nose is dirty he's going to pick it." He turned and paced toward his window, turned back and gazed across at me. "You'd better spend the next several days learning about the battalion. You'd better find out about the troubles we've had." His tone was now a little more sympathetic. "He's unusual, Hanlon. His methods have been unorthodox, to say the least. Keep your eyes and ears open. Don't let him destroy you."

"Destroy?"

He'd begun to return to his chair. He stopped and turned. "Destroy," he said definitely. "That's the word I used, isn't it?"

"Yes, sir."

He gave me instructions: "Take a jeep. Use it as you wish for the next week. Find out all you can. What you learn may surprise you. Now, if you have questions, you may ask them."

"There was something, sir, about the firing, though this may not be the appropriate time to bring it up."

"Bring it up," he said, waving his free hand at me. "Good questions make good officers. What is it?"

"It's not exactly a question but more an observation." I paused, realizing it might be better for me to make it a question. "Maybe it *is* a question, after all."

"What?" he said impatiently.

"Well . . . do you think there might have been something unusual going on at the range yesterday?"

"What do you mean by that?"

"Well, I've been told that around here the guns have been giving everyone trouble. Even when we got to the range they acted up. But then they suddenly began to operate very well. Does that seem strange to you?"

"Not at all, not at all." He put the broken cigarette carefully down in his ashtray and leaned toward me. "The major makes us perform maintenance on them every day, two or three hours a day. Oh . . ." He tilted his head and rolled his eyes like a person about to faint. "Those guns are wily beasts, that's for sure. You have to work with them constantly to tame them. We did that. Orientation and synchronization. Radar and computer checks. Muzzle and loading-mechanism checks. Everything came together at the right time." He paused, his mouth twisting into a knowing smile. "But how would you know that, not having been here? You were here only for the fun part. The rest, my friend, has been tedious and troublesome. But it paid off."

"Then why, just before the shooting started, couldn't the batteries get some weapons even to point toward the water? I mean, several crews were having a lot of trouble."

"That's because we'd just towed them across part of England to get them to that beach, for God's sake! A lot of bouncing and jiggling. It takes a while to get the tubes and wires settled. Some of them we couldn't fix, of course. Too bad."

Five of the battalion's twelve weapons had acted up so badly they hadn't even been fired. Two were from each of the other gun batteries and only one from A, Ball's battery. The scoring had been done by only seven guns. Didn't that surprise Ball? "There were very few direct hits," I went on, "yet a lot of the target planes blew up and went down."

"Shrapnel," he explained. "That's what flak's all about. Foul up the engine. Knock off a stabilizer. Hit the gas tank. We hit a lot of gas tanks. It was beautiful!"

Had I not overheard Shea and South I'd have believed too. There were few explosions that didn't occur close to the target planes. It wasn't hard to understand why Ball and possibly the other COs were sure their guns had done the job.

"Do you think I shot them down with my forty-five?" he went on. "You were there." He was annoyed. "You saw for yourself what happened."

I nodded.

"Hanlon." He peered across at me. "There are good questions and bad questions. For your own sake, I don't want to hear you asking the bad ones. You have cynical eyes. I'll bet you're the sort of person who doubts the sun rises, even when you're looking right at it."

"No, sir. I'm really not."

"Then don't bring up stupid things. Hear?"

"Yes, sir."

New possibilities were occurring to me:

Shea knew I'd been at the tower door listening and was laying a trap, waiting to see what I'd do with the knowledge I had.

Ball had figured out that there'd been a conspiracy between Shea and South and was now protecting himself, me and everyone else by talking me down.

The conspiracy included Ball and the other battalion officers, everyone but me, who couldn't, at least couldn't yet, be trusted.

"Let's make that an order, shall we? I don't want you raising questions about the only good thing that's happened around here lately." He moved around his desk, stopped a few feet from my chair, regarded me sadly. "Yesterday, for the first time in a year, I was able to relax and catch my breath. Please don't do something that will cause it to be knocked out of me again."

"I'll try not to, sir."

"I appreciate that, Hanlon. I appreciate that very much."

I sat there waiting for him to say more.

But he gazed at me blankly. Apparently it was his way of letting me know he'd finished.

I stood and moved across his office, then across the orderly room to my desk. When I sat down I looked back to see him smiling at me. A man relieved. He held his cigarette between his forefinger and second finger, high, near his shoulder, an elegant pose with a single flaw: about an inch from his fingers it had broken, and the remainder hung vertically, dangling from a strip of paper. Still smiling, he stepped back and closed the door softly behind him.

Seven

⁊⁊⁊⁊⁊⁊⁊

*I*took the captain's advice. From the moment I began work each day I listened as though I were a spy. When someone mentioned equipment that didn't work, I made notes. When another told of an unpleasant encounter he'd had with the CO, I asked for details. I hurried to the gun site of a crew chief who was said to have located a part on the seventy-five that no one had known existed. I began tuning in on the complaints of enlisted men, particularly those who'd been in the battalion longest. In the afternoons I toured the gun sites, where my ears opened to all gossip and complaints. At 1700, quitting time for most, I took my jeep to the officers' club, and there, beneath gray uncertain smoke, above ice cubes rattling nervously in glasses, amid rasps and curses, I heard anecdotes, rumors and stories that confirmed a dominating message: the 46th Antiaircraft Artillery Battalion, once nicknamed by brigade "the Fumbling 46th," had, until Shea arrived, been one of the saddest outfits in the European Theater.

"Now you take Smathers," Gilley said. "If you want to know about this battalion, you've got to start with him."

"Who's Smathers?"

"Lieutenant Colonel Jamie Smathers, the CO who was here before Shea. By God, I've met a lot of cards in the Army, but that man was a deck and a half all by himself."

"The last of the great gentlemen," said Major George Perkins, a puffy man, the oldest of the officers who sat in the bar area each afternoon.

Gilley smiled. It was the first time since the firing that I'd seen his face express anything but bewilderment.

Gentleman or no gentleman, he pointed out, Smathers had been lethargic. He rarely held an inspection, exercised little discipline and didn't give a damn about the troublesome gun. Perkins agreed, recalling Smathers's only statement of policy: "This is my battalion and, within reason, I intend to make life here as pleasant as possible for everyone."

The colonel's pastime was watching movies at the base theater. He ordered many himself. He preferred musicals made before 1940. His favorite actor was Dick Powell, his favorite actress Ruby Keeler. "When those two got to making music," the chief said, "you could look over and see his head bobbing like a kid's rubber ball. Jesus, he was happy!" While few shared the colonel's tastes, all appreciated the movies for another reason. The last film was never over before 0130 hours, which meant that the colonel got home late and, as a result, didn't arrive at battalion headquarters before 1000 the following morning. This gave everyone a measure of extra time. The enlisted men, for example, did not begin rolling in until 0900, the sergeants around 0930 and the officers about 0945. Perkins noted that they all could have taken longer, for it was rarely that the colonel finished drinking his coffee and reading his morning *Stars & Stripes* before 1100, when he set out on his morning stroll. Now and then he scheduled a walk to the gun sites.

"That was a big event," Gilley said, "not only for him but for the gun crews too." Enlisted men got out of bed with flu bugs and sprained ankles and various occupational ailments. The crew chiefs made their men wear their best uniforms. It wasn't really necessary. Most of the men dressed well for the colonel without being told. Some even shaved, which was unusual. They shined up the gun tubes, trimmed the grass around the Quonset huts and picked up unsightly scraps left by the skeleton crews the night before. "It's a nice day, isn't it sergeant?" the colonel would say when he arrived at a site. The sergeants would agree even when the weather wasn't tip-top, for they found it hard to take issue with anything "Gentle Jamie" had to say. Rarely did the colonel glance at the guns. He'd kick a paper cup into the open or pluck a weed. He talked about putting in a new entranceway at one site and a volleyball court at another. He spoke often about keeping the sites livable. He told one crew chief, "I'd like the mothers of these troops to be able to visit and not be offended by what they see." When he finished chatting, he'd return the crew chief's grateful salute and set out on foot for the next site. "Walking saves money on gas," he once told Perkins, who'd been his exec but whom Shea had later demoted to S-1. "Lord knows we waste enough on paper and ammunition and that other nonsense. Let's do what we can to economize." No one could recall the colonel so much as stepping on the pedestal of a seventy-five. "I find that overwired thing repulsive," he once confided to Perkins, who was eventually asked not to mention the gun in his presence.

"Wasn't he concerned that the guns, what they do, what they're supposed to do, are the reason we're here?"

"Not old Jamie," Gilley said. "For him they were reminders of war, which he'd seen enough of."

For all his lovable qualities, Smathers struck me as a commander no better than Shea, or the Shea I thus far knew. For neither of them did it seem to matter that the guns couldn't shoot down planes. The memory of Shea's conversation with South had been throbbing through me constantly. I now wondered which was worse: to make it falsely appear that the weapons could do the job they were put there to do, or to fail to acknowledge their existence.

Naturally the colonel's attitude, like that of all well-liked commanders, began to rub off on his men. The crews kept away from their weapons as much as possible, and therefore little maintenance was performed. After a disastrous day at the range when the weapons didn't score a single hit, the brigade commander said, "I hope a Russian spy ship wasn't sitting out there observing what happened. If it was, Smathers, you can be damn sure they'll go right after *your* base as soon as the war starts." Perkins said Smathers gave a start. "I certainly hope we won't find ourselves in a situation like that." Perkins said the brigade CO spit, almost hitting Smathers's shoe, then turned and walked away.

Perkins recalled that the former CO had had at least one moment of achievement. A few weeks after the unhappy firing, a major general from Headquarters, U.S. Army, Europe, flew onto the base with an inspection team. All day he led his team, in and out of the radar van, over and under guns, through orderly rooms, across barracks and finally into battalion headquarters. Exhausted, the general sat down behind Smathers's desk and looked up at the CO. "I hope that's all you have scheduled," he said. Smathers replied, "No, sir. There's one more event, the battalion parade." The general winced. On his way to the parade grounds Perkins overheard the general say to his assistant, "After what I've seen, I expect to find the men in this battalion marching sideways." But Smathers liked parades and had had the battalion practicing for a month. He stood proudly as his men filed past him and the general: crookedly, brokenly, zigzag, but forward.

"It was inevitable he couldn't last," Gilley concluded. I asked, why inevitable? He said he figured an officer's mind is like a supply room. "There are a lot of things that, even though they're nice, you get gigged for having there. Old Smathers never got the wrong things out."

"Someone realized he wasn't doing his job?"

"Probably. But I'm talking about something else."

"What?"

"The movies."

A war movie, one of my childhood favorites, *Wake Island*, mistakenly got pinched in between a couple of Smathers's favorites, *Honeymoon Hotel* and *Swing Time*. The chief believed that the shock caused by the Japs charging across the screen and William

Bendix shouting and all those grenades going off was what did him in. Whatever the cause, he was found slumped over in his chair at intermission, a tortured look on his face.

Both said the tears that flowed in the battalion afterward were genuine.

"That man was like a father to us," Gilley said.

Perkins nodded. "You hardly knew you were in the Army."

Eight

.r.r.r.r.r

T hat the Army would find someone like Shea to repair the damage done by Smathers seemed to all, at least in retrospect, inevitable. Everyone present a year and a half earlier remembered vividly Shea's arrival in the battalion. No one, I was told, remembered it more clearly than Sergeant Effram Y. Benson of C Battery. I spoke to Benson and others who'd been present that Friday night.

The major drove himself onto the base a little after 2200 in a sedan borrowed at brigade, shot up the hill to battalion head-quarters, screeched to a stop in the parking lot, got out and rushed into the building to find Benson, the sergeant of the guard, asleep at the desk of Major Perkins.

"What's your name?" Shea demanded as Benson raised his head from the little pillow Perkins had let him use.

Benson told him.

"Call the Air Police detachment and have them send someone to arrest you."

Benson gazed up. The flame-haired giant before him seemed to have leaped out of one of his nightmares.

"When you hang up, call the battalion sergeant major and have him send someone to replace you. When you're done with that, call the officer of the day and tell him to hang on. Now where's the CO's office?"

"At the other end of the hall, sir."

"Put me on the line when you have the officer of the day." The major turned and rumbled out of the office.

Benson said he sat there for a few minutes and shook like a baby. He said he almost cried thinking of the bad luck of it. It wasn't easy but he managed to make all the calls.

First Lieutenant Stan Pryzbyskowski, then assistant operations officer, now a battery commander, happened to be officer of the day. He popped up in bed in his room at the officers' club. The sound of the telephone ringing after duty hours was unusual. He, too, had been asleep. When he picked it up he heard Benson say, "Juh . . . juh . . . just a minute, sir." He next heard a growl that he said reminded him of two things: a bear that had come up to the car window once when he and his parents were vacationing in Yellowstone National Park and a nun he'd had in grade school in Chicago who made that sound when she cleared her throat. The growl turned to words: "I'm your new commander. Call a meeting of all battalion officers at twenty-three hundred in my office."

"Tonight, sir?"

Wham!

Pryzbyskowski stared at the crackling receiver, finally got the message. He put the receiver down, picked it up again, and started making the calls.

All the officers sooner or later found their ways from the officers' club, houses, taverns, poker room (in the basement of Air Force headquarters), and other places, including a Reading whorehouse called Darlene's (where Captain Buckles, the battalion supply officer, liked to hang out). Each, amazingly, was seated on a folding chair in front of the major's desk by 2300. Gilley said that many, including himself, came with shirts buttoned wrong and caps wrinkled and without insignia. But he emphasized that all got there, as though, for officers of the 46th, this was itself remarkable.

Shea told them who he was and said, "I'm holding an inspection of all batteries in one hour."

Chairs squeaked.

No one spoke.

"A complete full-dress inspection of all men and equipment."

According to Gilley there then came from the back of the office a polite, troubled, almost whispered comment: "But . . . we've *never* had a night inspection before, sir. The men aren't used to it."

The major asked the speaker's name.

He was told.

Shea squinted as though he'd found a spy in the room. "Are ·you a battery commander, Ball?"

"Yes, sir."

The skin on the major's face went tight. "Yours will be the first unit inspected."

The inspection began on time. No battery passed. Ball's scored lowest but no battery even came close. Sergeant Grey told me, "It was like this heavy tank appeared and began firing at liberty. We was liberty." There were rasps, moans, and a rising barrage of curses. No matter. Another inspection was scheduled for 0200. No one expected to pass that one either. No one did.

The inspections went on all through the dark morning, Shea marching through orderly rooms, supply rooms and barracks, then climbing into his sedan, racing out to radar and gun sites, coming back. He found something wrong everywhere he stopped.

He was apparently at his toughest around the guns and radars. Lieutenant J. C. Maxwell, in charge of the big acquisition-radar van, recalled a conversation between Shea and a noncom in his crew that took place at 0310:

"Who left the broom up on that antenna?"

"I did, sir. I was dusting it off for you, sir."

"Dusting off an antenna, for Christ's sake!"

"Yes, sir."

"Go up and get that broom and stand with it at right shoulder arms until I get back here again."

The soldier did what he was told, stayed where he was until 0545, which was when Shea returned.

Most figured the new CO would wilt sooner or later. Who could keep going at such a pace? Surely not this heavy wheezing lunatic. The enlisted men watched him like kids ogling a fast freight about to fly off the rails. It didn't. They, not he, were collapsing. Grey remembered a conversation he had with PFC Billy Lee Richards:

"My feet are growin' one whole size per hour, sarge. Can I sit down?"

"Ain't nowhere to sit. The officers got all the chairs, the noncoms got all the desk tops, and ain't nobody gonna sit on a bunk or a footlocker till the new CO gives us his okay."

"I'll kill him one of these times, sarge! I swear to God! How many years do you get for killing a major?"

" 'bout four hundred," Grey told him.

Shea remained alive and the inspection went on. Finally one battery passed. It was Charlie, Captain Vernor's outfit. The time was 0630, a little after sunrise. Citizens in Newbury began calling base headquarters to inquire about the shouting and screaming up at the base. When the men in Charlie quieted down, they smuggled in beer from the PX and sat around cursing the red invader until they ran out of words and energy.

Another battery, Baker, passed at about 0830, then Headquarters, a little after 0900. Men in Headquarters, Baker and Charlie, too strung up to get back to sleep, watched as Shea returned to Able again and again. Able seemed doomed. The soldiers in the other batteries began to root:

"C'mon, you spazdiks! Get yourselves over the top!"

But Ball's men moved like rusty robots as Shea appeared and disappeared. Crawford said he finally had to help the weakening captain out of his chair every time the major's sedan turned into the battery parking lot. Ball told me he hadn't prayed for years, but that day he prayed. Finally Shea gave Able a passing grade. Everyone in the battery except Ball celebrated. He had a driver take him to the dispensary, where he got three kinds of pills from Doc Michaels, the base surgeon—two for nerves and one, incredibly, for sleep. He said he went home, took an extra amount of each and stayed in bed for thirty-six hours.

For the next two days members of the 46th were hard to find anywhere. They lay across beds, chairs and desks; hung out windows and over gun tubes; were curled up on toilets and spread out behind bushes. Sleep was like a precious black-market item. They took chances getting it wherever they could. It would take them all, from Ball at home to Benson down at the stockade, a long time to catch up.

Nine

,·,·,·,·,·,·,·

The Skysweeper had been the main defense at Greenham Common and a number of Strategic Air Command bases for about two years before Shea took command. According to Gilley, officers everywhere were befuddled by it, nowhere, he suspected, more than at Greenham. "Before Shea got here, there wasn't a single day when all twelve guns in the base's defense were properly oriented and synchronized."

O&S—orientation and synchronization—was performed on each weapon each morning. The radar antenna was made to point to a distant fixed object like a tower on a hill. Then the gun was pointed at the same object. The azimuth and elevation of the object were known in advance. When pointed at the object, the radar dials and the gun dials, as well as the computer dials (taking information directly from the radar), were all supposed to show the known azimuth and elevation. If they did so, the weapon was properly oriented and synchronized. On paper it was a reasonably simple job. But not in practice.

On one weapon the radar and gun dials would read alike but not the computer dials, as though the radar, which fed its information to the gun *through* the computer, had magically taught itself to skip that step.

On another the computer would give the gun reverse azimuth

readings. If, for example, the radar picked up a low-flying plane in the north-northeast, the computer sent information that positioned the gun tube in the south-southwest.

Every weapon had, it seemed, its own eccentricity or eccentricities. At the firing range I'd enjoyed shooting the old World War II forty-millimeter guns, even the cumbersome nineties and one-twenties. With those, there was some relationship between what one intended to do and what actually occurred. But the seventy-five, part of the new wave of military electronics, turned the human actor, whether officer or enlisted man or even electronics technician, into a comic bit player.

Even before Smathers came along, Gilley said, weapons danced crazily or sat like boulders refusing to move, let alone fire properly. At an early firing one weapon lowered its muzzle to the sea and began letting go at a pleasure craft, which was, fortunately, out of range. There were many such stories, all rendered as if the seventy-five were a living creature full of whimsy and malice.

Sergeant Byrne's seventy-five had an antenna with a habit of flipping toward anyone walking near it who was carrying metal. A faulty radar, some crew members claimed, but others pointed out that the radar had performed as well as any other during practice tracking missions. It must have been something else. No one seemed to know what, including the technicians. "She's a screwball, all right," said Byrne. "And it isn't only our helmets. See her raise that antenna sometimes when an Air Force jet makes its approach for a landing. Then the gun tube follows and pretty soon she starts slamming the loading arm into her breech. Follows the damn plane to the end of the runway, throbbing and jumping like she's mad that it got in safe." Byrne peeked over the top of the pit, looked at his gun. "Sometimes you wonder whose side she'd be on if we got ourselves in a real wingding."

A weapon of Captain Vernor's reportedly began sinking into the dirt in its pit. Day after day it went a little deeper until finally the radar and computer could not be seen from outside the sandbag walls. The tube had to be increasingly elevated. "This baby's digging itself a hole," Vernor's crew chief told him. Vernor had to order the piece removed to the gun park, which had a concrete pad. There then arose speculations. The most popular seemed to be that beneath the hard ground on which the gun had rested there lay an ancient well that could no longer take the pressure from the modern heavy weapon that was perched on top of it. According to this theory, the ground would one day have opened up and swallowed gun, crew members and all. Those who believed that it had a mind, like Byrne, said the weapon had simply grown tired of the tight little pit and was making trouble so it could get itself a vacation in the gun park. "You watch," Byrne told me when the weapon had been placed in a new gun pit after the latest firing, "she'll start digging in as soon as she needs a rest." I visited the old gun site and saw the depression the weapon had left in the earth.

Another weapon was mistakenly left plugged into its generator after O&S. Those who told its mysterious story said it remained still and silent all day as if keeping the mistake to itself. That night the sergeant in charge of the skeleton crew was awakened in the Quonset hut by a strange noise and got up to investigate. He opened the hut door to see the silhouette of what appeared to him to be a giraffe raising its neck toward the sky. He was sure he heard crying. He stood there frightened for a long time, until finally he figured out that the main power cable was still plugged in. He crept to the generator and pulled out the plug. The gun then lowered its tube. The computer went on whimpering, however. This should have been impossible. No power was being fed to the weapon. For nearly an hour the sergeant sat on the gravel in his shorts, listening until the whimpering finally subsided.

I drove out to the gun site in question. It happened to be one of Battery A's and therefore one Captain Ball might be planning to assign me. I told the sergeant, Rivera, the story I'd heard and asked him if it was true. He twisted the toe of his boot into the gravel walkway and said, "It's no joke, lieutenant. I had to switch my crew chief to another gun the next day. He was too scared to be around her at night. He won't even come here for visits anymore."

Officers said that during the morning maintenance sessions they'd seen weapons lower their gun tubes and point at each other. Once, Gilley said, each picked out a partner and pointed at it, so that had all been fired simultaneously, all would have been destroyed. "Not a bad idea when you stop to think of it," Perkins commented. Gilley, who'd spent a lot of time since the firing puzzling over the results, now admitted the possibility of intelligent communication between computers. Others had explanations of their own for the pairing off. Many thought it was the work of members of night crews who wanted to provide others in the battalion with work to keep them occupied during those gaps in the day when there was usually nothing to do.

Everyone, it seems, had a favorite theory about the behavior of the seventy-fives. While these theories varied, in fact often contradicted each other, most were based at least to some extent on a belief in the otherworldly, the mystical. Few explanations, in fact, struck me as even remotely possible scientifically or technologically. It was refreshing now and then to hear a theory that at least veered toward assumptions of the times.

Sergeant First Class P. I. Peters, a slight blond who had fought in the Korean War when he was only seventeen, walked me around his gun site and said, "I figure there's a Communist back in the factory where they make these crappers and he has this Einstein brain by which he fixes them so they'll mess us up whenever we turn around. He's put an electronic device and an explosive in each one, and all the devices are set to blow up the guns one day." He rubbed his knuckles across his small nose. "Just as these devices blow up, in comes this Ruskie parachute unit and it's got us deader'n hell. What do you think?" I told him the theory was farfetched. He nodded. "That's what Lieutenant Pryzbyskowski said when I told him we ought to take them apart and try to find those devices." He looked at the gun, then at me, and laughed. "But the damned thing makes you wonder, doesn't it?"

Shea had been in the battalion for only a short time when

Sergeant Akamuro's seventy-five acted up in his presence. The major was examining the loading mechanism when the pedestal on which he was standing began to move. "What the hell!" he said, jumping off. He then walked cautiously around the gun, bending down, peeking here and there. Finally he turned to the civilian technician, asked him to check the circuits from terminal to terminal and find out what was wrong, then left the site. The technician did what he was told. It was an old story: he couldn't find the trouble, let alone the solution. Shea came back and told him to try again. He tried again, the major standing beside him with arms crossed. Still the technician failed. The major then took off his jacket, opened his collar and said, "Start to finish, once more." The technician, with a diagram spread out before him, once more did some troubleshooting while Shea held his tools. When the sky darkened, Shea ordered portable lights brought in and turned on. On went the civilian, with his snorting assistant at his side. Late that evening, at about 2000 hours, the technician saw a wire that wasn't illustrated on the diagram. He connected it to the nearest open terminal. The weapon, which had been making growling sounds as it moved, now began to purr and stay still.

Shea put aside a whole week to supervise O&S. He began at sunrise each day and remained at a weapon until radar, computer and gun were pointed where they should point. He treated each weapon as though it had a mind and will of its own. Each technician and crewman and officer was assigned to watch a dial, a circuit, a gear or something. Each gun chief was to notify him whenever anyone saw even the slightest deviation from normal. It must have proved very frustrating, for often after supervising a satisfactory O&S, Shea was called back again. "More than once I saw him go behind a Quonset hut and talk to himself," Gilley said. But he didn't go under, and on Thursday, just before supper chow call, he had every major component on every weapon pointed to a single distant object and all the readings on each weapon agreed with one another and with the predetermined readings of the distant point.

Peters and the other crew chiefs were pleased that the gun had chosen to shoot at target planes and not something else during the recent firing. No one, not the crew chiefs or crewmen or officers, showed signs of suspecting that there'd been anything devious. In fact, they all seemed sure that Shea had taken decisive control over the weapon. Though they didn't understand how, they were grateful.

I wanted to say, "Nothing has changed. The gun is the same as it's always been." No one would have believed me. Its real powers were even more impressive than those being attributed to it. Whether by design or accident, it was providing a means of keeping officers and men from thinking about more important matters: why they were on this base, how useful the weapons really were, the truth about the firing. No one, save perhaps Shea and Captain South and, of course me, doubted that the weapon had finally been subdued. All were now passive and relieved, not at all suspicious.

Ten

"What's a swagger stick?" Ball asked as he, Crawford and I stood before the bulletin board inside the entrance to the officers' club one day before lunch.

Pinned before us was the directive that had prompted his question. It appeared the day after Shea had visited a nearby British regiment.

Swagger sticks will hereafter be carried by all officers in the 46th AAA Battalion. They are intended to add dignity to your appearance. Any officer seen without his swagger stick will be considered out of uniform.

"One of those leather things that look like a long thin pretzel," Crawford said. "The English officers use them. Some have a strap on the top to go over your wrist."

"I'll be darned." Ball scratched his cheek. "What are you supposed to do with it?"

"Just let it hang down, I guess," Crawford said.

"For Christ's sake. Is that all?"

"Swing it when you walk maybe. I don't know."

Ball looked up again as though there might have been something he'd missed. He frowned and turned to Crawford again. "Maybe point to things."

"Guess it's possible."

"Or tap a soldier when you want something."

"Look." Crawford was pointing.

A hook had been screwed into the polished mahogany wall near the bulletin board, and from it hung something that fit the description Crawford had just given.

"That's a swagger stick."

Ball squinted and gazed. "Well, I'll be a son of a bitch!" He turned, smiling. "Let's go eat lunch."

Strange, the things that interested the captain. He'd spent the whole morning worrying about who was going to stand guard in the battery parking lot. Guarding the parking lot was a special assignment. The captain was fearful of surprise visits by Shea. Every day Ball stationed someone at the lot's entrance to keep his eye on the road leading from battalion headquarters. If the sentinel saw Shea's sedan he was to run to the orderly room and shout a warning. The last time a warning was sounded, the captain hurried to his office, spread some papers out on his desk and pretended to be reading them. Crawford came awake, went into the supply room and began to examine equipment. Ball told me to hurry upstairs to the battery classroom and remain there until I was told to come down. "I don't want you making a dumb remark and fouling up an outfit I've taken months to square away," the captain explained. Sergeant Grey got on the phone to the motor pool or one of the gun sections and started shouting. Two minutes after the guard ran into the orderly room, battery headquarters seemed a very busy place. So far there had been several alarms, but the major never arrived. The sedan often came down the road from battalion without turning into the battery parking lot: Shea was headed for the PX or off base. Still Ball continued the procedure. It was like having a clock with a faulty alarm that's liable to ring at any time of day; it kept you expectant, anxious.

We ordered three iced teas. When they arrived the captain

picked up his glass and took a sip. He drank in a strange way, holding his head way back because of his long nose. It was a thin nose, only slightly convex, and, despite its length, somewhat attractive. It only looked odd on his face, whose other features were small and pinched together. He took another sip, and when he swallowed he stretched his head toward the ceiling like a crane drinking water. He put down his glass and looked at me. "Well, Hanlon, now comes the action."

"Pardon me, sir?"

"It's been quiet lately. It's been very very quiet." He was grinning at me. "This swagger-stick business is going to perk us all up. I can't think of a better way for you to get used to the rigors of life here. Not that it'll prove you out one way or the other. At least it'll keep you on your toes."

The captain had told me several times that I'd have to prove myself. I now stared across at him and said, "Seems like more harassment to me."

"What do you mean by that?"

I turned to Crawford. His eyes were on me but making no comment. Neither he nor Ball had been happy about my questions regarding the battalion. Since I'd asked him about the firing, Ball didn't seem to trust me at all. I turned back to him. "Maybe I shouldn't have said anything. I just don't see that swagger sticks are going to make this a better outfit."

Ball gave Crawford a troubled look.

Crawford's indifferent expression didn't change.

I said, "Nothing important."

But Ball clamped his eyes on mine, waiting for me to say more.

"Well," I finally went on, "I just wonder if we shouldn't be more concerned about why the guns sometimes work and sometimes don't instead of worrying about . . . how we look."

The captain's eyes, now anguished, swung to Crawford. "Speak to him at length about what he's just said, Mike, but not now, not in my presence." He finally turned his attention to his menu.

Ball and Crawford were a perfect team. The captain constantly darted about the orderly room while his executive rarely left his chair. Ball was often chattering; Crawford said little. When the captain went too far in speech or action, the exec pulled him back, just as when Crawford sank to lethargy, Ball raised him with an assignment: "There are some clean rags in the supply room. Why don't you deliver them to the gun sites." Often he'd add, "Take Hanlon with you."

Ball and Crawford were the ones I'd have to rely on during the coming months. I wasn't comfortable with either. Most of the time I was invisible to both. When I arrived at work in the morning, Ball was usually sitting on Crawford's desk, looking over the day's memos, directives and orders. "Says here to check the spares on the jeeps. Hah. We do that every day, don't we, Mike?"

Crawford would be in his chair, his long legs spread-eagled under his desk. He would yawn and raise his eyes to Ball's. "Every morning, captain. First thing."

Ball would smile, put the directive down and go on to the next sheet.

Sometimes when he commented to Crawford I nodded or shook my head. Once I even tried to break in to make a suggestion. The captain's hand flew up like a traffic cop's, and, blinking rapidly, he went on reading the memo. I'd wait for hours, hoping for a chance to speak to him. He spent much of each day in his office, behind his closed door. One day I went in with a training schedule for him to look over. He was in his chair facing the blank wall behind his desk. "The schedule, captain," I said.

"Leave it." He didn't even turn around.

I saw on the desk a big bottle with pills about the size of mothballs. In large red letters were the words *Cool Tummy Antacid*. I'd heard noisy wet chewing sounds from the office on several occasions. I supposed they were the antacids, though several smaller bottles of pills always surrounded the large one like sentinels. I put the schedule down and left the office.

After we'd ordered our meals, the captain left the table. When our salads arrived, Crawford sent me to tell him lunch was being served.

I found him in front of the full-length mirror in the foyer. He'd removed the swagger stick from the wall and was standing sideways, holding his right arm straight at his side, twisting the stick this way, then that, then swinging it slowly back and forth, stopping, holding it straight again, looking to the ceiling thoughtfully, then again at the stick, swinging it in a longer arc this time, looking up, puzzling, finally smiling to himself.

I felt embarrassed, as if I were peeking at someone urinating. I told him lunch was being served, then turned around and went back to the dining room.

"What's he doing?"

"Standing by the mirror inside the front doors. He's . . . sort of practicing with the swagger stick."

Crawford nodded, as if that was just what he'd expected the captain to be doing.

Ball finally came back to the table. He was smiling. He sat down and said, "Mike, that business about looking dignified. He's right. Those things are really going to sharpen our appearance."

Crawford nodded.

"What's on the schedule this afternoon?"

"Oh, the usual, captain. Checking equipment, mainly. Grey's supposed to have a report from the gun sergeants on the availability of grease-nipple paint. I think we're running out."

"I didn't know that. Damn."

"I was going to have Hanlon here throw a coin on the mattresses of some of the new men. The sergeants say they haven't been bouncing."

"That's not good."

"And I was wondering if you might want to give a little talk on hygiene to our mess crew. Grey said he saw that new cook picking his nose."

"New cook?"

"The one with the big Adam's apple."

"Oh, *that* dog!" Ball made a spitting sound. "I could tell when I saw him he was worthless. We get all the weak ones." He looked at me. "It's not fair."

"Oh shit," said Crawford.

"What?" Ball said in a panicky voice.

"That new cook is on duty in the parking lot this afternoon. I just remembered."

"Jesus Christ! Not him, Mike!"

"Sorry, but his name came up on the roster. I'll skip dessert and go back and replace him with someone else."

"No," Ball snapped. "I won't enjoy eating my fish unless I know that moron isn't in the lot. Go call Grey. Have him put someone else in the lot right away."

"Yes, sir." Crawford left to make the call.

After a brief silence I saw my hand swing out, toward the captain, and stop only when it struck a water glass, knocking it over onto the small plate containing Crawford's bun. "Whoops," I said. "An accident."

Anger had surged through me and ended up in my hand and my hand had shot toward Ball. It had moved the way a head turns at an unexpected sound or a foot is stamped in disappointment. After a few seconds the anger silently verbalized itself: what do parking-lot guards and faked firings and grease-nipple paint and coins on beds have to do with defending the country?

"What is *wrong* with you?"

I looked across. "Nothing."

"Are you that clumsy all the time?"

"No, sir," I replied mechanically. "I have to go to the bathroom." I didn't but wanted not to be near him.

In the bathroom I withstood the disgusted look of the person inside the mirror, nodded after he spoke to me, saying, "Get control of yourself, for God's sake!" I felt a need to wash and dry my hands, did so, and returned to the table, where I switched Crawford's bun for mine and said "Sorry" to Ball.

"While you were gone, Hanlon, I was thinking how very tough Shea's test on you is going to be."

I'd several times heard about new officers being tested but had taken testing in a general sense: each officer had to prove he could perform the duties assigned to him. Ball was speaking specifically, however.

I waited until Crawford returned before asking about the test. I'd addressed the lieutenant, but Ball answered.

"He gives a different one to every new officer. A make-or-break thing. Second johns get the hardest tests. Yours is going to be bad, Hanlon. It's because you're . . . you're very cynical." He turned to Crawford. "Isn't he, Mike?"

"More than most, I'd say," Crawford replied as if he'd been considering the question for a long time. Crawford gave the captain what he wanted to hear. If Ball had asked if I looked like an Argentinian, Crawford would have agreed.

"I'd say a *lot* more." Ball turned back to me. "The old man smells out qualities like that."

I'd been taking extreme measures to avoid Shea. On the way to the battery each morning I drove around the battalion headquarters area, not through it. When at a gun site I saw his sedan turn onto the airstrip, I got into my jeep and headed back to the battery area. If I heard Shea was coming to the officers' club for a meeting or social event, I remained in my room until, peering through a window at the front of the manor house, I saw that his sedan was no longer in the parking lot. Sooner or later I'd have to face him. I suppose I should have guessed he'd be coming after me. I asked for more information about the test.

The main course had arrived. Ball turned to Crawford. "Take him aside sometime and explain it to him." He looked at the salmon sitting before him, then back at me. "I will *not* talk about unpleasant things when I'm trying to eat."

"Yes, sir."

Only lately had I recognized that my fear of Shea was as much a fear of myself, that tendency in me to speak up about the wrong things at the wrong time. It had gotten me into trouble when I was in college and later when I was at officers' basic school. Only minutes earlier I'd stunned Ball with my ill-timed remark about the swagger sticks, then startled him by knocking over the glass. All of my remarks, and now, apparently, my movements, seemed ill-timed. Still troubled about what Shea had done at the firing range, I might in anger blurt out what I'd overheard. The consequences, I was sure, would be terrible.

After taking only a few bites of fish, Crawford excused himself and left for the battery. "I'm going to make sure someone reliable is in the lot."

"Good, Mike. Good."

It wasn't until Ball was wiping some chocolate pudding from the tip of his nose that he seemed to notice me again. He smiled. "It puts me in the pink. You know that?"

"The salmon, sir?"

"The swagger-stick business. We've been on edge since the firing, wondering what he's going to do next." He spoke enthusiastically. "Now we know." He scraped the last of the pudding out of his bowl, took a sip of tea and said, "Let's go back and do what we're being paid for."

He signed the check and we left to do whatever it was we were being paid for.

Eleven

.r.r.r.r.r.r

*L*ater that afternoon, when Crawford and I were alone in the orderly room, he told me about the tests. "There's no way to avoid them. He aims at your weaknesses, or what he thinks are your weaknesses. He puts you in a sort of make-or-break situation to see how you'll hold up. Some don't."

A lieutenant named Cleary had arrived in the 46th with a record showing poor mechanical aptitude. Nevertheless Shea assigned him to the motor pool and instructed him to teach a brush-up course on engine tune-ups. Most of the noncoms and other enlisted men at the motor pool were able to do tune-ups blindfolded. In Crawford's view, Shea's purpose was either to humiliate Cleary or give him a chance to correct his greatest weakness. Whatever the purpose, Cleary fumbled and froze. He instantly gained a reputation for incompetence. "Even today, when something goes wrong on a vehicle or a gun, someone will say, 'Get Lieutenant Cleary.' That brings a lot of laughter." Crawford believed Cleary was a good officer, yet for his remaining tour of duty, about eighteen months, the enlisted men mocked him openly. His life in the 46th became an ongoing humiliation.

"In making an officer look weak, isn't he lowering morale?"

"He'll sacrifice one officer to keep all the others on their toes."

A brash first lieutenant named Minelli who'd been transferred from a seventy-five battalion in the States made the mistake of bragging about his ability to make radar and computer repairs. Shea waited until a difficult problem arose. Not surprisingly, one soon did: the radar on one of the guns just wouldn't allow itself to be synchronized with either the computer or the gun itself. The representative from the gun manufacturer recommended having the entire unit replaced. "Not yet," Shea told him. The major ordered the lieutenant to the gun site. "Stay out there until the damned thing works," he said. The lieutenant confidently went to the site. At the end of the first afternoon, he'd made no progress. "I'll get it tomorrow," he announced. The phone in the officers' club soon rang. It was Shea calling Minelli. Crawford heard the lieutenant say "Yes, sir" about ten times. Minelli hung up, finished his beer, went to his room, got his sleeping bag and returned to the site. He stayed there for two weeks, sleeping in the gun shack, taking his meals with the crew, returning to the officers' club only to clean up and change uniforms and have a beer. He never did solve the problem. Eventually the radar system was replaced, and Minelli was transferred.

I asked Crawford what he thought my test might involve.

He didn't know. "I agree with the captain, though. He's lining you up for something big. The reason is that he's waited so long. The longer he waits, the tougher it usually is."

I'd begun to put together fragments of gossip ("The boss was in the office to look at your personnel file the other day, Hanlon," Perkins said), rumors ("Hear the major asked for a second lieutenant from West Point and got you instead," Ball informed me one morning) and even direct evidence (Shea had recently sent Gilley a memo which the chief showed me: "Does Hanlon know anything about the seventy-five's computer?"). Since the incident at the firing tower not five waking minutes passed when I didn't think about, worry about, Shea. At times I felt as certain as daylight that he knew I'd overheard him and South and was laying for me. The reports did nothing more than reinforce the fear already in me and growing like a bad case of hives.

Worried about my own impending test, I asked about Crawford's.

He'd been sipping from a cup of coffee. He got up and poured himself more. Unless he was walking in or out or pouring coffee, he sat in his chair, usually slumped down, often with his feet on the desk and his cap pulled low over his eyes. Back from the coffee machine, he didn't slump down but sat at the edge of his desk and gazed through the window. "Bad," he said. After more staring and a little coffee-sipping, he told me why.

The first time he'd gone to the firing range a corporal had come up from the rocky beach in front of the line of guns and said he'd seen a strange-looking metal object sticking out among some stones. Shea halted the firing, went down to the beach himself and took a look. What he discovered was an old British land mine. Fifteen years earlier all the beaches in that part of the country had been mined in anticipation of an invasion by Hitler's army. The beaches had been cleared after the war, but now and then a stray mine had appeared. Shea ordered Crawford to dig out the mine and carry it half a mile down the beach where there was an old concrete blockhouse. He didn't want it near the men, guns or, especially, the ammunition.

"The truth is, explosives make me nervous, which is why I spend a lot more time in the orderly room than out at the guns. Shea must have noticed me backing away from the weapons when the crews were removing rounds from the packing cases. I guess he figured me out. Whatever his reason, he gave me the job of moving that mine.

"All the way to the beach I remembered warnings I'd heard about not touching mines, particularly old ones. Yet here I was, ordered to carry one half a mile down a rocky beach. I stood over it for at least five minutes with the whole battalion watching from the knoll above the guns. Some of the enlisted men were cheering as if I were a football team. I went numb, didn't think I could do it. I looked up and saw Shea staring at me, just waiting for me to blow myself up. Maybe him looking is what did it. Anyway I carefully removed stone after stone and picked up the mine. Behind me everyone went silent. Step by step, over the roughest damn surface I've ever walked, I carried that thing, as wide as a dinner plate and as thick as my forearm. It must have weighed fifteen or twenty pounds. On the top was a little button, still shiny, the detonator. If I touched it, or even jiggled the whole thing too much, I might return to the knoll in little pieces. There was, of course, the chance, a good one, that I'd trip and fall. Somehow, despite itches and sweaty hands and several little stumbles, I kept myself going. It wasn't courage or anything like that. The only thing that took guts was picking up the mine. After that, I had no choice to make except the choice of getting it to the blockhouse. And I did." He closed his eyes and let out a little groan. "I still don't know how I did it."

"But you did *do* it," I said, moved by his achievement.

"You know, all the time I was walking I tried to persuade myself that the mine was dead. I couldn't, or I might not have been so careful in walking. And thank goodness I couldn't. Later, when we were waiting for a British ordnance team to defuse it, the vibrations of one of the gun carriers set it off. Shrapnel and rocks flew out of peepholes in the blockhouse and sprayed the beach."

"How has he treated you since?"

He paused, staring into his coffee, finally raised his eyes, nodding. "Not bad," he said. "In fact, I'd say he likes, or at least respects, me. He doesn't harass me like he does some of the others."

Crawford then told me the lieutenant I'd replaced had been given one of the hardest tests. His name was Williston, but everyone called him Whitey because of his light skin and blond hair. His troubles started before he arrived in the battalion. He'd been in the hospital at Fort Bliss for most of the week during which instruction had been given on the large acquisition-radar set. The T-30 was an early-warning system located in a big van, one of which was assigned to each battalion. (I saw our van every time I crossed the base, a huge awkward-looking cube on wheels with a curved antenna which circled constantly.) That week of missed instruction became Whitey's vulnerable point. Another commander might have kept the young officer away from the complicated radar set, at least until he'd had some on-the-job training; not Shea. The lieutenant had passed the officers' basic course and was officially qualified to supervise activities on every piece of equipment in the battalion. Shea assigned him to the acquisition radar.

Each day, Whitey oversaw maintenance and operations in the great van. As long as one of the two radar specialists, trained technicians, was present, the lieutenant was safe. If either of them was absent when an emergency arose, the lieutenant was likely to have trouble. He attended the set dutifully, trying to learn as much as he could from the specialists. He weathered several small crises.

The one he didn't, the worst and final one, occurred predictably on the day one of the two specialists reported for sick call. The second was on pass, and there was no one but the lieutenant to conduct operations. He had with him a corporal and a private, both nearly as helpless as he. As Williston hopped about, trying to make the numerous daily checks, he began to feel queasy, then dizzy. Sure that no one would believe him if he said he'd gotten sick on the same day as the specialist, he tried to stay on the job. Soon he could no longer keep his eyes focused well enough to study the screen, fill out forms or read dials. Finally he left the corporal in charge and had the private take him, in the jeep assigned to the radar set, across the base to the infirmary, where he hoped to get medication that would temporarily relieve him. The corporal, trying to do two or three things at once, let some wires heat up under the control panel. Williston or he had failed to make sure a blower was turned on. A fire started, and before the corporal could get it out, much damage was done.

"It was the corporal's fault," I said, as if Williston had been I.

"Doesn't matter," Crawford replied. "The officer in command is always responsible."

We'd been told that many times during ROTC and officers' basic classes. But Williston seemed to have been put into an impossible situation. "What happened to him?"

"Shea ordered an investigation."

"And . . . ?"

Perkins was put in charge. The investigation lasted for several weeks. Everyone knew that in some way Williston would be found responsible. The only question was how responsible. Shea monitored the investigation closely. Whitey suffered silently throughout, but everyone could see that he was being affected: "He lost a lot of weight he couldn't afford to lose, kept getting even whiter all the time. He didn't want to talk about what had happened. He was letting it eat him up, almost literally." Finally Shea reported the results: Williston was found pecuniarily responsible in the amount of $43,543 and would have to pay. The decision was later upheld at brigade headquarters, at Headquarters, U.S. Army, Europe, and at Department of the Army.

I'd gone rubbery in the chair beside Crawford's desk. "How could he afford to pay all that?"

"Don't know. Neither did he, I guess. The Air Police found him wandering about the grounds in back of the officers' club a night or two later. He was mumbling and spitting up blood. They took him to the base hospital. Later he was flown back to the States."

"That's it?"

"He's at Walter Reed Hospital in Washington. Some say he's had a nervous breakdown."

"Even a general doesn't have money to pay for a thing like that."

"They'll probably make some sort of arrangement with him before he's discharged, give him five or maybe ten years to pay, collect a payment every month."

I had a few other questions, but I saw Crawford was pushing his cap over his eyes and sinking in his chair. "Happy I told you all that stuff?"

"No," I answered. "I think I'd have been better off not knowing."

"So do I."

He was soon asleep, leaving me to picture and picture again the troubles that had led to Williston's downfall. The more I tried to identify differences between me and him, the more aware I became of similarities: age, rank, training and, as if it mattered as much as all the rest, blondness. I left the orderly room and took a walk around the battery area, trying to distance myself from Williston, from Shea, from myself and my fears.

Twelve

˙ /˙ /˙ /˙ /˙ /˙ /

Within a few days every officer in the 46th was carrying a one-and-a-half-foot leather stick wherever he went. Some got them caught in closing doors, some stabbed passersby, some sent them accidentally into moving parts on guns, vehicles and radars. There were reports of near-losses of eyes and hands. I heard grumbles and curses, but no one dared complain.

Each morning Sergeant First Class Leo Bronowski, our battery's supply sergeant, sat on a trash can at the edge of the parking lot, arms crossed, watching Ball, Crawford and me as we stood twisting our sticks while we waited for Grey to call morning formation, give assignments and dismiss the battery. I'd have been less conscious of my swagger stick if it weren't for Bronowski. Every time one of the three of us moved his stick the sergeant's eyes leaped toward it like the tongue of a lizard. Because of Bronowski I started keeping my stick locked under my arm. With little else to do, I began, like him, to be a student of the sticks of the others.

Ball's stick, like the captain himself, was always in motion. He used it like a balancing device. If he spoke to an enlisted man, he leaned back, pushed the stick out in front of himself and gestured. "You there, um . . . um . . . ." Crawford would whisper the man's name to him. "Stillman. Pick up that Snickers wrapper."

76

With each of his words the stick made a darting movement, a jab upward or to the side, a quick visual imitation of the word itself.

Crawford was always, without success, trying to find a place on himself to deposit his new appendage. He tried his back pocket for a while, but the stick didn't go down deep enough, and he had to grab it to keep it from falling out. I suggested he hold it under his arm; he ignored me. He tried sticking it in his belt like a dagger or sword, but when he moved too much it slipped down. One morning he put it in his mouth, clamping it between his teeth at the very center. He looked like a cat with straight whiskers. With both hands free, however, he seemed at last to relax. He looked ridiculous. I hoped he'd pull his stick out of his mouth and start laughing because of the joke he'd made on us. But he didn't. At last his stick had found its place.

Bronowski was hypnotized.

I tried to ignore Crawford. The other officers didn't stare at him, laugh or make comments; why should I? Yet his actions with the stick made us all seem like characters in a Gilbert and Sullivan operetta.

"Watch Flu," Ball said.

Merrill Flu, sluggish and soft-looking, was battalion intelligence officer. I watched. He was certainly the most devoted swagger-stick wearer. Ball claimed he'd passed Flu's office and seen the stick strapped to the captain's left fist while, with his right, he wrote out a memo. At lunch his stick sat on his lap. Sometimes the stick began to slide down, but he grabbed it before it went to the floor. Why he kept it with him every moment I didn't know; at the club the rest of us deposited our sticks on the shelf above the coat rack. Perkins reported that he'd driven past Flu's rented house one evening and seen the captain in his garden wearing civvies. "I waved. When he waved back, the stick was in his hand."

"I hear he polishes it," Captain Buckles, the battalion supply officer, said.

Some said Flu had never excelled in anything during all his years in the Army, and now, a short time before retirement, he was, by God, going to come out on top just once. Others said Flu had simply gotten to like his stick the way people get to like pets. Gilley, whose office was beside Flu's, said he knew for a fact that Flu took the stick to bed, in fact used it to shut off the alarm clock in the morning. There were many stories about Flu.

"The man scares me," Captain Vernor said.

Mark Vernor, a battery commander, was the battalion's only black officer. He often sat alone, eyeing others from behind large round glasses with transparent rims as he puffed on a long-stemmed pipe. When he wasn't present, others spoke of him admiringly. "He's probably the only one around here who isn't afraid of Shea," Gilley told me. Vernor did more listening than talking.

Someone asked Vernor what the remark about Flu meant.

"If Shea told him to make another hole in his head, he'd do it."

"There's truth in that," Gilley put in.

I wondered what Vernor would say if I told him what had happened at the firing range. He was so inscrutable I made no attempt to speak to him, yet was comforted to know someone existed who might not fear the major.

Perkins came up with a joke about Flu: "Flu's wife likes his swagger stick better than him." The first time he spoke it, several officers laughed. Unfortunately he kept saying it, except when Flu was present. He wasn't at all bothered by the others' lessening appreciation.

I found the joke stupid, even offensive, and one day, after he spoke it, I said, "We're all just as ridiculous. Why make fun of him?" I was sure Shea laughed to see his officers prancing like puppies with sticks they'd retrieved. Perkins's joke was nothing compared to the joke the major was pulling on us. Even Vernor, commenting only on Flu's excessive zeal, hadn't questioned the "value" of the sticks.

"What in hell you talking about, lieutenant?"

"The sticks. I don't see how they . . . improve anything, even our appearances."

"That so?" Perkins looked at me as though I'd just told him I'd put molasses in all the gun tubes. I expected a righteous lecture. Instead he snatched up his stick and left the bar area.

Everyone stared at the table or at his beer.

Finally Vernor caught my eye and tilted his head toward the latticed windows in the turret overlooking the lawn behind the bar. I didn't know what he meant until he got up and walked over to the windows, then stood there, looking out.

I got up.

Others at the table, caught in their daydreams or worries, didn't seem to notice.

"What is it?" I said, coming up behind Vernor.

He was, or seemed to be, looking at the tall rushes that surrounded the pond beyond a slope not far from the window. With great deliberation he removed a pipe from the breast pocket of his Ike jacket, tapped it, then reached into his pants pocket and removed a pouch of tobacco. He spoke as he loaded the pipe. "You'd better learn who you can talk to and who you can't."

"Not Perkins?"

"Not Perkins." He was still looking out. We must have looked like a couple of spies exchanging information at a train station. "You show a lot of irritation. What's it all about?"

"I don't think it's irritation. It's . . . something else." I was starting to trust this man, not only because of what I'd heard about him but because of the way he carried himself and the calm way he was now speaking to me. Why couldn't he have been my battery commander? It seemed as though several minutes passed—it may have been only a few seconds—before I said, "I saw, I mean heard, something unusual at the firing range, and I haven't been able to get it off my mind."

He grunted in a way that told me he wanted to hear more.

"I was a witness, I think . . ." I hesitated, eyeing him. ". . . to something . . . well, not in line with regulations."

There was a wooden window seat around the inside of the turret. He'd raised his foot to it, and, with elbow on knee, was still looking out, still seeming to ignore me. "About the way the planes were brought down?"

Did he know too? "Yes," I said. "That's right. It has to do with . . . how they were destroyed."

Now he looked at me. "Do *you* know?"

"I think I know."

"You *think* you do." His eyes seemed to penetrate my forehead. "What's that mean?"

"I heard something, between Major Shea and Captain South. It was sort of . . . well, what the major said was—"

"Stop!"

"Pardon?"

He tapped the air with his pipe. "Don't tell me what you heard. Tell me who else heard it."

"No one else heard it."

He nodded and looked back at the rushes. "Then you didn't hear it." He brought his leg down, checked his watch, looked at me for a second time. "You didn't hear it, and you didn't start to tell me you heard anything, and you're not going to tell anyone else you heard anything. Got it?"

"Why?"

"Because no one else heard what you heard. There are no witnesses."

"Except the major. And Captain South."

"Think about that. Then put the whole thing out of your mind." He stared at me, challenging me, saying with his eyes that I could throw any response at him and he'd give me back the same one he'd just given me. "Understand?"

I knew he wanted me to protect myself. And though I said "Yes," in some deep way I did not understand.

"Good." He reached out and gave me a sharp pat on the upper arm. He smiled, held the smile until I gave him one back, then turned and left the bar.

When I returned to the table only Gilley was there. He soon said something that reinforced Vernor's message: "For Christ's sake, Tom, you're going to have to be careful who you say things to. Perkins is one of the CO's sniffers. Besides, don't you realize what we'd be doing if we weren't busy learning how to live with these things?"

"No."

"Crawling around on some hill out there, pretending to be planting mines under English farmhouses. Or maybe at the gun sites, having contests to see whose battery could make the gun tubes go around fastest. Or maybe seeing which battery could do the best job of painting its grease nipples red. I'd rather take these things." He looked fondly at the stick, which was on his lap, then at me. "I mean, wouldn't you?"

I was sharply disappointed over my near-miss with Vernor. "No," I snapped. "Nothing could be crazier than these goddam sticks." I picked up my check and headed for the cash register.

"Tom," he said from behind.

I turned.

"You think too much. In the Army you've got to know when not to think, which is just about all the time."

Thirteen

◦◦◦◦◦◦◦

During the next few days Vernor's and Gilley's advice sank in. I first resolved not to worry about the swagger sticks. Just as sensible to worry about stripes, hash marks, oak leaves, eagles, stars, braids, patches, medals, crests, belt buckles or even flags. In the Army that would not only be futile but crazy.

I then joined the others. When Shea set up a competition among the batteries to see which one could come up with a Battalion Standing Operating Procedure for the proper display of swagger sticks during inspection (the Army had nothing published on the subject), I didn't smile. I even made suggestions.

"When we come to attention we could do something more original than just holding it out in front of us like a rifle. We could point it toward the sun, wherever that happened to be." I probably wouldn't have made the suggestion if Crawford hadn't earlier come across with one that seemed no better: having the officers stand beside the gun when brigade or European Command inspecting officers came by, then salute by raising the stick at the angle at which the inspected gun was pointing.

Ball had been considering Crawford's suggestion. Now he thought about mine. "Suppose it's after sunset?"

I said, not certain, "Are there ever outdoor inspections after dark?"

His face seemed to sink, which meant he was thinking hard. "I guess not," he said. "But suppose it's raining?"

Crawford reminded him that inspections were held indoors when the weather threatened.

"That's true." He sat down in Crawford's chair, and his eyes circled the room. "But it still doesn't solve the problem. If there are clouds or if you're indoors, how would you know where the sun is?"

"Shouldn't an officer be able to know where the sun is at all times?" I said.

They looked at me but said nothing. Within minutes Ball took himself out of Crawford's chair and walked slowly to his office. He kept the door open, which meant he felt no great crisis, was just mulling over something.

Crawford went out to one of the gun sites, to stand beside a weapon and test his inspection theory. He came back with a disappointed look. "No good," he said. "If the gun tube happens to be pointing away from the entrance to the gun pit and you turn and point your swagger stick that way, you'd be turning your back on the inspecting officer."

Ideas were coming out of me like machine-gun bullets. "You point the guns toward the entrance to the gun pits, so that both the gun and the officer are saluting toward the arriving inspector?"

"No good," said Crawford, who'd opened his shirt collar and sent his stick down his back to scratch it. "You can't point a weapon at a superior officer."

"How about *above* the inspector?"

"No. Our gun tubes tend to shimmy down." He took Ball's place in his chair. "I'm kind of soured on my own idea anyway," he went on. "An arm would get mighty sore holding a stick straight out for any length of time."

Ball came out of his office, his mouth sliced into a smile. He sat down on the side of my desk. "You were right about that, Hanlon," he said.

"About what, sir?"

"Knowing where the sun is supposed to be at all times. Every officer should. Especially if he's responsible for planning an attack or defending against one. You just *have* to know. Watches don't tell you exactly where the sun is. You never want to attack into the sun, if you can help it."

Crawford listened, frowning. "What the heck are you talking about, captain?"

"The way to salute with the sticks when there's no sun."

Crawford nodded as if he understood perfectly.

"Anyway, Hanlon, I have the solution." He explained that Battery A's proposal would be to keep the swagger stick snappily under the left armpit while at attention, then to bring it horizontally out to the front with the right hand at the command "Present arms," thereupon bringing the left hand over the top of the right and sliding it smartly upward along the stick, finally stopping and holding the stick toward the inspector.

"Yes!" said Crawford. "The inspector could reach between both hands and snatch it."

Ball snapped his fingers. "Exactly."

"But I don't know," Crawford went on. "There's still something wrong with it."

"Well, for God's sake, tell me what!"

"I don't know. I have to think about it."

Ball and I watched Crawford think.

"Oh oh," he said suddenly.

"What?" said Ball, alarmed.

Crawford looked up. "I'd rather not say."

"Say!"

"I'd prefer not to."

"Say it!"

"Well, captain . . ." He looked about to be sure we were the only ones in the orderly room. "When you slide that left hand up the stick, it'll look like . . ." He leaned toward Ball and me and whispered: " . . .you're playing with yourself."

"Damn!" Ball wheeled around. "Damn!" He shuffled to his office and kicked the door shut behind him.

Crawford turned. "Didn't he ask me to say it?"

I nodded.

Crawford and I sat at our desks, separately working on the procedure.

Finally the captain's door opened. He stood in the doorway. "We're going to stay with my method," he announced.

"I'm relieved," said Crawford.

So was I. The God I sometimes believed in surely didn't want me to spend any more time worrying about how to present swagger sticks, probably didn't even want me to have one.

"Write up a swagger-stick drill, Mike. We'll practice it before sending it on to the major."

On my way to the latrine a few minutes later, I heard a gun sergeant say to Bronowski at the supply-room door, "What the hell was the exec doing out at my gun site this morning?"

"Dunno," said Bronowski, speaking, as usual, in near-grunts.

"He told my radar man right in the middle of morning orientation to turn the gun tube this way and that, and his hand was up with that thing in it, moving it around the sky."

"What thing?"

"That brown thing they've all been carrying around lately. Looks like one of those long, fake cigars people sometimes have as a joke."

Finishing at the urinal, I heard Bronowski's voice come booming through the walls: "Goddam craziness!" he shouted, speaking very clearly for once. Then he said something else, several things, just as passionately, but I couldn't make them out.

Ball was standing at the supply-room door when I came out. "What in the world is going on in there?" he asked Bronowski.

"Nothing," Bronowski replied politely. "Just banged my head on something hard."

"Well, control yourself, sergeant. Language like that sets a bad example for the other troops."

"Yes, sir," Bronowski mumbled.

Three days later there was big news at the officers' club: the manual of arms for swagger sticks submitted by First Lieutenant

Stanley Pryzbyskowski and Battery B had been approved by Shea.

The first lieutenant and his assistants had come up with a simple method: at the command "Present arms!" the officer raised the tip of the stick to his forehead straight up from the side, cutting down on the possibility of hitting someone.

Perkins and Gilley took turns standing and practicing beside the 46th's table until finally Gilley struck his eyeball instead of his forehead.

"What do we talk about now?" someone asked anxiously.

Ball suddenly turned to Perkins and said, "Let's guess what he's got planned for us next."

Everyone turned to Perkins.

"He's been staying in his office," the captain replied with a frown. "Acting very private."

"Why?" said Ball.

"He's been reading a lot of stuff from brigade. Probably classified. Otherwise he wouldn't close the door. He's been keeping the door closed."

"I've seen it closed," Gilley put in. "I don't like the look of that."

"Maybe we're going on a field exercise," Ball said. "God, I *hate* field exercises!"

"Me too," said Flu.

"Does he seem angry?" Ball wanted to know.

"He seems . . . what's the word? You know, when someone's thinking a lot."

"Pensive," I said.

Perkins turned to Crawford. "I knew the kid had something positive to contribute once in a while. Anyway, I haven't seen the boss that way before, so I don't know what it means."

"Maybe it has to do with Hanlon's test," Ball suggested.

Suddenly they were all looking at me.

I tried to appear indifferent, though my guts were tightening.

"I'd hate to have anyone, especially him, spending that much time working on a test for me." It was Ball, ever reassuring.

"I doubt it has to do with him," Perkins said. "It probably has something to do with the stuff he's been getting from brigade."

"That means it has to do with all of us," Ball suggested.

"I'd say so."

I wasn't much relieved. Sooner or later I'd have a test. The sooner the better.

There followed not only silence but stillness, as if the world had frozen and we were stuck forever in place. I imagined explorers from another planet landing. Their Earth scholars, having received information from spaceship scouts for decades or maybe centuries, would quickly determine we were a bunch of officers having after-duty drinks. What it would take them years to figure out would be the kind of expression they found on everyone's face. Finally an Earth scholar would enhance his reputation by defining the syndrome: "Unfocused apprehension: nervous energy dissipated in air; a condition unique to *Homo sapiens*." My fantasy was broken when Gilley slid his chair back, making it screech.

"This may surprise some of you," he announced, "but I'm having another beer."

"May as well get a pitcher," said Perkins.

There were nods. The others started putting scrip on the table.

I stood and left.

I walked around the manor house to the garden at the back. The sun was reaching, speckled, through the leaves of an ancient oak which stood about twenty yards beyond the latticed windows of the bar. The lawn descended over a mound to a small pond. I'd frequently looked at it from my window. From there the water, full of shiny lily pads, seemed clean and still. I moved down the far side of the mound and stood at the edge of the pond. I couldn't hear voices from the bar or the sounds of planes or vehicles on the air base. A cooling breeze spread upward, bearing with it a faint sweet fragrance. For several minutes I forgot that I was on a military installation. I imagined I wasn't in the Army at all. Finally the harsh laughter from the club bar broke over the mound and into my reverie. I turned and started back to the club.

I was very tired. There seemed no reason to return to the bar. I went up the broad staircase and down the narrow hall to my room. I took off my uniform, put on my soft civilian pajamas, ones I hadn't worn since arriving at Newbury. They were far more comfortable than my olive-green Army long johns, woolly uglies I'd purchased at Bliss. I fell asleep quickly.

Fourteen

"Ah ha," said Ball from his office the next morning. "Here it is." He signaled to Crawford and me by waving a memo he'd plucked from the morning mail and read. "Come in here. Close the door behind you."

By the time I'd closed the door and was seated beside Crawford, the captain had moved to his window and was gazing out, nodding.

"What's it all about, captain?" said Crawford.

Ball turned the sheet around and pushed it across his desk. We leaned over and read:

On orders from headquarters, 32nd AAA Brigade, the 46th AAA Battalion will prepare selected 75-millimeter weapons for transfer to other battalions within Brigade Command. These weapons will be exchanged, one for one. Exchange will be completed five days from the date of this memorandum. Lieutenant Thomas Hanlon, 2nd Lt /Arty, will be convoy commander. Other directives follow.

"The test," Crawford said without taking any time to think about it. "This is Hanlon's test."

It seemed an immense assignment. Yet I felt no fear, no anxiety. If anything, I was relieved. "How many guns are involved?" I asked.

Neither knew. "We'll be getting information little by little," Crawford told me. "That's the major's way. Unfold things like in a mystery novel."

The captain gazed at me. "I'd hate to be in your shoes."

I often felt the same way about him.

"You know what kills me, Mike," he went on. "This means we'll probably have to give up our best guns and get some dogs in return."

"They just want to make sure the defense is all evened out," Crawford explained. "It's because of the firing results. They're taking some of our good guns and exchanging them for some of the others' bad ones."

"It's not fair," said Ball. "Let those other bastards work on their guns and get them to function." He was looking at me, for support.

Unable to tell him what I knew about our guns, I only shrugged. It was a gesture he probably expected, a second lieutenant's gesture.

He sighed, and his eyes fell once more to the memo.

If Shea's deception was resulting in the exchange of our weapons for those now in other battalions throughout England, there'd surely be other consequences. Maybe Shea would be asked to write guidelines to be used in seventy-five units all over the world.

Ball paced about his office.

Crawford reread the memo.

Maybe the brigade commander, having been persuaded through Shea that the seventy-five was an effective antiaircraft weapon, had canceled plans to request more effective weapons of some sort, presuming such existed.

"Why are you tapping at the bottom of my desk, Hanlon?"

I hadn't noticed.

"Do you have to go to the bathroom or something?"

"No, sir. I was just thinking about . . . my new assignment."

"Oh." He nodded, as if he understood. He was walking a groove into the floor. "The whole thing is disgusting, isn't it?"

"It *is*," I said emphatically.

He came to a halt, gave me a troubled frown, went on pacing.

Now and then, reading a textbook or hearing an instructor lecture, I'd pass over a crucially significant word or phrase, not know it was significant until it recurred in the textbook's or instructor's summary, or on a test. In a required political science course taught by a fiery Jesuit at the University of San Francisco, The Dynamics and Tactics of World Communism, we were told, again and again, that the imperialist intentions of World Communism, directed from the Comintern in Moscow, never varied; they were and would always be the total subjugation of humanity to Atheistic Communism. I'd not only heard Father Glynn say that but had read it in the textbook he used: *When Do We Face Them? Now or Later?* Even the illustration on the dust jacket—a bald eagle tearing through a red hammer-and-sickle flag—reminded me. I began reading "outside material," newspapers and magazines that took a more liberal, and, I thought, rational, view of the Soviets. Father Glynn and my liberal "outside" readings had so soured me on a monolithic view of Communism, each for a different reason, that I decided to work for the election of the more liberal of the two Presidential candidates, Adlai Stevenson. In any case, when the priest gave his midterm test, one of the multiple-choice questions was "How often do Communist intentions vary? (a) always, (b) never, (c) frequently, (d) occasionally." Caught between Father Glynn and his textbook on the one hand and my developing liberalism on the other, I circled (d). When Glynn returned my test, I saw, written small at the top, "Grade: 96"; but several inches below there was a large red circle around the word "never." His circle made all the answers I'd gotten right seem less important than the one I'd gotten wrong.

Yet even if I'd been right, even if the Soviets were only an occasional threat, what right had Shea to mock the defense of the SAC bases in England by perpetrating through fraud the false notion that our antiaircraft guns could shoot down enemy planes?

Crawford read the memo again. "It's a rotten job," he said, looking across at me. "Dangerous and dirty. You've got to haul those monsters all over England, plant them in gun pits, pick up and secure the ones they replace, then make your way back. I'd rather lead the whole battalion to the firing range. On this job you've got to wiggle through unfamiliar towns and cities to get to the other bases. All sorts of chances for things to go wrong."

"You're a great comfort," I told him.

His remark about the towns and cities reminded me that American military higher-ups weren't the only ones being deceived about the seventy-five. So were the British. Our secondary mission was to defend them. Some defense! I decided that the notorious British atomic spy Klaus Fuchs could not, through his years of deception, have carried his haunted knowledge more fearfully than I at that moment was carrying mine.

"Captain," I said, having felt stomach pains I was sure were like pains Whitey had felt, "I don't feel very good. Do you mind if I go back to my quarters?"

"Hanlon," he replied flatly, "right now I don't give a damn where you go. Just be sure to take your stick."

I picked up my cap and swagger stick and moved out of the orderly room as quickly as my cramping stomach would permit.

Fifteen

~~~~~~

"**S**tand at ease, Hanlon."

Pinned to the wall behind the major's desk was a map of England. A transparent overlay had been placed on top of it. In red grease pencil someone had drawn a thick oval-shaped line. At the bottom was a dot and beside it were printed the words GREENHAM COMMON. On the lower right part of the oval was another red-printed identification: UPPER HEYFORD; near the top another: BRIZE NORTON; toward the left another: FAIRFORD. These were the U.S. Strategic Air Command bases in Great Britain, the locations of seventy-five-millimeter Sky-sweeper battalions.

After telling me to stand at ease, the major used the tip of a pointer to move about the oval. "Normally this trip could be made in twelve or thirteen hours going at convoy speed," he said, sounding impatient. "Because of the drop-off and pickup of weapons—four to go, four to come back—it'll take longer. I'm giving you twenty hours. Here are the papers showing the men and equipment you'll be taking." He took several sheets of paper from the open folder that lay on top of the desk. They were mimeographed and stapled together. "Sit down and take a look at them." As I was lowering myself, he said, "Where's your swagger stick?"

"On the coat rack outside your office, sir."

He nodded, leaned forward and began fingering through other sheets in his folder, speaking to me at the same time. "You'll have less than a week to prepare. I want a progress report from you each day."

He slid papers from the right side of the folder to the left, back again, looking for something. I'd noticed dark pockets under his eyes. His hair seemed grayer than it had last time I'd seen him up close. He was breathing noisily. He found the paper he was looking for, and with a mechanical pencil made changes on it. Finally he looked up.

"Atomic-bomb protesters have been active in Oxford recently," he said, "so we've arranged for a police escort there. Nothing those folks would like better than to jam up your convoy on one of the narrow streets."

We'd passed through Oxford on the way to the firing range. I'd looked from the jeep's windshield and plastic side windows but had seen only a few dark stone buildings.

"Any questions?"

"No, sir. But I would like to make a request."

"What request?"

"I really don't think I'm the right person for this assignment and ask that you find someone else."

He threw the pointer onto his desk with a pushing motion. "What in hell kind of a statement is that?"

Only minutes earlier, as I'd walked from Battery A to battalion headquarters, I'd decided to ask to be replaced. I knew that if he granted my request, my later test would be even more difficult. I didn't care. "It's not a matter of the job being too hard. It's a matter of . . . well, I'll have to say, conscience."

"Conscience?" he said as if he'd never heard the word.

"It's something I'd rather not have to explain. It has to do with . . . the guns. I'd prefer just to leave it at that."

He paced around his desk, stopped behind my chair. I could feel his eyes on my skull. "Conscience," he repeated. He returned to his desk. "Man comes in, says, I want out of a job, says it's a matter of conscience, then says, heh, I can't tell you why just now except that it has to do with the guns. Have you suddenly become a conscientious objector?"

"No, sir. Maybe, at some later time, when I, if I . . ."

". . . feel more relaxed?"

"Something like that. I would like, sometime, to explain my position."

He slid his swivel chair toward me and said, "I promise you'll get the chance. Now . . . have you looked over those papers I handed you when you came in here?"

I glanced down. "Just briefly, sir. I . . . was sort of concentrating on . . . my request."

"You've had plenty of time to go over them." There was no urgency or threat in his tone. He was simply informing me. "I'm going to have them distributed as they are." He stood, brushed something off the front of his Ike jacket, went to the coffee machine, on a small table at the side of his office, and poured himself half a cup. "I want you to make an inspection of each of the guns I designated for transfer." He came back, put the cup on his desk. "Do that today, then tell the crew chiefs involved to make necessary repairs. Tomorrow morning hold a meeting of the personnel I've assigned to you and go over their assignments. You've got a few days to get ready. You'd better make a schedule and show it to me for approval. Use the jeep from Headquarters Battery outside this building. Use it until your convoy assignment is completed. Any questions?"

It all seemed clear and precise, but what did that matter when the entire gun exchange shouldn't even be taking place? "I don't, about your instructions. I do about what I was saying a couple of minutes ago."

"You want out of the convoy."

"Yes, but not just to get out of work or anything."

"Conscience."

"Yes, sir."

"Denied," he snapped. "Now, unless you intend to refuse to take the convoy assignment, in which case I'll have you court-martialed, please leave my office and start making preparations."

The mention of a court-martial chilled me to silence. I found myself nodding.

"Dismissed," he said coldly.

I rose, saluted (he didn't even see me), shuffled out of his office and made my way to the parking lot. The jeep he'd mentioned was parked there. I got into it, started it and pulled out of the lot. I intended to go to the gun sites but had driven about twenty yards when I noticed the papers he'd given me lying on the seat beside me. I realized I'd better read them carefully before going to the sites. I turned back and swung the jeep into the snack bar across the road from battalion headquarters.

Louis Prima's voice was coming out of the juke box, singing "When You're in Love." I liked the song but just now couldn't appreciate it. Every other male in the place seemed to be ogling a pretty auburn-haired girl busing tables. I purchased two dough-nuts and a cup of coffee, took them to a small table near the counter, then noticed that the table had no sugar dispenser or cream container. I didn't bother searching for another table, just sat down and began sipping the coffee, black. My great issue of conscience unresolved, I began looking at the papers the major had given me.

Four guns were to be transferred. All of the weapons in the battalion had numbers, and I recognized them from the numbers that Shea was sending the most troublesome of the weapons that had scored passably at the range. There would surely arise problems when we removed them from the gun pits, problems when we towed them, problems when we tried to put them down on the other bases. And if all that could be done, there'd be problems when the other battalions tried to make them work.

I turned to the second sheet, which contained the names of the other convoy personnel, saw immediately that Sergeant Bronowski, sullen Leo Bronowski of Battery A, had been named assistant convoy commander. He communicated in grunts and seemed to hate all officers. Other names I recognized included a corporal in Battery B known as "the Drunk." (He'd been arrested twice in Newbury, and once each in Reading and Lon-

don, each time for causing disturbances in public places.)
Another was a corporal from C who periodically had nervous fits
resulting from nightmares in which he saw his wife making love
to other men. (She'd twice traveled to England to be with him,
but both times he had terrible attacks, resembling nervous
breakdowns, and refused to see her. The attacks lasted until she
got on a plane or boat and went back home; as soon as she left, he
recovered. Soon he sent for her again.) Another, a private first
class from B, had chronically gone AWOL and, as a result, had
spent nearly half his time with the 46th in the guardhouse.
(Would I have to chain him to a truck?) Finally I saw the name
O'Hara, and recognized the cook Ball refused to let stand guard
in the parking lot. He was probably the worst.

There were many stories about O'Hara. The most recent I'd
heard had to do with the latest brigade inspection. The inspecting officer had ordered every soldier in the battalion to disassem-
ble and lay out for viewing the three major parts of his M-1 rifle.
O'Hara must have missed the "three major parts" section of the
order, for when the inspecting officer arrived at his barracks,
there sat the cook with every little screw and wire and spring
from his rifle sitting on the kitchen apron that lay across his lap.
The tiny pieces of the separate major parts were never to be
taken apart except by trained ordnance people. Not aware of
what had happened, O'Hara's battery commander at the time,
Captain Bottoms of Headquarters Battery, led the inspector to
O'Hara's bed at the corner of the barracks and, surprised to see
O'Hara sitting down, shouted, "Attention!" O'Hara, startled,
jumped to his feet. Hundreds of minute pieces of the rifle flew
across the room, some finding their way into cracks in the floor
and openings in heating vents. The rifle had, of course, been
ruined. Now, on each payday, ten dollars was being taken from
O'Hara's paycheck for the purchase of another.

I closed my eyes and tried to enjoy the music now coming
from the juke box. It was from the movie *Shane*, pleasant music,
but I couldn't relax. I tried to distract myself by watching the
pretty serving girl, who was again picking up empty coffee cups

and plates. If she approached my table, I'd say something about the weather. She didn't approach and soon vanished into the kitchen area. Somewhere nearby, someone, maybe she, dropped an armload of plates; they made a great crash.

I got up and left.

Sixteen

.·.·*.·*.·*.·*

T
he worst of the guns to be transferred was Sergeant Rivera's. Its radar and computer acted up even when the power switch was turned off. It was usually the last to be oriented and synchronized each day. Sometimes O&S couldn't be done. With the help of South and his hidden button, however, it had achieved a passable score.

After the firing Rivera's gun wouldn't lower its gun tube to less than forty-five degrees.

Gilley had spent several days trying to get the tube to go down; he couldn't. "This is like looking for an answer when you don't even know what the question is," he said at the officers' club bar, when he was saturating himself with beer the evening before he had to report his failure to Shea. "The power drive's okay, the gears don't seem to be broken, and it's had plenty of lubrication. It just won't go down." After he'd had about a dozen beers, Gilley's conversations became extended monologues, which bar companions or passersby could tune into and out of as they wished. "You think he's going to believe that? He's not going to believe that. He's going to say, 'Gill, you're ordnance, for Christ sake! An ordnance man is supposed to fix guns.' He's liable to put me out there with a sleeping bag like that Manilla or Minolli. Huh. He can put me out there all year, and I still won't be able to make that tube go down. . . ."

I nodded a couple of times, but I don't think he noticed me.

I stopped at the site of the gun with the tube that wouldn't descend.

"Are you sure the CO wants this one?" Sergeant Rivera said.

"I'm sure," I told him. I showed him the order designating his gun for transfer.

"It's hard to believe," he said, shrugging. "Who's going to take her?"

"Maybe no one."

What was I supposed to tell Colonel Potts, the battalion commander at Upper Heyford, scheduled to receive Rivera's monster? "Perhaps this is a special model, sir. It only shoots at high-flying aircraft."

"Bad as she is, I bet the next one will be worse. Anyway, I don't want to have to dig her out again." The sergeant's wrist was taped. He'd suffered a sprain while trying to hold down a pedestal arm during one of his crew's several attempts to get the weapon back into the pit after the firing. He saw me looking at his wrist, said, "You think this is bad? I got two guys still in the infirmary, one with a broken foot and one with a torn muscle in his stomach. She fought us all the way down. Hate to see what she's gonna do when we try to get her up again."

I told him I'd ask Shea whether or not he'd substitute another gun for his.

"The crew and me will appreciate that, lieutenant. I guarantee."

I spent most of the afternoon moving from site to site. The sergeants and crews whose weapons had been chosen were, in general, resentful. "What are we gonna get in return?" Sergeant Curry asked. "Something that works? No way! Why don't they just leave well enough alone?" I didn't dare tell him his gun was no better than the one for which it was being exchanged.

At the end of the day I left Shea a memo requesting that another weapon be substituted for Rivera's. If Shea said yes, I might ask for other substitutions.

Yet my work was wearying and pointless. In the end, I was

sure, the defenses at Strategic Air Command bases would remain the same. The guns didn't work. Wasn't there a seventy-five-millimeter battalion commander somewhere in the world willing to pick up a phone and call his brigade or division commander and say, "Let's just stop the nonsense and admit we've been slicked by a gun manufacturer"? Why didn't I pick up my phone and say that to Shea? Fear. Fear, I supposed, was everyone's excuse. I pictured myself calling *Stars & Stripes* and the *London Times*, telling them to send reporters to the base, then taking them from gun to gun, showing them how bad the weapons were. Headlines would follow:

WORTHLESS GUNS
WASTE MILLIONS

Army Lieutenant
Uncovers Fraud

For a while I was brave in my vision, but soon I imagined an aftermath: arrest, trial, conviction. A year earlier the Rosenbergs had been convicted and executed as spies. My imagination took flight. What the government had done to the Rosenbergs they could surely do to me:

TRAITOR HANGED!

I advised myself back to reality, which meant turning off my mind and preparing worthless guns for a meaningless exchange.

Sergeant Bird surprised me by saying, "I don't think my gun got all the hits he gave it credit for." Round and red-haired, he stood beside his tool shack, opened the breast pocket of his fatigue jacket and removed a pack of Lucky Strikes. He smoked continuously. Even when he was in the gun pit, there was a smoking butt balanced on something outside. He held the pack toward me.

I shook my head. "What do you mean, you didn't get all the hits you were credited for?"

He lit his cigarette, held it in the air between us, then slightly raised the hand with his lighter in it, pointing it toward the cigarette. "Say this lighter is the gun." He lowered his eyes to the lighter. "And say this is the target plane." He raised his eyes to the cigarette. "Now look at the way I got them moving." He was moving both the cigarette and lighter horizontally. "What do you see?"

"The lighter is pointed at the cigarette, whereas it should be pointed ahead and a little above or below, depending on whether the cigarette is going up or down."

"You got it, lieutenant. But this is the way it looked to me when my gun was shooting. Nearly every time. Even when I was able to pick up the tracers, they looked like they were going in behind the plane." He tilted his head thoughtfully. "I admit it was hard to tell. My gun wasn't ever the only one firing at a given time. But when I saw my own tracers—I'm pretty sure they were mine—they weren't going anywhere near the target."

I asked him if the other crew chiefs had the same impression as he.

"If they did, they weren't talking about it," he said. "Most of them bragged like their guns got the planes they shot at. Maybe they did. How do I know?"

"Did you mention your suspicion to Lieutenant Pryzbys-kowski?"

"Why take away his happiness? He worked hard for us. I don't want him to feel bad that his gun isn't as good as he thinks."

After listening to him for a few more minutes, I realized he wasn't really interested in who shot down what. Like Rivera, he didn't want himself or his crew to have to dig out his gun, send it to another base, then dig in the one he'd be given to replace it. "Maybe the boss can find someone else's."

I told him I thought there was little chance Shea would change his mind. I said I'd requested that Rivera's gun be replaced but had gotten no reply. I doubted I'd produce anything but anger if I appealed for him as well. "Maybe," I suggested, "you could make a direct appeal to the CO." As I saw it, that was Bird's only chance.

"Are you kidding?" He flipped his cigarette onto the gravel between us, crushed it out with the toe of his combat boot. "You know what I do when I see that man coming anywhere near me?"

"What?"

"I turn all the way around, no matter where I am, all the way around so I'm facing the other way, and I make myself smile. Then I turn back around. I want him to see me smiling, like I'm saying to him, 'Yes, sir, this is Sergeant Bird, a happy man, happy in his battery, happy in his battalion, happy in his brigade, happy in England.' I figured him out, lieutenant. If you look like you're weak or sick or sad or anything like that, he goes after you. He goes after complainers especially. That's why I'm not going to ask him to leave my gun here." The comment had turned into a speech, and he was gesturing now with both hands. He flapped the hands toward himself. "I got a wife and a little tiny kid, a girl, with carrot-colored hair just like mine. They're back in the States. I haven't seen the kid since she was two months old. Also, I only got another year to go. That's all, just one."

"Okay, I get the point."

He went on, "I can't talk to the man. Not only about my gun. About anything. All I can do when I'm around him is try to smile." He smiled at me to demonstrate. He had brown teeth with spaces between them. His smile was a mournful grimace. If Shea had noticed the smile, he must have thought Bird had just received bad news.

"It looks like your gun has to go," I told him.

"Why?" said Sergeant Berman at the next site I visited. "These guns, every single one of them, sir, have personalities. I mean they're actually sort of people themselves. That's the real problem with transferring them. I know every quirk this baby has. I'll give you an example. In the tech manual it says, 'Lubricate the rotating gears before performing O&S.' But with my gun, you don't do it that way. If you do, grease squirts all over the place when you do O&S. That doesn't happen with Peters's gun or with Bird's gun or with Rivera's or with anyone else's gun. Just with mine. Theirs don't squirt. They can lubricate before O&S. I've got to lubricate afterwards."

"Maybe there's something wrong with the gears, or the lubrication you're using."

"No, lieutenant." He was short and wore thick glasses. Because of his stocky build, he reminded me of a football coach. He looked at my feet and held up one finger. "Try to understand. It's the same with everything. Take paint. Other guns take paint straight out of the cans they give us. Not mine. I have to mix the paint they give me with a lot of thinner, almost fifty-fifty. If you take a close look, you'll see that my gun shines a little differently than the others. That paint in the can is supposed to be pre-mixed. It doesn't stick on my gun."

There was no gun close enough to his for me to compare.

"Also, one of the sections of my platform is loose, and when you set the gun up for firing, you have to put an extra bolt in so it doesn't wobble under the gunners' feet. You have to put it in a special place. I know just where to put it."

"I see."

"Also, one of the two cylinders that feeds live rounds to the loader-rammer works a little more slowly than the other." The cylinders were part of the gun's magazine, each alternately feeding a round to a mechanical arm, which rapidly shot the round into the breech. "As a result, I have to have one gunner stand with his hand on the fast cylinder during firing, making sure it moves at the same speed as the other one. If I didn't do that, two rounds could be sent to the breech, one on top of the other, then—boom!—I've no longer got a gun or crew. Or me."

"You'd better write that down," I told him. "The crew chief who's going to receive this weapon needs to know that. Those other things too."

He shrugged, hands open. "How am I supposed to get her ready and write everything down, lieutenant? It'll take me longer than we have. Weeks. Listen, who is supposed to figure out that with this gun on a cold day you have to put a heating pad, like the kind you use for your back, on top of both the azimuth and elevation power controls before switching on the power from the generator? Two heating pads, therefore. On no other gun do you have to do that. Only on this one. I had to buy the heating pads myself at the PX. This gun has arthritis."

I wondered if the brigade commander or Shea or whoever had the power to make a change ought to be reminded of the singular characteristics of each weapon and the danger of breaking up the more or less intimate relationship between it and its chief and crew. I shared the thought with Berman and added, "Maybe I ought to suggest transferring not only the weapons but the chiefs and crews too."

He jumped back, alarmed, as if I'd just suggested we light a couple of cigarettes, then go over and start filling the generator with gasoline. "Don't do that. Okay?"

"Just a thought."

He shook his head. "As hard as it's going to be to get used to another gun, I'll do it. I don't want to have to get used to a new CO. As bad as the old man is, he's like the guns: I know how he works; I know what to expect." He was holding one of my sleeves. "I'll get used to a new gun." He turned, pointed to his gun. "This one no one will get used to. But . . . that's their problem. Right?"

I said I supposed it was. I reminded him to write down all the special characteristics of his seventy-five and made a note to tell the other crew chiefs to do the same thing.

"I will, lieutenant," he said. "I'll start this afternoon." He'd given me wary looks after I suggested transferring chiefs and crews as well as guns. Before I left his site he said, "If you come up with any more ideas, why don't you try them out on me first? Maybe they'll be good. Who knows? Maybe not so good. It's better to try them out on someone first."

"I'll try them out on you," I promised.

Later I found Gilley at the far end of the bar. I started toward him, but Pryzbyskowski reached up from one of the tables and said, "Leave him be." I turned.

Vernor shook his head. "He won't even know you're here." I sank into a chair beside him.

"Been through hell," Perkins said. "The CO's door was open, and I heard a lot of it."

Looking across, I saw Gilley weaving on his stool and gesturing with both hands, drunk.

"You 'member what it was like caddying? We'd go down there that place near Teaneck. . . . Hell, you wouldn't know that. How would someone like you know about Teaneck?" On he went, telling Reggie, the regular bartender, what it was like growing up in New Jersey during Depression days, when he caddied for rich industrialists and, later, worked with convicts as a member of the Civilian Conservation Corps. He was miles and years away.

Reggie polished glasses and now and then nodded politely.

"It was a fearful session," Perkins whispered. "I could hear the boss comparing him to bugs and worms and banging walls and furniture."

For the remainder of the afternoon no one but the bartender said a word to Gilley.

The following morning I found a handwritten note on my desk:

Hanlon-
Rivera's gun goes. Don't ask about his or any others again. You'll be signing a statement at each base saying the "transfers" are combat-ready. It's in your interest to make sure they are.

Shea
CO

Here it was, just hours before I was supposed to leave with the guns, and nothing seemed right. I dragged myself and the bad news about substitutions to my jeep and once more set off to check on the condition of men, weapons and vehicles. I'd never been less certain that I could carry out an assigned task.

Seventeen

At 0420 on a chilly morning, Captain Arvin Cogswell, all 280 pounds of him, stood wheezing before the hood of the five-ton gun carrier parked just behind my jeep. "Start, you son of a bitch!" he shouted, grabbing the steel grating that covered the radiator, then pushing and pulling until the truck moved slightly. He turned and said, "You should have called me yesterday."

I'd tried calling him at the motor pool the previous afternoon. His dispatcher said he'd gone home for the day and didn't want to be disturbed.

I told him about yesterday's call.

"I'll fire that stupid dumbbell," he said.

Sergeant Bronowski and I had minutes before walked the line of parked vehicles. We'd found the Drunk, Private Billy Harwell, missing. Bronowski had sent two Battery B crew members to the barracks area in the food carrier to search for him. We'd also found a flat tire on Bronowski's trailing jeep. Now the lead gun carrier, a five-ton, wouldn't start.

"What do we do, captain?" I said, trying not to sound anxious.

He coughed loudly, spraying a cold mist over my face, removed a wrinkled half-pack of Pall Mall cigarettes from his field-jacket pocket, lit one of the cigarettes with a stick match, coughed again (this time I evaded the mist) and, through the cough, said, "General Motors carburetors aren't worth a damn!" Smoking and coughing, he managed to add, "I'm waiting for that brainless grease-ass Turner." Turner was one of his motor-pool mechanics. He mumbled something else, but the cough was so bad I didn't hear what he said.

I'd called Cogswell from a runway phone after the gun car-rier's driver told me he couldn't get the five-ton started. I myself had listened to the truck's ticka-ticka noise and could make no sense of it.

I checked my watch. Two more minutes had passed. "I have to be off the base in less than seven minutes," I told the captain. There was no time to unhook the gun and bring another truck into place.

"That's your goddam problem," he said.

Departure time was important because of the arrangements for escort through Oxford and traffic arrangements at other places.

Worry had kept me awake until 0100. When I finally did sleep, I kept waking up. At 0230 I stayed awake, rattling off the names of checkpoints, times of arrival and departure, names of convoy personnel, British traffic regulations, radio call signals, etc. I hadn't anticipated a missing man or a truck that wouldn't start.

Though Cogswell had minutes ago slammed shut the truck's hood, he was now hammering it, trying to get it open.

Even if Turner or someone did fix the five-ton, would it hold up until we returned?

I'd been warned that breakdowns on the narrow English roads were often disasters, producing clogged traffic, angry English-men and furious commanding officers. A few days earlier Perkins had told me about a lieutenant who'd been riding in the cab of a lone truck towing a seventy-five. His driver had increased his speed, wanting to get back to base in time to change and meet his girlfriend at a nearby pub. He'd taken a turn too fast, causing the gun to topple. The radar antenna and the loader rammer had been crushed and there was internal damage to the computer. After a Report of Survey, the lieutenant (who else?)

was found pecuniarily responsible for the astounding amount of $210,000. I was carrying four guns, not one. Four times $210,000 equaled $840,000. And the damned things didn't even work!

The food carrier, a three-quarter-ton, came speeding across the main runway and screeched to a stop beside me. The driver leaned out and said, "Lieutenant, they got Harwell back there." His thumb was raised toward the truck's bed. "Passed out. What do we do with him?"

"Uh . . . put him in back of one of the troop carriers. On the floor so he doesn't fall out."

"They think he's going to throw up pretty soon."

Let him fall out, I thought, but I said, "Put him near the tail-gate."

"Yes, sir." The driver spun the truck into a turn and headed down the line of vehicles.

I turned, surveyed the jagged line, saw, near the end, the weapon with the locked gun tube, pointed disdainfully upward. I saw a headlight flickering. I heard the men in the troop carrier nearest me arguing violently. (Suppose a fight broke out when we were traveling and injuries resulted. Would I have to pay for those?) Someone in another vehicle shouted, "When are we gonna get this show on the road?"

I checked my watch. Four minutes remained before scheduled departure.

I might have to have the five-ton and its gun pushed to the side, go without them—a failure before I'd even started.

Another minute fled by.

Corporal Turner appeared, running toward us from the motor pool about a hundred yards from where we were parked. He was carrying a toolbox. He wore no hat, and his yellow hair was twisted to one side. When he got closer I saw that his fatigue jacket was on inside out and his eyes were only partly open. He made his way to Cogswell, who was at my side, snorting. "Not my fault," he said, ducking past the captain. "Start it," he told the five-ton driver.

As the driver tried to, Turner opened the hood, climbed onto the bumper, lowered his head over the spinning fan as if he intended to decapitate himself. "Again," he said. I heard only ticking sounds. Turner's toolbox was still in front of the truck. He removed a screwdriver from his pocket. Using the screwdriver's handle, he hammered something. He then reversed the screwdriver and started twisting it. He reached around the screwdriver and slapped something. He raised his head and said, "Again."

The driver pressed the starter. The engine hummed.

"Gun it!"

The driver pressed the accelerator and the engine roared.

Turner put his screwdriver back into his pocket, jumped off the bumper and closed the hood. He made a shadow-boxing move in front of Cogswell, darted around him and picked up his toolbox.

I looked at my watch. We had, amazingly, two minutes left.

"Sir," I said, "I'd like to take Turner with me." Not a single motor-pool mechanic had been assigned to the convoy. Until now, I hadn't thought I'd need one. And this Turner seemed to be a miracle worker.

"You should have been smart enough to ask for him. Too late now."

What else or who else had I forgotten to ask for?

I hoped Bronowski's flat was fixed. I hoped Private Harwell was settled on the floor of the troop carrier, near the tailgate. I hoped there'd be no more engine troubles.

I reached into my field-jacket pocket, pulled out my flashlight, pointed it toward the vehicles behind my jeep, then blinked it on and off five times.

Engines sputtered.

I opened the jeep's canvas door and got in beside Jimmy Miller of Battery A. He'd been the lead driver when the battalion had gone to the firing range. According to Crawford, he was the best driver in the battalion. I'd felt confident when I arrived on the runway and found him studying the route maps.

"Ready?" I asked.

"Have been, sir," he replied.

"Let's go." I reached out, raised my hand, slowly lowered it. Our jeep crept forward.

I kept my head out, looking back, until I saw that all the vehicles were moving.

"Using the back roads until we get near Oxford is going to be a problem," Miller announced the moment I'd snapped the door shut.

"Why?"

"It's dark. We might not be able to see all the markers. With those roads I'm going to have to depend on markers."

Guides had left an hour earlier, with instructions to place the markers wherever there might be doubt as to which turn to take. "I'll help you look," I said.

The problems I'd just encountered—a missing person, last-minute vehicle troubles, no mechanic—made me wonder how much greater my troubles might be after I took the convoy off the base and onto the roads.

After we'd cleared the base and were on the road that skirted it, I opened the door and looked back. Vehicle intervals seemed to be the proper forty-five feet.

"Who's the spectator?" Miller said after I closed the door. He was nodding toward the front.

I looked ahead, saw parking lights shining from a space at the side of the road at the very top of the hill we were beginning to climb.

Peering out as we passed, I saw that the vehicle was the battalion sedan. As Miller drew closer I made out the unmistakable buffalo-shape of Shea, his arms locked over the top of his steering wheel. He didn't seem so much to be looking at us as staring through us. His eyes remained still as our jeep passed his gaze. I looked back, saw him staring through all the other vehicles too. He was the professor, standing over me as I took the exam, expecting me to foul it up, waiting for me to.

"He's headed back to the base," Miller said after glancing into his rearview mirror.

Was he just going back for coffee before coming to follow us again? Would he appear and reappear all the way along? Whether he stayed or followed, his presence was expanding.

Miller began whistling.

"Please don't do that," I said.

He frowned but stopped.

"Sorry," I said a couple of minutes later. "I guess it's him. I thought he trusted me, but there he was, checking."

"He doesn't trust anyone," Miller said flatly.

Eighteen

"**W**ake up, lieutenant."
The jeep's bouncing movements had already awakened me. I sat up, saw that the road we were on was narrower and bumpier than the road on which we'd started.

"There was a detour sign back there. But I don't know . . . this doesn't look right."

I turned, noticed the gun carrier behind us creeping with exaggerated motions.

"There was no detour on the map." Miller had slowed to five miles an hour. "When I turned off back there, this road was paved. Then, after about fifty yards, it turned to dirt."

"How long have I been asleep?"

"About a half-hour."

A beeping noise came from the ANGR-5 convoy radio perched on the backseat. I grabbed the handset, pressed the transmit-receive button.

Bronowski's voice sounded: "What in *thee* hell is going on, lieutenant?"

"Don't know," I told him. "Miller turned at a detour sign. It looked like a good road. But . . ." I was looking at the vehicle behind. "This one is barely wide enough for the jeep, let alone trucks and guns."

"I saw the damned sign too. The so-called guides that went out last night to plant 'em must've screwed up."

"Right. What about the trucks in front of you?"

"They're bouncing all over the place. The guns keep sliding toward the ditches on either side. The road's gonna give out soon."

"We'd better stop and try to back up."

"Can't do that, lieutenant."

"Why not?"

"You ever try to back up a five-ton with a gun attached to it, even on concrete?"

"No." The last vehicle I'd backed up was my eight-year-old Pontiac, to put it in my mother's garage before leaving for Fort Bliss.

"They jackknife all over the place. One of the guns gets both its wheels in a ditch, and we'll be here all day pulling it out."

At the firing range Shea had been careful to see that the gun carriers brought the seventy-fives into their firing locations head-first. I now understood why.

"Ain't nothing to do but keep going."

I looked ahead. Hedgerows crowded the banks on both sides. Between us and the hedgerows lay ditches. Though not terribly deep, they were soggy. They might trap the wheels of the guns and trucks.

I picked up the map, searched it. Miller leaned over and pointed to the last village we'd passed. He moved his finger slightly. "This must be the road we're on," he said.

I followed the line his finger touched. It ended an inch or so from where it began and didn't connect to anything. "Dead end."

"Looks that way."

"Are you sure that detour sign was one of the 46th's?"

"Yes, sir. It was just like the two others we came to when you were asleep. Red letters on cardboard about three feet by two. They were real easy to see, which is why I didn't wake you up to help me look for them."

"Keep going," I said. "Maybe the road isn't a dead end after all."

"Look!" Miller was staring through the windshield.

I raised my eyes.

About thirty yards ahead of us, straddling the grassy hump that ran down the middle of the road, stood a woman in an apron. She was about fifty years old and had straggly gray hair, which the breeze was tossing about. She held a hoe upside down, and beside her, jumping about and barking, were two large sheepdogs, one on each side. One of the dogs had predominantly brown markings, the other predominantly black. The brown one was making thrusts toward the jeep and baring its teeth. The other was simply hopping about in place. The woman's cheek rested against the hoe's blade. Her fists were wrapped around the neck of the hoe. She was peering at me over the jeep's headlights.

"Parking lights," I said.

Miller pushed the light switch in halfway.

The dimmed lights seemed to calm the brown dog somewhat, for it pulled in its teeth and stopped making thrusting movements.

The woman took a step toward us.

The scene before us darkened as other drivers, following Miller's lead, cut down their lights.

The woman now trudged forward. Her dogs trotted beside her, noses going to the ground in search of scents. The dog with black markings swept to Miller's side and crouched across the ditch from him, eyeing him and growling. The other swung to my side and took a pouncing stance beside the ditch, its shiny eyes on me, daring me to step out. I opened the canvas door slightly and spoke into the air: "Would you mind telling us—" Before I could finish, the dog leaped against my door, slamming it shut, then fell back and went into its crouch.

"George!" the woman bellowed.

The brownish dog hesitated, turned and moved slowly to the front of the jeep.

The woman raised her hoe and pointed the handle at me over the top of the hood. "Kindly remove your army," she said in a loud voice.

Again I opened the door, just slightly. "We're friendly!" I called.

She held the hoe steady, spoke over the top of it. "If so, why are you invading this property?"

"We're not invading, ma'am. We're—"

"You *are* invading! Take these monstrous machines of yours and leave!"

"Isn't this a public road?"

"No, it's a private lane. Mrs. Willicut's!"

Why had we been routed onto a private road? There was no time to figure it out. "May I please speak to Mrs. Willicut?"

"You *are* speaking to Mrs. Willicut."

The dog with black markings was now clawing at Miller's door, trying to get it open.

"Please call off your other dog," I said.

"Albert!" she shouted.

The dog leaped back. Recovering, it glanced toward the front of the jeep, then at Miller, finally moved toward the woman.

Signaling the dogs to stay, she stepped across the ditch, moved to the side of the jeep and stood beside my door, scrutinizing me. "If you meant to give me a fright, you've done so! I want you to remove those cannons before my lane gives way!"

"We were on our way . . ." I paused, remembering that the order from brigade had been marked "Secret." ". . . to another place on a . . . an assignment. But it seems we've gotten lost."

She tilted her head. Her frown softened into a curious stare. "What is your name, please?"

"Second Lieutenant Thomas Hanlon, United States Army Reserves."

She looked at the vehicles behind, squinting.

I pushed the door fully open, made sure the brown dog was still in front of the jeep, then looked back.

Curious faces under helmet liners stuck out from the canvas

canopies of the troop carriers. Pulled together as they were, the trucks and guns and men did look like an invading army. You couldn't see the end of the convoy. For all she knew it went on for kilometers.

"There are only a dozen vehicles, counting the guns," I assured her.

"I was afraid you were Soviets," she said.

Both dogs were peeking at me cautiously from beyond the jeep's front tire, the head of the black one hanging over the head of the brown one.

"You see over there?" She pointed the hoe handle toward a hill about a quarter of a mile away. "That's where I captured the last intruder. His plane crashed. In 1942. His name was Brinker."

"You captured a German pilot?"

"Yes! I rang up Mr. Gardener. And he rang up the constable. But, you know, we had him in hand before they got here." She turned to me, her face as plain as the earth around her. She snapped her head, for emphasis or maybe warning. "Mr. Gardener and I, just the two of us!" I noticed she was wearing men's boots, too large for her. What I'd first taken to be shouting was apparently her normal volume, for she was speaking as loudly a few feet from me as she had been from the front of the jeep. "They had a ceremony at the end of the war. I have a medal to show for it."

"Mrs. Willicut?"

"He liked my buns. I gave him some while we waited for the constable. He didn't take to the ones with the raisins in them." She smiled. "*Nor* do I. Isn't it odd how one remembers such things?"

"Yes."

"All of which comes to this: if you don't remove your soldiers rather soon, I'm going to call the constabulary once again. Mr. Gardener is dead now. But I have no fear, you see."

In a text on this region I'd found in the small officers' club library I'd read that the people of Berkshire were provincial, sometimes resentful of intruders, including tourists. The explanation the author gave was that Berkshire had been and was a kind of crossroads county, traveled over by Londoners on the way to the sea and back, by international travelers going from coast to coast, by university students moving to and from Oxford and Cambridge. While the county had fine inns, some dating back centuries, the Berkshire people had had their fill of strangers. Though I wasn't sure whether we were still in Berkshire or had crossed over into Oxfordshire, I decided that what was true of Berkshire people must also, to some degree at least, be true of Oxfordshire people. In any case, the woman before me was making it clear she wanted nothing more than to be rid of us.

"The problem with us leaving, the way we came in I mean, is . . ."

"Charles had no fondness for Yanks. 'They're all children,' he used to say. I myself never felt quite the same. That is to say, I do see the childish aspect, but I find the quality rather attractive. On the other hand . . ." She raised her hoe toward the vehicles. ". . . it does result in situations like this."

"Then you do realize that we didn't come down your road to occupy your land or anything like that."

"Ah!" She brushed back a twist of hair that had fallen over her eye, then squinted up at me. "You'd never get away with it, in any case."

"I only want to get us out of here." I mentioned the guides, said one of them might have put a road sign in the wrong place. "Where does this road actually lead?" I asked.

"To my house."

"Only to your house?"

The brownish dog had come from the front of the jeep and was barking at me. "Silence, George!" she commanded. The dog stopped barking.

"Hey, lieutenant!" someone called from one of the trucks. "Is this a piss call or what?"

I turned. "At ease!"

"But I got to go bad!"

What I didn't need was soldiers urinating on this woman's ditches, hedges and pastures. "Use the portable latrines!"

"But there's a whole damn field out there, and—"

"Quiet!" I turned back. "I'm very sorry. They've been in the trucks for quite a while and are getting restless. I'd like—"

"How many are there?" she said, squinting past me again.

"Twenty-six in all. The beginning of the road back there, where we turned off, was paved. It looked to my driver like a road that would go through . . . to somewhere. Are you sure . . . ?"

"They tried to make a high road and I wouldn't let them."

I'd wondered why British roads, even highways, wound about as they did. And why British vehicles, such as Jaguars and Austin Healeys and Morris Minors, were designed as they were. "You simply stopped the government from finishing the road?"

"I did indeed. They began, whereupon I made an appeal. *And* I defeated them."

If this woman had the power to stop her own government, she surely had the power to stop us, or, for that matter, help us.

"The gentleman from the Transportation Board was very nice indeed. Mr. Alcott-Davis. It turned out he'd once met Charles, during the war, before the bomb went off near Stonehenge. Charles, you see, was an aircraft mechanic. He wanted to fly in Wellingtons, but of course he was too old. Mr. Alcott-Davis was at the time in charge of repairing the airfields after the bombings. He wasn't there the day the bomb struck Charles's hangar, but, well, he told me . . . ."

I tried to think of a way out. In view of the road's dead-endedness, there seemed only one feasible possibility. When she finished, I spoke it cautiously:

"I wonder if you will give me permission to have my men take some of the steel plates from our guns' firing platforms and put them down to make a couple of makeshift bridges. That way we can drive over your ditch and onto your pasture, then turn around and get ourselves back to the road."

"What of my hedges?"

I glanced along both sides of the narrow road. There was no break in either hedge. "I guess we'd have to dig out a couple of sections. I'd be sure to have them put back."

She winced. "You will *not* use my ditches!"

"Yes, ma'am."

She glanced past me toward the line of vehicles.

I turned.

Men had stepped out of the trucks and were standing in the narrow spaces between the trucks and ditches, yawning, stretching, pushing each other. In the distance I saw Bronowski beside his jeep. He flung his hands desperately out in a what-do-we-do-now gesture.

"Follow me," she said.

I signaled Bronowski to wait.

Mrs. Willicut, dogs at her heels, had begun to make her way toward the rise in the road ahead. She was using her hoe as a cane to get her over the bumpy spots. She turned, saw me still standing where she'd left me. "Come along!" she said as if I were one of her dogs.

I hesitated, then called to Miller, told him to have Bronowski tell some men to set up the portable latrine. I hurried after Mrs. Willicut, who'd stopped at the rise to wait for me. "Quick step!" she said like a drill sergeant. "Quick step, please!"

Nineteen

.·.·.·.·.·.·

"**T**hat's Willicut Manor," she said as we stood on the
rise in the road. "It's not a proper manor house, of
course. But we always wished to call it one. And
therefore did."

Before us stood a sturdy-looking country home with numerous windows and two gabled wings. A circular driveway led
to the slightly elevated portico and was surrounded by a hedge,
which she was now indicating.

"Woodbines."

"Very nice."

"Yes. But you aren't here to bathe me with compliments, are
you?" She peered at me over the top of her glasses. "Please do
examine my drive-around and tell me whether or not you can get
your vehicles over it without damaging my garden."

The driveway circled a lush flower garden, which would make
passage difficult, as would the bordering bushes, whose leafy
branches hung over it. Further, the driveway didn't appear long
enough for all the vehicles. I gave her no indication of my rising
doubts, said rather, "Do you mind if I confer with my sergeant?"

"Of course not." She smacked the hoe on the ground, said
loudly, "Albert! George!" The dogs' heads popped toward her.
She turned. "I'm going to find my lambs and then put these
beasts in the barn." The dogs gazed at her, as if they were

thinking over her proposition. "Go!" she said loudly. The brown one bounded down the lane. The black one followed quickly.

I hurried to the top of the lane, which was about equidistant between my jeep and the house. I waved to Miller. "Send Bronowski!"

He stared for a moment, then nodded, opened the driver's door and leaned in to signal the sergeant on the radio.

I moved back to the house, believing at least for the moment that between us Bronowski and I would find a way out.

My hope fizzled fifteen minutes later when the sergeant, standing beside me after we'd walked together around the driveway, shook his head and said, "Can't do it. You couldn't get half of them onto this driveway, even if you lined them up bumper to bumper. We've got to call the base and have them send the wrecker to tow us out."

We'd already lost twenty minutes. Even if Shea agreed to dispatch the battalion wrecker to tow us out, we'd lose hours. I of course had little hope that Shea would allow the wrecker to come to our assistance. I turned back to the driveway, studied it again, was sure now that Bronowski's guess had been conservative.

Standing there, it struck me again, this time with a chill, that everyone in the U.S. Army in England, except Shea, myself and possibly Captain South, probably believed that these seventy-fives were an effective element in the defense of the Western World. That's why I'd been given exact deadlines. A gun in transit couldn't shoot down a Russian plane. The weapons I was taking had been uprooted—weren't able to "defend"—and the same was true of the ones I was to pick up. In the eyes of the brigade commander and all the other battalion commanders, the SAC bases were temporarily vulnerable. That's why there was such an emphasis on getting the guns to their new bases and returning with the exchanged ones as soon as possible. Major Shea was playing right along, pretending the movement of these guns on time was critical. I knew but couldn't prove that their movement made no more difference to the Western World and its future than the movement of Mrs. Willicut's sheep from one pasture to another. Less, I was sure.

"What you gonna do?" said Bronowski.

I walked away from him, stopped at the head of the cul-de-sac, surveyed it again. I came back, moved past the sergeant, stood at the end, noticed that the woodbine hedge was set back by a few feet. I pictured something. The picture started to become a plan. I returned to Bronowski. "Go back and bring the convoy up here."

"You're not going to call Greenham then?"

"No. Bring it up. Slowly."

His eyebrows curled to a cynical look.

The solution, I was inspired to believe, would be parallel parking, a practice I'd not only become familiar with but had mastered during college summers while working at a parking lot near San Francisco's Seal's Stadium. When I started at the privately owned lot, I'd see a space, guess it would hold one large or maybe two small cars, then watch the lot's owner, Jerry McGee, slip four and sometimes five vehicles into it. "A buck's a buck," he told me. "*You* learn to put 'em in like that." I did, so tightly that large people lost buttons getting out between vehicles.

Bronowski stood in front of my jeep, looking back. "You sure about this?"

"I'm sure."

Pretty sure, I thought.

The width of the cul-de-sac had ignited the inspiration. I'd bring the first jeep all the way around and park it at an angle, nose to woodbines. I'd then have the first gun crew detach its five-ton carrier from its weapon, drive the truck around and park it tightly beside the jeep. I'd then have the gun crew pull the first gun around and hand-park it parallel to the five-ton, and so on, in effect shrinking the length of the convoy by at least seventy percent. With all the vehicles tucked in, the approach road would be cleared. Then, beginning with the first jeep, I'd have all of them moved out, noses first, have the crews reattach guns to five-tons and return carefully down the lane.

I didn't share my plan with Bronowski because I didn't want him to talk me out of it. As he guided the jeep forward, he looked back suspiciously a couple of times.

I ignored him, complimented myself on the speed and simplicity of my plan, then realized there was also speed and simplicity in self-inflicted bullet wounds and leaps off high bridges.

Soon I took over from Bronowski and was walking backward in front of the lead jeep, guiding Miller forward.

I saw the gun carrier just behind the jeep slide and nearly go into one of the ditches. Bronowski, in front of the carrier, assigned a man to walk on the other sides of the two ditches, beside every tire, including those beneath the guns. That further inspired me. I assigned a noncom to walk backward in front of each jeep and truck, told each to have a team watch the wheels, one person for each wheel. Whenever a vehicle began to slide or waver in any way, the observer called, "Stop!" The sergeant was to analyze the problem—a wheel slipping toward a ditch, gun starting to veer away from gun carrier, driver going too much left or right—solve it and inch onward.

Soon all the vehicles were lined up a few yards from the driveway.

Bronowski, perspiring, came from the back of the convoy and stood beside me. "Now what?"

I described my plan.

The sergeant's stiff look reminded me of looks he gave Ball after the captain had ordered him to do something pointless. ("Some of our gas masks are less olive-drab than others, sergeant. See if you can trade with the other batteries until all ours match.") His shrug was also familiar. "Sir?"

"Let's just do it, sergeant."

I led Miller and the first jeep around the drive, carefully guiding him into the first parking space. Then, inch by inch, I guided the first truck around the driveway. The driver groaned each time I asked him to back up and straighten out. He found the parking even more difficult. Numerous times I had him back and pull forward. Despite his complaints he ended up getting the five-ton so close to my jeep that he couldn't get out on the driver's side. He started to slide toward the passenger side, but I said, "Stay there for a while."

Mrs. Willicut had stood on her front step watching. After we'd parked the truck without damaging her woodbines or garden, she told me she was in charge of the bakery booth at the East Isley Sheep Festival that afternoon. "I have spare buns. Do you suppose your gentlemen would like to have some?"

Everyone must have heard her, for there followed an assenting cheer.

She smiled, turned and went back into the house.

Buns or no buns, I was sure that if I got my little convoy jammed in her driveway, both she and the troops would be furious. I couldn't tell yet whether or not we'd fit. Suppose I failed. I'd read books and seen movies about mutinies, revolts, uprisings. I imagined Bronowski pronouncing me incompetent and taking over.

I turned and found a sullen crew watching me from beside its weapon. "You've got to pull it around," I said. For a few seconds no one moved. Finally a gun corporal, Collins, bent down and picked up the tow bar. One by one the others positioned themselves around the gun.

Despite the crew's complaints, the gun went around the circle with less difficulty than had the five-ton. After the crew had gotten as close as possible to the truck, I saw that the driver could, after all, get the passenger door open. I told both him and the crew to go to the house and ask Willicut if she needed help. I myself went back to the driveway.

The mystery sharpened as I watched each truck and gun being parked. Would they all fit?

Bronowski, after helping me guide the last gun into place, came up to me and said, "Look." He pointed. "I don't think you can get 'em all in."

There was enough space in the driveway for one more vehicle only, and there were two left, the three-quarter-ton food carrier and Bronowski's jeep.

"I'm going to do some measuring," he said.

Watching him pace, I was certain the jeep wouldn't fit. And if it remained on the road, it would block us as completely as if it were the Tower of London.

"Won't work," he said, coming back.

"I can see that."

"What you gonna do?"

"Don't know." I wanted to flee and hide.

Bronowski walked to the driveway, turned back, scanned the vehicles neatly tucked together around the circle, took a close look at the food carrier, moved to the jeep.

"I'll tell the driver to bring the carrier onto the driveway, okay?" he said, coming back.

"Why?"

"Don't ask, lieutenant."

"I'm asking."

"I got an idea. That's all."

"That's what *I* had and look where it put us."

"What do you say?"

I guessed he'd decided that though my plan was no good, we were so close to completing it we might as well finish it before going to something else, if there was a something else. I said, "Go ahead."

Not wanting to watch Bronowski bring my plan to its futile final end, I went over to the house. Two dozen sloppy-looking soldiers stood on the porch eating buns. I held my fatigue jacket over one shoulder and watched them eat buttered buns and drink lemonade from the truck. I felt sticky perspiration. My legs were weak from all the hopping around. My heart was beating rapidly. They were listening to Mrs. Willicut tell stories: dog stories, war stories, sheep stories and Charles stories. I began to feel light-headed, as though I might collapse and faint. I needed some of that lemonade. I headed toward the porch.

Some of the men were already helping Mrs. Willicut bring the trays back into her house. I watched others line up beneath her steps, waiting to use the bathroom, which she'd invited them to do.

I turned.

Bronowski had guided the three-quarter-ton into the circle, but there sat the jeep, blocking the rest of the vehicles.

The men around him slid doubtful eyes from me to the jeep, then back to me.

Desperately I thought about backing the jeep to the highway. It would be a long and tedious job, given the roughness and narrowness of the lane. Even driving forward, Miller had had a hard time keeping the light vehicle from slipping into one of the ditches. The bigger vehicles had the slight advantage of weight, which helped hold them in position, whereas on the road's soft surface the jeeps were more like tennis balls.

I recalled an incident Captain Murdoch, one of my college ROTC instructors, had shared with his class. Remnants of the German army had been left in disarray after General Patton's Third Army swept across western France in 1944. Nearly all the bridges, ferry boats and barges on the Seine had been destroyed by Allied bombings. Many thousands of the enemy had no apparent means of retreat. As soon as bridges appeared, Allied planes blew them out of the water. Yet somehow the Germans were escaping in hordes. How? The Allies didn't know. At one crossing, twenty-seven thousand troops fled across the river in three days. "Now that retreat should have been impossible," Murdoch asserted. "Can any of you figure out how they carried it off?" There were a few guesses. Murdoch shook his head to each. Finally he gave us the solution. "Pontoon bridges were hidden by the Germans in the woods beside the river during the day, but under the cover of night they were pulled out and set up, allowing both troops and vehicles to cross; in the morning the bridges were removed."

I searched for ways to apply the principles of the German escape to our situation. Nothing came to mind.

"Need some men," Bronowski called. He began to spout off names. "Over here!" He was standing beside the jeep.

Several men moved off the porch and toward him.

I followed. When I reached him, I said, "Why do you want them?"

"We're going to pick up the jeep and turn it around."

I wasn't certain his plan would work but knew that the only other possible solution, backing the vehicle out, would take an enormous amount of time.

He stationed three men at the front, three at the back, three on each side. He hopped about, a mad choreographer. "Jensen, you're too tall. Get out of there. O'Brien, you stand where he was." He had them practice the lift twice before he had them actually do it. "If you fall when we walk around, you pull your ass right out of the way." Finally he had them ready. "All four wheels up at the same time, around together, all four down." Then he gave the signal. Up went the jeep, slowly but smoothly around they went, and they put the vehicle gently down. In my enthusiasm I yelled, "Terrific!" Several of the jeep movers frowned at me. Bronowski, however, took a bow.

After the jeep had been turned around, the sergeant opened one of its doors, reached in, got something, stuffed it into the back pocket of his fatigue pants, then signaled me to follow. He led me behind the woodbines, removed what he'd taken from the jeep—a paper bag—opened it and revealed a small bottle of an off-brand vodka. "I know this is against regulations, but I . . ."

"Never mind," I said, nodding toward the bottle.

He uncapped it and handed it to me.

I took a couple of swallows. They went down as easily as spring water. Only moments later did I feel the fire, and a new but welcome dizziness.

After taking several swallows, he put the bottle back into the paper bag and the bag back into his pocket. "You first," he said, pointing.

We moved back to the front of the driveway, where Mrs. Willicut was sadly bidding the others goodbye.

Bronowski interrupted, announcing that there was still work

to do. He meant getting the vehicles out of their parking places, hooked up and back onto the road.

We'd lost nearly two hours. Maybe we could make it up. Nothing now seemed impossible.

Mrs. Willicut was telling one, then another, "Do come back and visit me. Oh, do come back!" She complimented them to me and said she hadn't minded being invaded at all.

I thanked her for the use of the driveway, the hospitality, especially the buns.

"Some of the boys are interested in seeing my poochies," she said. "Do I have time?"

I told her I'd rather they didn't since we had to work fast to try to get back on schedule.

"Ta," she said.

Within twenty minutes we had all the vehicles out of her driveway and were moving cautiously toward the highway.

I was in front, walking backward, guiding Bronowski's jeep, the one they'd picked up and turned, now in front of mine. It stopped. The driver pointed to something beyond me. I turned and saw people of various ages squatting in the lane, holding hand-painted signs, gazing out of stern faces. I put up my hands, waited for the muffled squeaks of brakes to stop, then turned all the way around to face the people who'd clearly trapped us.

Twenty

WARMONGERS! said one sign. BRING THE ARMS RACE TO THE FINISH LINE, read another. ENEMIES OF CIVILIZATION! declared the most comprehensive. But the most alarming was the largest, held by a short man with a swath of hair on each side of his bald sunburned skull. He sat at the center of the group and his sign said:

ABANDON YOUR WEAPONS!
STEP FORWARD!
SURRENDER!

Bronowski, who'd been guiding the second jeep, came up behind me and, angrily eyeing the protesters, said, "I thought this was a friendly country."

I was afraid the men would peer out of the trucks, see what I'd seen and come out to brawl. I told Bronowski to go back and keep them all where they were. "I'll signal you if I want you to bring the convoy forward. By patting my left thigh."

Bronowski grunted and went back.

Twenty-five yards separated the front jeep from the front rank of squatters, about forty in all. As I moved toward them, the short man stood and came out about five yards. He'd released his sign to one of the others, all of whom had remained seated. He reached to the inside pocket of the wrinkled jacket of his dark blue suit, removed a folded sheet of paper, opened it and held it until I stopped, a yard or so before him. Then, in resonant but trembling voice, he read:

"You are transporting dangerous weapons across the territory of a free nation!

"Those weapons are being used to defend bases containing aircraft which carry nuclear bombs!

"You are therefore parties to the possible destruction of mankind!

"We arrest you in the name of mankind!

"Please remove all weapons contained on your persons and step away from your vehicles!

"The Committee for Nuclear Disarmament."

He lowered the paper and raised his tired eyes to mine. He was no more than thirty years old, younger than most who sat huddled behind him. There were as many women as men, even a few children. They reminded me of refugees waiting at a border. They were unarmed and did not appear menacing. Yet the statement, whose phrases kept sounding in my mind after their spokesman stopped reading, seemed momentous, like the Declaration of Independence.

Those B-47s which took off from and landed on our base every day weren't just carrying melons. I and other officers of the 46th rarely talked about the jets or what was in them. I myself had been preoccupied with the battalion, had given little thought to the Strategic Air Command. But I knew that its commander, General Curtis Lemay, had boasted about having bombers armed with atomic weapons in the sky at all times.

I nodded and said, "I believe that at least some of what you say is true."

The spokesman's eyes rose in surprise. The white parts were so full of crooked red lines they looked like maps.

Behind him an old woman in a black cloth coat smiled.

Mumbles rose from others.

Apparently they were waiting for me to say more, maybe just "We surrender."

"We aren't carrying any ammunition," I went on. With no time to prepare, I'd have to let thoughts fall as I found them. "We're moving a few weapons from one base to others." That, it occurred to me, did nothing to counter the charges in their statement. "As for the atomic weapons, we are in the Army, and the Army doesn't have any . . . that I know of. Which doesn't absolve us from our connection with the Air Force. On their behalf, I must say that they have a rationale for those bombs which boils down to the fear of Soviet attack, not only on the United States but on Great Britain too. Yes, definitely. But . . ." I ran my eyes along the top of the hedge to my right, carefully thinking out my next remark, then said, "I guess I've wondered why a greater effort isn't being made on *both* sides—who's walking around with signs in Russia protesting?—to stop what appears to be a kind of worldwide suicide. Now that's about all I feel I need to say, except that I don't think I and the men behind me ought to be asked to surrender for acts we haven't committed and, I'd say to a person, don't wish to have committed."

There were several outcries from the crowd after I finished. I heard two distinctly:

" 'e's a load of gas!"

"I enjoyed that! Ask him something else."

They'd seemed ready to advance but didn't.

The leader turned around, as if for instructions.

Another man, about sixty, was frowning at me. He wore a Donegal tweed jacket with leather patches on the elbows. "Don't engage him in dreary debate," he said. "Arrest him!"

"He's admitting we've got a case," the spokesman retorted. "I think we ought to hear his full confession."

"I didn't mean to *confess* anything," I insisted.

"Arrest them all!" someone shouted.

That brought a loud assenting chorus.

The young leader said, "Have your soldiers step away from the vehicles."

He was closing off the possibility of negotiation. I'd at least have considered offering myself if they'd agreed to let the rest go. Now, I felt, there was no choice. I lowered my hand to my thigh.

I heard several engines growl.

I smiled at the leader, then reached into my back pocket, wanting him to think I was going for my identification. I heard the first jeep shift into gear. I removed my empty hand and shouted to the protesters, "You'd better get out of the way!"

"Ai! He's trying to trick us!"

As you tricked us, I thought.

I darted toward the convoy. As I approached the first jeep, Bronowski climbed into the backseat and leaned forward, holding open the canvas door on the passenger side. Miller slowed. I caught the handle of the door, turned and hopped along until I finally pulled myself in.

"Go," I said, "but stay slow and stop if you're in danger of hitting someone."

I turned to see the protesters scattering, some on all fours, leaping and diving toward the banks. The road was wider here than it was near Mrs. Willicut's house.

A dirt clod smacked against the windshield.

A can of yellow paint splashed open against the plastic window of the passenger door.

Children, who had climbed or been pushed up past the hedges and into the bushes, were safely out of the way. Some, in fact, were throwing stones.

One of them struck metal at the back of the jeep.

There was no way for me to contact the vehicles behind. I had to hope that the drivers and riders wouldn't do impulsive things like stop or jump out or hurl things back.

I watched through the small rear window.

The others were getting through without harming the protesters and apparently with little damage to the vehicles.

"Let's celebrate," said Bronowski, taking the bottle from under the seat I was in.

I waved it away and asked the driver how far we were from Upper Heyford.

"An hour at the slowest convoy speed, a half-hour at the fastest."

"Go the fastest."

The jeep jumped to a higher speed.

Twenty-one

....

The commanding officer of the 4th Antiaircraft Artillery Battalion sported a perfectly trimmed mustache and reminded me of a short Errol Flynn. After marching from his sedan at the edge of the side runway to which I'd taken the convoy, he snappily returned my weary salute and said, "Potts. And you?"

I identified myself and lowered my hand more sharply than I'd raised it.

"You're late, Hanlon," he shot back. Before I could tell him why he said, "Let's take a look at the weapon you're leaving me."

"Yes, sir." He was to get only one, and Shea had assigned him Rivera's.

"Which is it?" He turned toward the line of vehicles to his left and my right.

There was Rivera's gun, with its tube sticking out like a risen middle finger. "It's the one at the end, sir."

He started down the line. Many of the men were lying alongside the vehicles, tired and disheveled. None bothered to stand and salute him. He didn't seem to care. As we neared the end he said, "Why is the tube sticking up?"

"Well, sir . . ." I hurried to keep up. "We're not sure."

"But you intend to leave it with me?"

"Well, it's the one I'm supposed to leave you, sir."

One side of his mustache twisted downward. He ordered a couple of men standing near the weapon to remove the canvas cover. He bent down at the base of the gun and examined visible parts. He rose, turning. "I won't accept the weapon with the tube in that condition."

"But this is the weapon Major Shea ordered me to leave here, sir."

"I don't doubt it. And it's Colonel Shea."

"Sir?"

"He's been promoted to lieutenant colonel. The news came in this morning's mail from brigade." He watched me, as if wanting to note my reaction.

I doubt I appeared happy. The promotion would strengthen Shea's hold on the battalion. Life would be even more difficult for all of us.

"As for this gun, lieutenant," Potts went on, "I'd say you're someplace between the frying pan and the fire."

I turned, looked for Bronowski. Where? Then I thought, What good is Bronowski? He probably had no more experience with this sort of situation than I. He wasn't even a gun sergeant. I turned back. "I doubt Major . . . Colonel Shea would let me take the weapon back, sir."

"I'd say you can be damned sure of that. If I were you, I'd repair it," he said firmly.

I'd never even oiled a part on the seventy-five. I don't think I could have turned on the radar or computer without the help of a technician. And certainly I couldn't have supervised a firing without the help of a gun sergeant. Now he was suggesting I do a job that had befuddled a specialist like Gilley. "I don't know that I can manage it, sir."

"I'll assign my ordnance man, First Lieutenant Delsey, to assist you."

What could he do that Gilley hadn't tried?

"Time, sir. I'm several hours behind schedule already. You see, we were trapped and for some time delayed by peace protesters, back there on the other side of Oxford."

"What's this?"

I told him the story, beginning with the discovery of the changed road signs and ending with our getaway. It took me nearly five minutes. He nodded throughout, and, when I finished, said, "I think you ought to be proud of yourself and your men. Now, go to the Air Police headquarters at the north end of this runway and file a report. In the meantime I'll tell Delsey to meet you there. You and he can take the gun to site number five, where it will be put down if you can get it fixed within—I'd say for the sake of your deadline as well as my own—two hours." He stepped back and put his hands on his hips, waited until I looked at him, then added with great emphasis, "If the gun isn't in working order by then, you take it back. Understand?"

I nodded.

He then did something Shea, perhaps most commanding officers, wouldn't have done. He reached out, shook my hand, and said, "Good luck."

We saluted and off he went.

Twenty-two

,r ,r ,r ,r ,r ,r

I stood beside First Lieutenant Delsey at site number five and watched a skeleton crew from the 46th remove the wheels of the faulty weapon and carefully spread its supporting outriggers onto the moss between the gun pit and main runway.

After he'd found me at the Air Police station, Potts's tall flabby officer had done little more than puff on his unlit pipe and stare at me through his small wire-rimmed glasses. He'd wheezed noisily getting into and out of my jeep. Now he was breathing noisily as he watched the crew set the outriggers.

"We don't do it that way here," he said.

The gun was nearly in place; I made no reply.

The crew had been filling the air with spiced comments.

I took the toolbox from the weapon's storage area and asked Corporal "Skinny" Bagdell to elevate the gun tube as far as it would go.

"That ain't the problem," he said in his nasally voice. "Problem is getting her down."

I didn't bother to explain. "Take it all the way up," I said.

He began to turn the elevation handle.

Delsey had been sent to help. Why wasn't he making suggestions? I turned to him and asked, "Isn't this what you'd do?"

"Not sure, Hanlon," he said. "Haven't analyzed it. Haven't had time."

"But wouldn't it seem logical that something in the tube, attached to the tube, would be the cause?"

He put his hand out to one side, tilted his head and let out a massive sneeze. "Gun grease," he said, backing up. "I'm allergic to it."

"And?"

"I'm not supposed to get closer than fifty feet to those things, and here I've let you bring me . . . about twenty feet from yours."

I'd moved closer to the weapon, and he'd followed. Now he was backing up. Which meant he wouldn't be close enough to give me advice, at least advice that depended on his being close. He reached into his pocket and removed a large clean handkerchief. "It's logical, yes, to check the gears. There is a possibility . . ." He paused as he peeled the handkerchief open, raised it and blew his nose, one long and three short blasts. ". . . you'll find a broken gear tooth. On the other hand there's an even greater possibility . . ." He stopped and tried to refold the damp dirty handkerchief. He did a bad job but stuffed it back into his pocket anyway. ". . . that it can't be fixed."

"That's it?"

"As I see it."

Would I, in failing, be doomed to roam the landscape with the unacceptable weapon, a lieutenant without a battalion, a Don Quixote minus dream, cursed, perhaps, with this oversized Sancho Panza, Delsey?

I removed a flashlight from the toolbox and climbed onto the pedestal. I was soon lying across the grated platform, pointing the flashlight and poking my head into the cavity beneath the gun tube, which was now pointed nearly straight up.

"You'd better be careful putting your head in there like that," warned the first lieutenant from his distant place. "That tube could come down and turn your skull to mincemeat."

Defiantly I lowered myself as far as I could into the cavity.

His voice sounded again: "There's also the danger of bolts coming loose and the torsion spring snapping and the emplacing chains giving out."

"Give me a better way!" I shouted up at him.

He didn't reply.

How could I tell whether or not a gear was broken unless I looked at the gears? Though I'd winced when Delsey said "mincemeat," I didn't know enough about what it took for a gun tube to fall or an emplacing chain to snap to be afraid. I'd see what I could see and extract myself as quickly as possible.

I directed a beam of light along the outside edge of the elevating gear, which was a large-toothed wheel, quartered. None of the teeth appeared to be broken. I couldn't see all of them, however. I edged downward so that now my entire torso was in the cavity. I focused the light beam on the receiving gear. The teeth on that gear, those I could see, weren't broken. I raised my head slightly and called to Bagdell. I soon felt him step onto the platform, just behind me.

"What you want?"

Before I could answer him, I heard a cracking sound from below.

"First, what was that noise?"

"I didn't hear anything."

I hoped it was nothing more than an adjustment the newly emplaced pedestals were making to his added weight. "Can this gun tube be raised any higher?"

"It's straight up."

"All right," I said impatiently. "I don't mean higher, then. I mean 'go beyond the vertical.' "

"Like we're gonna make it point backwards?"

"Yes."

"In gunnery school they said you can do that but it's dangerous."

"But you can do it?"

"I've never done it, but . . . well, you can do it, about two or three degrees." He paused, shifting his weight. The shifting brought the cracking sound again. "Trouble is, you get beyond a certain point and that one gear comes off the other and then, whappo, the big sucker of a gun falls right down and smashes everything in its way."

"I would *not* do that, lieutenant," Delsey said urgently. "The weapon is in your jurisdiction until Colonel Potts accepts it. I therefore can't order you not to order your corporal to move the tube further. But I advise you not to do what you're thinking of doing."

"Duty," I called back. "I want to perform it in an easier way. Give me an easier way!"

"I'd have to have more time to study the problem. You rushed forward. Now you find yourself—"

"Time!" I said. "Time is *part* of the problem. Your CO has given me two hours. That was forty-five minutes ago. I've got an hour and fifteen minutes."

"A year ago," he said, "out at the practice range in New Mexico, I saw one of those tubes fall and turn a couple of crewmen into pancakes. If they'd lived, they'd have spent the rest of their crippled lives paying for what they'd damaged."

I was twisted into an uncomfortable position, about to descend again, but I stayed long enough to repeat something: "Give me an alternative." I waited, hopeful.

He said nothing.

"I'm going to do it my own way. Corporal, crank the tube up until I tell you to stop."

"I'll get Jefferson to come on and help."

"No! Every time you move, the platform makes a strange noise. I don't want anyone else on the platform."

"The higher you raise a gun tube, the harder it is to crank. It's a hell of a job for one person."

"Then do a hell of a job."

"He's right, Hanlon," offered Delsey.

I ignored him. "Bagdell?"

"I've got hold of it."

"Turn it, slowly."

The gears, under my flashlight beam, began to move. I saw gear teeth I hadn't seen. All were clean, meshing nicely. But then I saw something else.

"I'm looking at the elevation dial, lieutenant. I can give it about another half-crank is all."

"Stop."

"Okay. I stopped."

What I saw stood out because, unlike other parts, it wasn't dark and greasy but shiny and clean. "I'm going to go into the cavity between the radar and computer as far as I can."

"What you want to do that for?"

"Because I have to."

I waited for Delsey's comment. There was none.

I wiggled forward, pulled myself down into the cavity, which was just wide enough to accommodate me, twisted and squirmed, going as far as I could go. My toes were locked to the edge of the pedestal's grillwork. If the gun collapsed straight down all there'd be left to bury would be my feet. I reached forward, touched the shiny object, felt it move slightly. Both of my arms were extended fully. There wasn't much room to move either one. I turned the flashlight upward, aimed the beam, saw crushed metal. Clearly that metal wasn't part of the weapon. I tugged at it, twisted it, pulled it. It wouldn't come out. "Bagdell!"

He didn't answer.

My body jammed into the cavity had prevented me from being heard. I exhaled to make more space between me and the cavity, then yelled as loud as I could.

I heard him reply, muffled: "Ypph, spphh."

"HAVE A GUNNER BRING THE LARGEST PAIR OF PLIERS IN THE TOOLBOX!"

"Ypphh, spphh."

"HAVE HIM HAND IT TO YOU! AND YOU SLIDE IT DOWN MY BACK!"

"Bkk?"

"BACK! YES!"

I was sure I couldn't remain in the position I was in much longer without suffering cramps. I pulled at, tugged at and twisted the object; it wouldn't move. There was a slight quaking movement of the platform, followed by the cracking sound. The cracking sound was being made by the object, for as I heard the sound, I felt it move. Soon the pliers came icily down my back, stopping when they reached the base of my skull. I guided one arm back, curled it like a snake toward my neck, where, reaching with fingers, I took hold of the tool. With it firmly in my grip, I returned my arm over the same route to the extended position. Because of the flashlight I had to use one hand only to turn the pliers around and open them. Then I reached forward and closed the pincers on the metal object. I pulled with as much leverage as I had. The object didn't come out. I twisted it and pulled again. Still nothing. Finally I twisted it only, around and around, until, snap, it came loose. Aching, I exhaled, turned my head and called, "Pull me out!"

"Yes, sir!" He'd left the crank and knelt down near my butt. He now seemed not far away but on top of me.

Even without the flashlight in one hand and pliers and metal object in the other, I'd have had a lot of trouble squeezing out of the cavity. With the pliers I couldn't use my hands at all. "Can you pull my feet and help me get out of here?"

"I'll try, sir," said Bagdell. And he did, but I was jammed tightly in at a bad angle and he couldn't get me even partway up.

"Have someone help you."

He called Jefferson, said, "Hurry!"

In a moment the pedestal quaked again. There was no cracking sound, however, assuring me that the cracking sound had been made by the metal object. I felt hands tighten around my ankles. I heard tearing sounds, pictured my fatigue trousers and jacket being ripped, worried that my skin would soon be torn. "Pull steadily."

They began to pull, not very steadily. After the first tearing sounds there were no others, however, and despite continuing jerky movements, they soon had me near the top. I reached back, helped myself get all the way out, then stood, feeling woozy.

A cheer arose.

I looked out and saw the gun's makeshift crew, three or four, caps in hand, waving.

Delsey stood right where I'd left him, puffing on his dry pipe.

"Nice work, lieutenant," said Bagdell.

"Thanks."

Someone pointed to the object in my hand.

I looked. It was most of a tin can. It wasn't just flattened or twisted. It was nearly pulverized into a metal ball. A bit of lettering was visible, a script capital *P* and a small script *a*. It took me a moment to realize that it was or had been a Pabst Blue Ribbon can. I raised it and wiggled it in the air. How could it have gotten trapped that far down in the seventy-five?

The crew applauded.

I stepped down from the platform, walked over to Delsey and raised the smashed can. "Look at that."

He shrugged, reached for his handkerchief and said, "The problem isn't solved yet, you realize."

I looked back at the gun, then knew he was right. I'd removed the pulverized can, but it was possible that something else had caused the malfunction. It was also possible that the can had done some permanent damage to the gears. Possibly part of it was still jamming them. I wouldn't know until we tried to get the gun tube to come down, all the way to the horizontal position. Anxious, I climbed back onto the pedestal. I wanted to crank the gun down myself, but my hands were suddenly shaking.

"You crank it down," I said to Bagdell.

He did so, slowly. When he reached fifty degrees, he turned the handle more slowly, as if to increase the suspense, got it down to forty-eight, forty-seven, forty-six, then to the critical forty-five. It kept moving. "Ya-hoo!" he said.

I wasn't comfortable until he'd lowered the weapon all the way to the horizontal position. When the dial hit zero I said, "Let's go eat."

As one, the crew, minus Bagdell, raced toward the food carrier and began scrambling into the back of it.

I followed with the corporal, stopped when I reached Delsey, whose hand was up.

"One problem solved, another to come," he said.

"What's that?"

"Colonel Potts will of course want me to go over all the other major parts of the weapon—radar, computer—and assure him they're in good condition before he signs the exchange sheet."

"You do that, then, lieutenant," I said.

He moved his pipe and gave me a lips-only smile. "Not without you and your men. I'm not supposed to be up on the piece touching the parts. Doctor's orders."

I reached out, raised Delsey's hand, put into it the flashlight I'd forgotten to lay back in the toolbox, said "C'mon" to Bagdell, and headed for the food carrier.

"I'm not going to inspect this gun alone," Delsey snapped.

"Call the doctor," I told him. "If he won't give you permission, ask him to come out and give you a hand."

"What a swift comment!" said Bagdell as he parted for the back of the truck and I for its cab.

Swift or not, I was regretting it before the driver had the vehicle started. Like me, Delsey was caught in this remote pocket of the military world, in one of these absurd battalions, with one of history's most ridiculous weapons. Developing a sneeze every time you came near one of the monsters was beginning to seem an ingenious way to cope with the impossible. I didn't admire Delsey, but was on the verge of liking him.

Part Two

Twenty-three

./・/・/・/・/

S hea handed me three wooden darts, their bluish feathers faded and frayed, and told me to take a few practice throws. As I was checking the darts, he pressed the top of his hand lightly against my chest, easing me back. "There," he said, pointing down, "don't step over that line." Beneath me, nearly invisible in the wooden floor, was a painted red stripe about two feet long. The dartboard before me was filled with tiny holes, most of them in the sections marked with the higher numbers.

"Ai, Frank! You've got yourself a prota-gee, I see," said an old man at the bar, a few yards to our right. He had a sharp chin, a long nose bent in at least two places and three visible brown lower teeth, each standing half a tooth's distance from its nearest companion.

"I'm not claiming him yet."

"Not yet!" The old man laughed.

I studied the board and was about to step to the line when I remembered something. "Congratulations on your promotion."

He nodded. "Thank you, lieutenant. Now quit stalling and throw the dart."

I did.

It landed in the dark area at the middle of the section numbered 18. I'd played darts only a couple of times but knew about scoring. The area I landed in amounted to three times the number, or 54.

"There you are!" said the man with brown teeth. "You'd best put a claim on him now!"

There were hums of approval from several men who appeared to be farmers, sitting around a table near the entrance. When we'd come in, they'd called greetings to Shea, and he'd stopped at the table with me at his side and said hello to each. He'd introduced me as "one of my lieutenants."

"Let's see you put another one in there beside it," Shea said in a way that let me know he knew, or at least suspected, I'd been lucky on my first throw.

"I think I'll try for a different number," I said. I didn't think I could get the second dart to land near the first one.

The waitress brought our drinks. I took a long swallow from my mug and studied the board again.

"Which number?" Shea wanted to know.

"Do I have to tell you that?"

A couple of others laughed.

"You don't have to tell," Shea said. "But you've just let us know you don't have any idea what the hell you're doing."

"You'll see."

The section numbered 19 looked easier to hit than any of the others. When the laughter subsided I said firmly, "Nineteen."

"Good!" said one of the men at the table.

Over the top of the dart I sighted on the space I wanted. I concentrated as I'd been taught to do during marksmanship training at Bliss. I took a deep breath, waited until my hand steadied, then released the dart. It landed in 19, just a hair off the triple area for which I'd aimed.

"Be careful, Frank," said the old man. "He's a chance to put you away."

"No one's going to put Frank away," said one of the men at the table near the door.

"Doesn't matter anyway," Shea told them. "We're not playing

a real game. I'm just finding out what he can do." He turned to me. "All right. This time name the place you're going to put it."

"You mean . . ."

"I mean specifically name the number and what part you plan on hitting: double, triple, bull, whatever."

"How about the bull's-eye or the little circle around it?"

"Which? Pick one or the other."

"The . . . bull's-eye."

I heard skeptical murmurs.

No wonder. The bull's-eye alone was no larger than the nail on my little finger. Further, neither it nor the circle around it gave room for error. I felt I'd made a mistake, but it was too late to change. I stepped to the line, took a deep breath and aimed carefully. I released the dart too quickly. It dipped before reaching the bull's-eye, veered into a lower number, stuck there for an instant, then fell to the floor.

"Bad luck!" said the old man.

Shea shook his head and moved to our small table. "A couple more, Norma."

"I'll try another," I said after him.

"Skip it," he said.

I waited for at least some of the others to encourage me to go on, or call on him to encourage me. No one did. I put down the dart I was holding and followed him to our table. I'd felt good about overcoming numerous obstacles during my convoy assignment. Now I felt like a failure just because I hadn't made a dart stick in a board.

At 0246 that morning, only two hours and forty-six minutes behind schedule, I'd arrived back at the base with the full complement of exchanged weapons. After supervising the delivery of each weapon to its designated site, I went to my office and fought sleep long enough to type out for Shea a report of what had happened during the convoy assignment, including summaries of the adventure on Mrs. Willicut's property, the encounter with the protesters and the solution to the problem Colonel Potts had presented. I trusted that these difficulties, plus a few less serious, would explain my tardiness. I took the jeep to the club, went to my room and, without even loosening the laces on my combat boots, fell across my bed and sank deeply into sleep.

On awakening at 1040 I leaned over to turn off the lamp beside my bed and saw a piece of red plastic cut into a shield. Beside it lay a sheet of paper with handwriting. I leaned farther over and read:

Second Lieutenant Thomas Hanlon is hereby awarded the "Survivor" medal for passing one of Colonel Francis P. Shea's life-or-death tests.

                                        CWO Gilley

I smiled, was about to pick up and examine the "medal" when I noticed another note on the far side of the little table. I reached across and saw that it was typed and on officers' club stationery:

Lieutenant Hanlon:
    Colonel Shea called to say he'll meet you in front of the club at 1930 this evening. He asked that you wear casual civilian clothes. Also, he said you don't need to report for duty today.

                                        Sp/4 D. Ivy, USAF
                                        Clerk, Officers' Club

I was surprised by the invitation. "He hardly ever does anything socially with anyone," Gilley had told me. The exceptions were events related somehow to official duties, like the party after the firing. Even then, Gilley said, he'd been the first to leave.

I rolled back for more sleep, thinking I'd wake up in midafternoon, but I didn't come to until 1830 and had to rush. I showered quickly, dressed, had a cheese sandwich and milk and, feeling both flattered and apprehensive, went to the parking area, getting there only seconds before he arrived in a new-looking silver Karmann Ghia. "We're going to a place called the Crown and Spear," he said as I got in beside him. He spoke casually, as if we went out drinking together every night. In the lingering light he pointed out places of interest: the famous Newbury racecourse and Gray Lion's Inn, one of the oldest in England. We passed a Lavender Lane, at the end of which, he said, was his rented cottage. Though he didn't mention the convoy, I felt sure he was taking me out to reward me for the job I'd done. I wore my only sport coat, light blue, and my best slacks, gray officer's dress pants. His expensive-looking rust-colored Harris tweed jacket contrasted with an open-necked black shirt. After ten minutes of driving we reached the pub, an ancient-looking building about a quarter-mile from the highway at the end of a dead-end road.

"All right," he said, raising his mug. "Tell me a little more about that detour into the old woman's farm."

"Mrs. Willicut."

"How in hell did that happen?"

"Someone turned the signs around. The peace group, I thought. But it's possible the crew that went out the night before pointed one the wrong way."

He nodded. "The peace group, I'd say. And you got yourself away from them with no injuries, no damage?"

"None, I'm sure."

He raised his mug, waited for me to raise mine, clicked his against mine so hard I expected them to crack and to see beer splashing. They held together, however, and before he lowered his to the table, he consumed what was left in a single swallow.

My pleasure over the convoy results was chilled by my awareness of how pointless the whole operation had been. Even if the guns I'd delivered had been fully functional, capable of destroying all attacking aircraft within their range, my pleasure probably would have been no brighter. I was already recalling the children among those who'd been waiting for us at the mouth of Mrs. Willicut's road, eyeing me with the same looks of hatred I and my friends in grade school during World War II had laid on Helmut Dantine and other actors who played Gestapo officers in the war movies. Would there be pleasure in any remaining work I'd do in the battalion?

Norma saved me from having to struggle for an answer to the gloomy and possibly unanswerable question by appearing with two more ales.

My first, which I'd just finished, had reached my brain at the speed of light. I wasn't ready for a second yet and shook my head, but she didn't see me and put the bottles on the table.

"It's about time you brought someone in here besides yourself, Frank," she said. "I was beginning to wonder if you had any friends up at that base of yours."

"I don't," he said, straight-faced. "He's here only because I ordered him to come along."

"Is it true?" She looked at me.

"Not exactly. I mean I wanted to come."

"Well, you're young and nice, and you must come again." She put the beers on the table and tossed me a wink. "With or without him," she said playfully.

"He's too young for you, Norma."

"There are few too young for me," she replied.

She picked up Shea's empty bottle. She was thick and shapely and made swishing sounds as she wiped the table.

Shea was now conversing with the men near the door. They were all, I figured out, sheep farmers, and he was asking the oldest-looking one how much he'd want for his land, making it clear that if the farmer would sell, he might consider buying it as a place of retirement after his years in the Army.

"We pass these places down from father to son," the oldest man said.

"And your son wants yours?"

"Your kind don't retire, Frank," said the man with the brown teeth. "It's not in you to sit still." He seemed to be the pub's philosopher, tuning in on conversations, capping them off with pronouncements, sipping his beer in the meantime.

As I was finishing my second drink, I began to watch Norma. She was leaning against the bar, twisting her hips this way and that. I'd liked her from the first. Now she turned and smiled at someone at a table near ours. Have fun, the smile seemed to say, for tomorrow we may all be in the ground. She brought Shea and me each a third ale.

The colonel was still talking, and she asked how old I was. "Twenty-one," I told her.

"A lovely age!" Her eyes rolled as she swept away the empties.

I decided then and there she was the kind I wanted to marry. Soon, in the grip of the ale, I further decided it was *she* I wanted to marry. The differences in our ages made no difference at all.

Having settled nothing regarding his possible retirement farm, Shea turned back. "I think it's time we got down to the important business of the evening."

"What business?"

"I want to hear about that problem of conscience of yours."

Why was he bringing it up now? Why hadn't he wanted to hear about it earlier instead of threatening me with a court-martial? Leading the convoy, I'd continually thought about what he'd done at the firing range. I felt no different about it than I had the day after I'd witnessed it. What was different was the depressing recognition he'd just now brought me to, that, in failing to take a stand, I, like the colonel, was now a participating member of a conspiracy against the Army, the government, the country itself. "I completed my convoy assignment," I said. "Do we need to bother?"

"Your problem hasn't gone away, has it?"

"No . . . it hasn't." My friends who'd been wounded in Korea came back with battle scars. Most would carry them for the rest of their lives. I'd seen no war. I'd seen other things. What? I come up with generalities only: waste, corruption, hypocrisy, stupidity and lies. But the generalities fit. I'd done nothing about these evils. *My* scars weren't going to be badges of glory like my friends but ugly emblems of guilt, invisible, unresolved and well deserved. I looked across, said, "I'm sure it never will."

"Norma?" He turned.

She came over, said, "You're not drinking. Is there a fly swimming in that ale or what?"

"I'm paying for these, and I'll want a bottle of Black and White—make it two—to take with me."

"Oh, stop being so serious, Frank. You just got here."

"Zip it up, Norma, and get me that booze. Put it all on my bill."

She turned to me. "What's bitten his bottom?"

Apparently me. I shrugged, wondering how much of what he was getting I was expected to drink.

He stood.

I had a drunk's or near-drunk's fantasy. I'd leap up, bop him on the head with my mug and pull him to a corner. I'd then discuss with Norma our future together. When he came to, I'd tell him he'd passed out. By then I'd have arranged to move in with my beloved. We'd live together until the end of my tour of duty, then marry. Mother would have to get used to a woman nearly as old as she.

"Hanlon?"

I looked up.

He was at the doorway. Under one arm was a wrinkled paper sack with the necks of two bottles sticking out.

I pulled myself up and made my way toward him. "The bar is just fine with me," I said.

He pushed the door wide. "Goodnight," he said to everyone but me. Then, with his foot, he pointed me through.

Twenty-four

"**S**pit it out."

It wasn't something easily spit out. Vomited out maybe, or drawn out like a fever. Yet I knew him and his impatience. After hesitating for only a few seconds, I said, "I'd better begin at the firing range. I overheard, accidentally overheard, the conversation you had with Captain South about arranging to have the target planes blown up."

There was only his heavy breathing and the crunching of tires on the graveled road. I was curious but didn't turn. I didn't want to see his face stretched in surprise or, worse, pinched in anger. He said nothing until we turned onto the highway.

"How many planes do you think South brought down?" he finally said in a tone so calm it startled me.

"I . . . have no way of knowing, sir."

"Guess."

"Most of them that came down, I'd say."

"That's as close as you can come?"

I hadn't added and subtracted. "Yes, sir."

"Who else heard South and me?"

"I was on the steps of the tower all by myself."

"And you've told no one?"

With Vernor I hadn't been specific.

"No one."

He went silent again.

Should I, to protect myself, have said, "There may have been another witness," or "Yes, I did mention it to someone—I don't remember who"? No. I wouldn't have been comfortable with the deception, wouldn't have known how to go from it to the next lie, then to the one after that.

The last of the sun's light had vanished. We were weaving through small hills. I glanced at the speedometer. It read seventy. He was slowing a little on the turns, just enough to get around.

"That conversation's why you didn't want to take the convoy?"

This time I hesitated, making sure I wanted to say what came to mind. "Yes," I finally replied. "It's influenced how I think about . . . nearly everything."

"Explain."

Again I hesitated to be sure, then said, "If the guns can't really do the job they're supposed to, only be made to seem that they can, then everything else, nearly everything, seems pointless. I don't, for example, feel I accomplished anything useful delivering our seventy-fives to the other battalions and picking up theirs. To me that was about as meaningful as . . . exchanging swagger sticks."

Once more he was silent.

I decided I could have left out the comparison to his precious swagger sticks. But the rest I didn't regret. Would I feel the same after the effects of the ale were gone?

He slowed abruptly, swung into a turn. As we went around I saw a sign: LAVENDER LANE. Though the road was paved, it seemed even narrower than the road leading to the pub. He accelerated, and the car began bouncing from bank to bank. Just after we'd turned onto the lane I'd seen a large moon ahead, but now overhanging trees were blotting it out. The door on my side scraped a hedge. We'd gone about a hundred and fifty yards when he cut his speed, so quickly I had to reach out and press my hand against the dashboard. I looked up. Before us, slightly elevated and partly visible through a break in a tall hedge, was a squat white cottage with a thick thatched roof. He turned the car, stopped it, then reached back, grabbing the bottles of whiskey. His movements were quick and forceful. He lowered a hand, snapped open his door handle.

"This is where we're going," he said over his shoulder as he slid gracefully out.

I couldn't get the door on my side all the way open because of the dirt bank. I scrambled over the gearbox, got clumsily out on his side, looked up and saw a bright three-quarters moon and, beneath it, him, standing in tall unkempt grass, looking back at me, his hands on his hips, each wrapped around the neck of a bottle. When I started toward him, he turned and headed for the cottage.

A dim light came on as I ducked under the small narrow entranceway. The place was made for people smaller than the colonel, who stood hunched in the doorway to what appeared to be the kitchen. He pointed the neck of one of the bottles toward a room to my right. "Go in there and sit down till I piss and get some soda crackers and find a couple of glasses."

I entered a low-ceilinged parlor, saw in the light coming from behind that there was or seemed to be only one place to sit, a lumpy dark green overstuffed chair. The other potential sitting places—a sofa with a pale green hue that clashed with the forest green of the chair, a pair of wooden chairs that looked old enough to be antiques, and a small bench set against the wall opposite the fireplace—couldn't be used because they were all piled with a variety of objects: unfolded Army and civilian clothes, books, magazines, and a scattering of other things including kitchen utensils, towels, maps and a military .45 pistol sticking out of a holster attached to a shoulder strap that hung over the sofa arm. Much of the floor was hidden by a chaos of books, enough to fill at least a couple of wheelbarrows. Titles included *Man's Fate*, *Witness*, and *All the King's Men*. Leaning against one mound of books were some record jackets. I could see and identify only the one on top: a Bach concerto by Glenn Gould, whose dour young face gazed at me over the top of his piano. On the floor near the albums was a black boxlike record player whose lid lay tilted over the turntable in a way that suggested the hinges might be broken. The sense of disorder was general and included the way the several framed objects hung crookedly on the walls, as well as the juxtapositions of subject matters within the frames— here a peaceful English rural scene but near it the 46th's battalion crest with its bright reds, oranges, yellows, blues and the shouted motto "Hit Them Hard and Sure!" As it was, this parlor couldn't have come close to passing one of the colonel's own inspections. In fact, it would have taken a fast worker a couple of hours to bring it even to a barely passing level.

A toilet had flushed, water had run in a sink, and now the colonel, shoeless, in bright yellow socks, shuffled into the parlor carrying one of the fifths of Black and White under his arm, and two tumblers and a bowl of soda crackers in his hands. He stopped beside me and told me to take one of the tumblers, then crossed to the sofa, raised his foot and forced open a space in the debris. After putting the cracker bowl on the floor, he sat down in the space he'd made and said, "Bring your glass over here, and put some booze in. I drink like the English—no ice. If you want mix, go look in the kitchen, around the sink. There might be some soda water there."

I didn't like Scotch, which I'd tasted only once, in college. I asked if he had any ale. "Scotch only," he said. I wanted to remain at whatever level of drunkenness I'd reached and decided to take some Scotch but sip it slowly and straight. I went over to the sofa and poured myself half a tumbler and returned to the big chair.

"Your brain was on go from the day you first showed up in my office," he said as he poured the golden-brown liquid into his tumbler, "and I'm not surprised you brought up the firing— somehow expected you to sooner or later—not that I figured out you had your ear to the door."

"It wasn't there deliberately."

"I heard you the first time."

He'd filled his glass nearly to the top. He took some, swished it through his teeth, then swallowed and looked across. "I've got no problem with you hearing what you heard at the firing range. You believe that?"

"It's . . . hard to believe, sir."

"But it's true. And not mainly because there were no witnesses besides you or because the evidence lies an unreachable forty feet under water. Or anything else. It's a good thing you finally spoke up. That conscience of yours was causing one momentous problem of communication between you and me."

"I agree." And it still was.

"If you'd come to me sooner I might have told you what I'm about to tell you." He dipped his hand into the bowl, closed it into a fist and brought it up with two soda crackers and part of a third. The extra piece was sticking out between his thumb and forefinger. "You see . . ." He turned his hand sideways, caught the broken cracker between his teeth and pulled it free. After poking it into his mouth with the back of his hand, he gave it a couple of chews and swallowed it. ". . . I made the decision to get some help from South just minutes before the shooting started. And, you may as well know, he'd given us some 'assists' a year ago. I'd hoped by this year we could achieve a respectable score without him, but after watching the guns during the prefiring checks, I was sure we couldn't."

His confession surprised me, but I was even more surprised by the ease with which he'd delivered it. He was like a fisherman explaining why he'd used lures instead of live bait. His tone helped free the question that had buried itself in me from the moment I discovered what had happened:

"Didn't it bother you that what you and the captain did was, might have been, unethical?"

"By whose standards?" he said as he finished off the last of the crackers he'd picked up. "Yours? God's?"

"I could have put that a better way: against regulations. Un-authorized."

"By the Army's standards, you mean."

"I . . . guess that's it."

He took a large swallow of Scotch. "You've got much to learn, lieutenant. I, you, and every other officer, and noncoms and enlisted men too, often find ourselves in a position where we have to interpret regulations, and—"

"I'm not just talking about interpreting—"

"Just a minute," he said sharply, poking the air with his glass. "I wasn't finished. . . . And are sometimes required to go beyond them."

"Required?"

"If you want to press me on it, which you obviously do, I'll come right out and tell you that means occasionally having to ignore a rule, stretch a regulation, sidestep an agreement, play dumb to an understanding, and so on. Every situation you find in those goddam military texts is clean and well-defined, but in reality none are."

He'd reminded me of one of my last classes at Bliss. The lesson for the day was Retreat. The teacher, Colonel Weaver, described what a battery officer was required to do when an artillery unit was being overrun. It was most important, he said, to render your weapons unusable, and, he added, "It's best to evacuate everyone except one enlisted man, who should set a quick charge and destroy both weapons and ammunition." He said that the enlisted man might be blown up by the exploding rounds. "So be sure you choose an expendable soldier." He went on to something else, but I kept thinking about that expendable soldier. Finally I put up my hand, and he called on me. I stood and referred to his earlier remark. "Isn't that deliberately taking one of your own men's lives . . . like murder?" The colonel seemed momentarily unable to respond. I waited, wanting to know. He was holding a pointer. He walked toward my desk, wiggling the pointer at me. "You have an interesting way of putting things." It wasn't the kind of response my questions usually brought. I nodded in appreciation. "War *is* like murder, isn't it? Think about it. They capture that artillery piece of yours and turn it around on you and you're going to see a lot of murders. Huh. Maybe even your own." He looked about. No one else was moving or talking. He ended by saying, "Ask yourselves, all of you, a couple of questions. One, what in hell are you defending? And two, are you willing to pay the price to defend it?" He nodded. "Murder indeed." He waited for me to sit down, then went on with his lecture.

"The history of the military is full of stories about individuals who went beyond the rules. I don't mean nobodies either. Billy Mitchell's theories of high-level bombing became the basis of long-range bombing strategies during World War II, but those very theories had caused him to be court-martialed and dismissed from the service in the twenties. Famous generals played free and easy with the rules when they had to: Grant, Sherman, Pershing, Scott, Rommel, MacArthur, Montgomery. And most war heroes wouldn't have been heroes if they hadn't broken rules: John R. Scott, Alvin York, Papa Boyington, Audie Murphy, many more."

I'd read about at least some he'd mentioned, was aware of how independently they'd acted. Indeed, many had been in trouble with superiors before they became heroes. In all, however, speaking up and taking chances and even breaking rules seemed with them exceptions, not rules.

"I inherited an ack-ack battery in Korea after the previous commander, Captain Barbaros, followed orders to the letter and got himself killed. We'd been ambushed and attacked in a pass north of Seoul. Ten besides the CO got it. Division ordered me to hunker down for the night, said planes would be sent the next morning to cover our retreat. I knew the gooks knew exactly where we were and requested permission for a night retreat. I was refused. After dark I took my outfit out anyway. Before daybreak, the gooks, using mortars, blew hell out of the positions we'd left. We had no casualties. For what I'd done I was awarded the Silver Star. If division had realized in the first place that to stay in the valley was sure slaughter, it would have saved itself embarrassment and the cost of a medal."

The story of Shea's Korean adventure stirred me, as tales of war often did, and caused me to put myself in his place and wonder how clear my thinking would have been and whether or not I'd have had the courage to speak up to division brass. Those of us who hadn't been in combat always wondered. Again and again we'd been told that we'd never know what we'd do until we faced the real situation. As a result, I, at least, partook imaginatively in battles I'd read about or created, many times over, now as a charging hero, now a fleeing coward, now calm, now excited, now terrified. Always I came out of them both alive and as ignorant of myself as when I went in.

"Listen," he went on. "I'll bet that if you're honest with yourself and me, you'll admit you were prepared to bypass standard procedures when you brought Rivera's gun to Potts's battalion. Tell me, if Potts hadn't been waiting to examine the weapon, would you have gone to him or his ordnance man and said, 'Well, I've just parked a damaged gun in your gun park— please accept my apologies'? Or would you have left the gun and gotten the hell out of there, letting Potts later battle with me over whether or not I should have had the weapon delivered?"

I told him the truth, that before leaving Greenham I'd planned to locate the 4th Battalion CO and inform him as precisely as possible about the condition of Rivera's old gun. But, I admitted, I decided a few minutes before pulling into Upper Heyford that I'd drop off the faulty weapon, avoid questions and get out of there as soon as possible.

"There you are."

"Not quite, sir. There were extenuating circumstances. I was exhausted after getting the vehicles off Mrs. Willicut's road and then dealing with the protesters and aware that we'd lost a good deal of time, but most of all had been put in a position by you that appeared to be impossible. Gilley had tried but couldn't get the gun tube below forty-five degrees. As Colonel Potts later put it, I was caught between the frying pan and the fire."

"There are *always* extenuating circumstances, aren't there, lieutenant?" he said, giving me a taunting smile.

"I wouldn't say 'always,' sir."

"How about 'often'?"

I gave him a reluctant nod.

"Even unreasonable ones, like me making you take Rivera's gun in the condition it was in."

"That *was* unreasonable."

He nodded. "As is the condition brigade puts on me every year when it says, in effect, 'Put your guns on the beach up there near Norwich and shoot down this or that many planes.' "

"No." Having sunk back in the chair, I now pulled forward. "It's not the same. The results of those firings affect brigade's, maybe the Army's, thinking about the defense of SAC bases in England, maybe all over the world. If they're led to believe the seventy-fives work, they'll keep them in place, try to get all of them in shape. They'll waste time and money and manpower trying to improve that which isn't improvable. The order to exchange some of our guns for some of the other battalions' proves you've kept brigade believing. Yet the weapon doesn't really work."

"What's the alternative to the seventy-five?"

"I don't know."

"I'll tell you. Nothing. They're now testing short- and medium-range missiles which are due to replace it in a couple of years. But the missiles are far from being ready, and they can't be made ready sooner, no matter how poorly our guns do at the firing range. Until they're ready, all the Army's got for the low- and medium-altitude job at Greenham and other places like it is the seventy-five."

"And you're trying to deceive them and everyone else into believing it can bring down Russian planes."

"Russian planes," he repeated flatly. He put his glass down, slid it aside and twisted off the sofa, going to all fours. He reached under the sofa and felt his way along, finally removing a shoe box. He then searched the mess on the sofa, eventually, with thumb and forefinger, pinching the tip of a worn-looking white cloth, pulling it free and placing it on the floor. He continued on his knees to the end of the sofa where he removed the pistol from its holster, held it, tilted slightly upward, toward the front wall to my right. He pressed the magazine catch behind the trigger, removed the magazine, and pulled the top slide of the weapon all the way back. He turned and gave me a hint of a smile. "Nothing to worry about, Thomas. I'm just going to give it a cleaning."

"I realize that, sir."

After inspecting the chamber to make sure it was clear, he laid the pistol on the cloth, turned and went on his knees to his glass, from which he took an uncharacteristically small swallow, then turned and faced me like a penitent. "Time for your military education to start, Thomas."

"Sir?"

"There aren't going to be any Russian planes."

"I don't understand."

"Of course you don't." He frowned, looking through me and the wall behind me, as if at some great puzzle in the universe. He shook his head and stood. "Be back in a couple of minutes." He plunged toward the doorway. I heard him thump through the kitchen. A door opened and closed. With a great roar he began to throw up. The sound was violent, I guessed like the sound a man would hear if he were lying under the exhaust pipe of a five-ton when the driver was gunning the engine. I put my hands to my ears, heard the roars again, several, muffled. Then, faintly, I heard a toilet flush. I lowered my hands. Soon came the sound of gargling. In a couple of minutes he came shuffling back. "I shouldn't have moved off the sofa so suddenly," he said in a growly voice.

He stood unsteadily beside the cloth, where he'd left his pistol, looked across and said, "There's no way you're going to understand that . . . brappp! . . . the guns don't matter and the Russian jets don't matter and the new missiles don't matter . . . until you acquaint yourself with Shea's Theory of the Cold War."

Twenty-five

"We're never going to shoot down a Russian plane because we're never going to fight the Russians," Shea continued. "The Cold War is convenient for both sides, an ongoing excuse for military buildups. By the way, as I'm talking, interrupt and ask questions whenever you want." He reached down, took a bore brush from the shoe box, picked up the pistol and pushed the brush into and out of the barrel three times, stopping each time to look at it and once (the last) to pick a speck of something off the brush. "I could feel that little demon," he said, holding the speck up. "Just didn't want to come out."

He'd said very little about his theory, but already I had at least a dozen questions. I spoke one: "If we and the Russians aren't going to go to war with each other, why do we build arsenals specifically designed to destroy each other?"

"To . . . breeeeep! . . . terrorize our own peoples and the rest of the world." He ran a dry swab through the barrel and, pulling it out, checked it. Satisfied, he took another swab, put a couple of drops of lubricating oil on it and ran it through, checking it each time.

"One of my philosophy professors would call that statement 'a vacuum cleaner,' meaning the most sweeping of sweeping generalizations."

"Good for him." He held the swab out, looked at it, rubbed it between his fingers, then tossed it aside. He ran a new dry swab through the barrel, raised and checked it.

"What I mean, sir, is that both countries have been preparing for years for a war with each other. Each constantly threatens the other, the weapons buildups on both sides accelerate, and neither side shows much interest in an A-bomb treaty or any other kind. The very reason our battalion is on this base is specifically to protect it and its B-47s from attack by the Soviets."

"It's just a game," he said, "and both sides play it credibly. Before I go on, remember this: since World War II there has been conflict, including threats and crises, like the Berlin Airlift, but no major direct confrontation."

"Because we've contained them with SAC bases, NATO, fleets and other forces stationed around the world. At least that's the government's explanation."

"It's propaganda. Governments never tell you what they're really up to. They tell you what serves their own purposes. Both sides have told their peoples there's a wolf at the door and backed it up by developing weapons to take care of the wolf and, as a result, have produced a lot of fear and patriotism."

"We've got the Russians surrounded and they have us surrounded. It seems to me there just might be real wolves at real doors."

"There are. But each wolf's true interest isn't breaking down the other's doors." He found a clean-looking white cloth in the mess on the sofa and plucked it free.

"They're not worried about war with each other?"

"Yes, but not to the extent that they're worried about other threats like resistance from within or the mice that are beginning to rise out of the grass. You can't, of course, overlook the crazy possibilities, like a blockheaded President thinking that with weapons designed for use against the Soviets, it might be fun to use them that way. Unlikely. The real threat is those mice."

"What mice?"

He went to one knee, set his pistol carefully down on the cloth and began rummaging through the shoe box. "The underfed, uneducated, ill-clothed, unrepresented, untended masses of the world." He stopped and looked across. "They're rising out of the grass in Africa and South America and the Far East, but also closer to home too. In . . . bbrrppp! . . . Mexico and the Caribbean and, hell, right there in the U.S.A." He found a small can of lubricating oil, removed it and, still on one knee, began looking for something else in the box.

If he was right, the small envelope of absurdity I'd felt myself enclosed in along with the impotent weapons and the silly swagger sticks and the humdrum conversations at the bar and the horrible tests and the pointless exchange of weapons and the frantic Captain Ball extended beyond this base into U.S. and Soviet foreign policies and the policies of many other governments and the attitudes of many other peoples, perhaps wasn't, finally, a small envelope but a huge sack in which all of humanity was stuck like a countless number of cats . . . and, I was now being told, mice.

"If the conditions they live under are so bad, how can they possibly give us trouble?"

"Throughout history colonial governments have asked questions like that. The British were asking that at about the time of the Boston Tea Party." He nodded at his observation. "There are ways, Thomas, and, while the U.S. and Soviets play nuclear volleyball, methods are being explored and even practiced. We're not preparing for them, and eventually we're going to be on the receiving end."

"We? Meaning the U.S.?"

"Not just the U.S." He took a small clean cloth from a folded paper bag he'd found at the bottom of the box, put a few drops of oil on it and began wiping the outside of the weapon. "We and the Russians and, I'd guess, some kind of united Europe—if they can get themselves united, possibly including Eastern Europe. You see, I think there's eventually going to be this alliance of larger powers that now, to one degree or another, are the Haves, dominating economically and in other ways control-

ling less powerful countries and peoples." He stopped wiping
and smiled across at me. "Geopolitical and military prognostica-
tion isn't an exact science, Thomas."

I nodded. "Almost everything you say is hard to conceive of,
let alone believe."

He gave a little burst of laughter, like a piece of popcorn
popping. "My father told me my great-grandfather had 'an ear in
the earth,' which meant he could lie down and turn his face to
the ground and hear vibrations or some damn thing and then tell
you where the sheep or horses were and whether they were on
their way or not. I've seen animals give signs before a storm or an
earthquake or, once, an avalanche—fussing and jumping and
such—but never saw a human being do what the animals could.
No matter. I've always felt a little like my grandfather was said to
be, only my ear isn't in the ground but in the air. I've always had
a feel for what's coming, as I did that night in Korea I told you
about." He laughed again. "Take you. If I hadn't had an instinc-
tive sense of your potential for leadership, I'd have written you
off long ago as just another second lieutenant stamped out at
Bliss."

"I appreciate that, sir, but it still doesn't make what you've
been saying any easier to understand or believe."

He nodded. With a clean dry cloth, he'd begun to wipe the
pistol clean. "Do care that you know my thinking but don't care
if you accept it flat-out. I want *you* to start thinking. I've got
enough head-nodding dummies around here who can't. You owe
it to yourself to find out what's happening in the world. I guess
I'm a kind of Marxist in olive drab because I believe that the
Have-Nots are soon going to be acting up all over the world. For
a preview, take a look at what the Vietminh did to the French last
year. Brrfff."

I knew the French had been involved in a costly war in Indo-
china, financed in large part by the United States, and that it had
lost its former colony after a crushing defeat at Dienbienphu.
"Do you see something like that happening with the U.S.?"

"We'll surely have opportunities to get ourselves burned somewhere."

"And in the meantime both sides waste time with the Cold War?"

Holding the pistol up to the light from the hallway, all he'd had to work with as he'd cleaned the weapon, he turned it one way, another, and finally, seeming to approve of his cleaning job, replaced its magazine and slid it back into its holster. "Thomas . . ." He turned, saw, then went over and picked up his drink. "The Cold War keeps the attention of everyone on the Soviets and the U.S. It's very good for both countries. It's like the distracting movements of the magician, the red handkerchief he waves with one hand while, with the other, he transfers a pigeon from his shirt to the sleeve." He cautiously took a sip of Scotch, then another. "Stay down, stay down."

I'd also been sipping, very slowly as planned, and didn't feel light-headed or as tired as I had when we'd arrived. The conversation was like a workout. Even when we weren't speaking, my brain worked at full speed. I was now connecting Shea's Cold War theory to the event that had set off the conversation in the first place. "I can see that if what you've been saying is true, what we actually did at the firing range, I mean whether or not our guns actually brought down as many planes as they were given credit for, doesn't really matter."

He closed his eyes, not the way one might after biting into a lovely piece of cake but the way one might after dropping it on the floor before he'd had a chance to take a bite.

What had I missed?

He took a mouthful of whiskey, held it, finally swallowed. "Whfffff."

"The red handkerchief," I said, finally making a connection. "That's it!"

"Brp."

"The guns appearing to do well was *your* red handkerchief. The weapon, acting up, had seemed . . . well, mystical, and you, showing it could be controlled, seemed even more invincible. You kept everyone's mind off the pigeon . . ." What pigeon? There had to be a pigeon. No. "There was no pigeon. No . . . war. No . . . anything. Not even guns that we could play war games with back at the base. You could produce nothing. Except . . . another red handerchief!"

"Which was?" he asked.

"The swagger sticks."

He raised his tumbler and said, "You're not much, Thomas, but you're the best I've got."

"And the gun exchanges, I guess, and inspections, all red handkerchiefs you've been using since the day you got here. You worried that if you didn't use them, someone might wake up and find out how empty and pointless—Jesus!—everything is."

Finishing what was in his glass, he tossed his tumbler onto a red-and-black-checkered wool hunting jacket lying on top of other things on the sofa and said, "Tomorrow there'll be another handkerchief, long and silky." He nodded. "I'll bring it out with a whip and a flourish."

"What's it going to involve?"

He stepped toward me, leaned down, and made his eyes go wide like someone pretending to frighten a child. "You!" It came out like "Boo!" He laughed at my startled response, then tilted his head toward the doorway, indicating it was time to leave. "Tomorrow," he said, "I'm letting you report in at one. When you do, go directly to battalion headquarters, not Battery A. I'll have a surprise waiting."

Twenty-six

.✒.✒.✒.✒.✒.✒

S hortly before noon I made my way dizzily into the bar
area, where about a dozen officers were scattered about,
all waiting for the dining room to open. Among them
were officers of the 46th—Gilley, Perkins, Perkins's new assistant, a Lieutenant Speer, others too—all of whom I wobbled
past, trying to get the attention of the young bartender.

I'd been awake for nearly two hours. The headache that had
begun to tighten as I'd made my way to the bathroom for a
shower had finally closed like a band of steel. Though I was
dizzy and slightly nauseated, I dared order the hair-of-the-dog
drink that Shea, anticipating my hangover, had recommended
before letting me off in front of the club: Scotch in milk.

The bartender winced when I gave my order.

I waited, eyes closed, recalling, as I had been doing frequently
since awakening, Shea's remarkable presentation the previous
night. I'd savored the colorful phrases—"nuclear volleyball,"
"mice in the grass," "red handkerchief"—marveled at the impressive display of knowledge, wondered over startling visions of
things to come. All had been integrated into a statement that had
jostled the foundations of my beliefs. I felt as I had after reading
great works like Plato's *Republic*, *Hamlet*, *Crime and Punishment*
and Swift's *Modest Proposal*. The world, the Army, life itself
seemed, in an instant, to have been inexorably altered.

The bartender, whose name, Harry, was sewn on his shirt pocket, watched with widening mouth as I raised the drink. He was still watching after I lowered the glass, half empty. "Will you live, then?" he said.

"I hope so." The unpleasant concoction didn't seem to be making any difference. I told myself to be patient.

When Harry moved off, I escaped into other recollections about Shea, remembered him calling himself a Marxist. It now seemed that the appropriate model wasn't Marx but one of the philosophers I'd read while searching for an antidote to Thomas and Aristotle: Friedrich Nietzsche. He'd been a screamer against the empty platitudes of his time, one who saw real distinctions between his "overman" (wrongly called, according to my professor, the model for Hitler's "superman") and the weak, degenerate and morally blind creatures who made up most of the world, those hopelessly out of touch with their own individualities. Shea was the "overman." For me he had provided a rationale for events that had seemed, until now, pointless, unethical, even cruel. Those included the arrangement with Captain South. What better way to assert the Nietzschean self than to create value out of the actions of those useless guns?

I opened my eyes, moved my eyeballs from side to side, felt pain.

Harry, hearing me groan, stopped wiping glasses in front of me, reached into his pocket and brought out a matchbook-size packet of Bayer aspirins. "My mother worked at a pub near one of your bases during the war. When I had my first job on a Yank base, she said, 'Carry some of these with you at all times.'" He opened the tin and dropped a couple of tablets into my hand.

I downed them with as little help as possible from the odd-tasting drink.

"It's best to be still."

I didn't intend to move any part of me until the headache subsided.

The aspirin, maybe in combination with the hair-of-the-dog drink, worked quickly. Moving my eyeballs from side to side didn't bring pain. Finally I turned, wanting to ask one or another of the battalion officers behind me what had been going on this morning. Surprisingly, the only ones who remained were the Air Force officers and a couple of captains from an engineer detachment that was extending one end of the main runway. I turned to the door leading to the dining room. It was still closed.

Where had they gone?

I had no idea.

I slid off the stool, paid for my drink, thanked Harry and made my way upstairs to put on my Ike jacket. My stomach was still queasy. I decided to skip lunch in favor of something from the base snack bar later that afternoon.

Twenty-seven

*A*lvin Carter, the sergeant major, led me to a small room with a desk and two chairs. The room was pinched in between the CO's office and personnel. "You're supposed to get yourself settled in here, sir," he said.

"For good?"

"Yes, sir."

"Why?"

He glanced toward the desk, then pointed.

I walked around, picked up the only object on the desk, a sheet of paper, and read:

> Second Lieutenant Thomas Hanlon is appointed Battalion Liaison Officer and Special Assistant, CO, 46th AAA Bn. Memoranda follow.
>
> Shea
> CO

As I was puzzling over the order, Shea, looking only a little disheveled, came into the office and said he'd sent it out early that morning after calling brigade to make sure there would be no snags in the appointment. "It's a 'bastard' position, but they've okayed it."

"Do I have enough experience for a job like this?" I said, dropping into the desk chair.

"No. No one does. But I need someone for special assignments. Don't have a damned executive officer because there's no one I trust for the job. Can't make you an exec. Your rank's too low."

"Isn't there anything less—well, I don't know—public?"

"What do you think this is, a grocery store where you can pick out a job like a cucumber?"

"No, sir, but I was thinking that maybe some of the others aren't going to understand why I . . ."

"Hell," he said, picking up my swagger stick, which was lying on the desk, "none of them will. But they'll get used to it just like they get used to everything else."

Had the 46th's officers walked out of the bar in protest over my new job? Would there be other reactions? I imagined Ball's bewildered response, including pleas to Crawford to explain why someone as clever as Shea could appoint someone like me to a job like this.

"They'll be talking about it for days. They'll argue over whether it's legal or not. It'll occupy every conversation. It's one reason I created the position."

"A red handkerchief."

"Red handkerchief. You going to be able to take the heat or not?"

"I think so." Did I have a choice?

"I'll check with you in ten days to two weeks and find out how the shoe fits. Maybe I've put you in one that's too tight."

Apprehensive about the position, I nevertheless wanted it.

"I'll try to *make* it fit," I said.

"We'll see." He looked through the office's only window for a few seconds, then nodded. "If either of us, you or me, don't think it's going well," he said, turning, "I'll have a new order cut that'll put you back in the battery of your choice. Let's talk about it in about ten days." He pointed the stick at me. "Fair enough?"

I'd, in effect, been guaranteed I wouldn't have to serve under Ball again. "Very fair," I said.

The convoy experience, Shea's speech and, perhaps most of all, the appointment he'd just made left me feeling more important than I'd felt since I joined the Army, maybe more important than I'd ever felt. Oh, there'd been moments of glory here and there, as when my father told me I was a better swimmer than he at the same age (eight), when the eighth-grade baseball team I captained won the city championship and when I received the only A grade ever given by the University of San Francisco's celebrated Thomist, Dr. Abraham J. Askew. There were probably others. But they were moments only. My new confidence was, or at least felt, permanent. I supposed a long time would pass before I knew whether or not I could adapt to Shea's imaginative and pragmatic approaches. But I wanted, desperately wanted, to shed habits I'd come to depend on like alarm clocks.

He began to tap the palm of his hand with the stick. "I'm going to give you an opportunity to establish a few credentials. I want evidence not only of command work like the convoy but staff work too. I'd like to be able to put you in for an early promotion."

"Really?"

"Really. After my tour of duty here, I expect to be given a plum of an assignment. Don't know where yet. But if things work out, I'll try to take you along."

"But I'm scheduled to be discharged in about seventeen months."

"You have a corporation back there waiting for you to take it over?"

"No, sir."

"Anything?"

"No." I'd considered law school or graduate school. But I felt no strong attraction to either. There had been no profession or line of work that drew me strongly to it, including the Army.

"Think about it," he said, tossing the stick onto my desk. "I looked at your file this morning. You came on active duty just after you turned twenty-one. You could be out with good retirement pay by the time you're forty-one. May seem old to you now. It's not." He turned. "You might be a full colonel by then." He stopped in the doorway and turned back. "Who knows? Maybe even a general."

After he left I asked questions I thought I could answer for myself.

Do you think you'll want to stay in the Army for twenty years?
No.
But nothing attracts you more?
Nothing. But something surely will before I get out.
You sure?
No.
Why not, then, consider an extended tour of duty, not twenty years, but a few, to get time to think about a possible future in civilian life and a possible future in the Army?
I might.
You should.

By 1530 I'd gotten most of the additional supplies I needed for the office. I'd had only a milkshake at the snack bar, and by 1630 I was hungry and returned to the club early.

Gilley and Perkins were among the several officers waiting for the dining-room doors to open at 1700. I slipped past others and approached them smiling. Together, as though they'd rehearsed the moment, they turned away. The snub was ridiculous. It left them both with their noses only inches from the dining room's two long doors. I waited, watching them, not averting my eyes when they looked at me. Finally the doors opened. I waited, then walked over to the table the two had taken and said, "Do either of you mind if I sit in one of those two empty chairs?"

Gilley turned away.

Perkins stared at me as if he might be laying a curse. "Some others will be eating with us," he finally said.

"Oh."

Gilley half turned. "You make some kind of deal with him for that new job of yours, Tom?" His face was tight and his ears red.

"No, I didn't."

He turned away, obviously not believing me.

Maybe Shea had gone too far. I wanted to explain why I thought the CO had made the appointment, say, "It's a reward for my work with the convoy." But to explain, I felt, would be to show weakness. It was important now that I not show weakness. I looked around but saw no one else I knew. I'd eat at the club snack bar. On the way out of the dining room, I encountered Ball.

"Who do you think you are?" He was blocking my passage.

"Excuse me, sir."

He was standing very close to me. He came even closer, whispered, "You're seeking power, aren't you?"

"No, sir."

Crawford appeared from behind him.

Wanting some kind of understanding, I smiled, said, "Mike, I want you and the captain to know—"

"Ignore him!" said Ball, moving on.

Crawford lifted his hands and shrugged as if to say, You know, I'd like to sympathize, but I don't let myself say or think or feel or do anything that might upset the captain.

I shook my head and went to the snack bar.

Twenty-eight

.r.r.r.r.r.r.r

T he snubs and insults flung at me in the dining room that afternoon were, it turned out, only a warning of troubles to come.

The next morning, when I went to Battery A to take personal belongings from my old desk, I noticed a small battered cardboard box lying on the floor between the orderly room and the supply room. Looking closer, I saw words scrawled in marking pen on one side: LT. HANLON'S STUFF. The box was so battered that when I tried to pick it up, a side fell off, and books, notebooks, pens, pencils and other items spilled onto the floor. I went to the supply room, where Bronowski found me a sturdier box. I complained to him about the one in the hallway. He told me he'd heard Ball tell Crawford to have my things put out there. "Said he didn't want any reminders of you around the orderly room." He shook his head.

I told him what had happened at the dining room the day before. "I guess they're bothered by my new job."

He returned to the tall stool behind his counter where I'd found him dozing when I walked in. He was like an owl the way he dozed on that perch of his without tumbling to the floor. "Maybe, maybe not."

"What else could it be?"

He crossed his arms and blinked slowly. "Convoy," he said.

"Worst thing you can be around here is competent. Nothing threatens officers in this battalion more than that. You did a competent job and threatened them."

What he said made at least as much sense as my explanation. I'd delivered the guns, led the convoy out of a trap and overcome protesters. I wasn't like Crawford, who'd passed his test by going onto a beach and carrying a live mine to a blockhouse. His act had been mindless and, despite what he thought, heroic. His they could applaud and then forget. Mine had been competent and had set a dangerous precedent.

Was that it?

If so, it explained Gilley's reaction to me in the battalion headquarters hallway about an hour after I brought the box to my new office. I was returning from the lavatory and smiled as we neared each other. "I've been wanting to say thanks for the medal you made for me," I said, hoping a conversation would result.

His eyes locked onto the hallway baseboard, and he skidded past me without a word.

He was the first friend I'd made after arriving at Greenham and the one whose coldness was affecting me most.

Soon no officer at battalion headquarters was speaking to me. Since my duties required that I deal with several face to face, the silences must have been as troublesome for them as they were painful for me. Perkins, for example, called his assistant, Sergeant First Class Gomez, whenever I went to personnel for information. Gomez would then point me to the filing cabinet containing the information I needed. Perkins managed all this without letting his eyes meet mine. Flu, Buckles, Captain Ewald in operations and the others handed me papers and took them from me, but never looked at me or uttered a sound.

The colonel had earlier asked if I could take the heat. I was painfully taking it, not sure how long I could go on without pleading for relief ("Send me to C Battery. Please!") or making the concessions necessary for me to become acceptable to my persecutors. This last was an option I instantly found repulsive and rejected. Soon the first seemed nearly as objectionable. The only condition that would cause me to back off in any way, I realized, was a collapse in my faith in Shea. And so far nothing threatened that. In fact, the punishment by silence I was receiving from the other officers renewed that faith, for it gave further evidence of their pettiness and of his incredible power over them.

Twenty-nine

.,.r.,.r.,.r.,.r.,.r

I heard my name and looked up from the seventy-five round I was cradling to see against the dying sun the unmistakable silhouette of Captain Vernor moving toward me from the gun pit's entrance, abruptly stopping when he saw what I was holding.

"Finish what you're doing," he said. "I'll wait outside."

He was honoring a brigade regulation: when ammo was being handled, no one except the handler or handlers was supposed to be in the gun pits. Vernor was strict on himself and others when it came to regulations, despite his reputation for attempting to have changed those he didn't like.

Recently the battalion had been sent a shipment of ammo. Soon afterward, a couple of gunners complained during one of Shea's tours of the sites that some casings were dented. My first assignment as special assistant was to spot-check the ammo at all the sites.

After I came out of the pit, Vernor guided me away from some of the crew lingering near the entrance, toward a flat grassy depression several yards beyond the gun shack.

"What are you doing at one of my sites, lieutenant?" he said. The sun had just fallen behind a distant hill, and, against the pale green sky it left, the captain was still mostly a silhouette.

I told him about the gunners' complaints and my assignment.

"You should have told me before you came here."

"The colonel didn't say anything about getting permission."

"It's not a matter of permission," he corrected. "It's simple courtesy. Do you know why he didn't send Gilley?"

"No, sir."

"Gilley's ordnance. Normally he would check the condition of ammunition."

He was right, I realized. In addition, Gilley lately had little to do.

"Or if it's a matter as serious as damaged ammunition, why didn't he inform me and his other battery commanders?"

I thought he had. "I don't know."

He turned and paced to the edge of the depression, looking to the right, then left, as if he were searching for one of those intruding planes Shea had said would never attack. He then gazed ahead, toward the bright spot in the sky where the sun had just descended, toward the last shimmering light.

A couple of days earlier Vernor had intercepted me as I was making my way to the snack bar and invited me to join him and two of his Air Force friends for lunch. I hesitated, but then, wanting company, said, "Sure," and followed. As he and the others chatted, however, I felt the eyes of my critics. I looked up and, sure enough, they—Ball, Perkins, Buckles—were, each in an unfriendly way, eyeing me. Within a few minutes Vernor had somehow figured out what was going on and said, "You'd better learn how to play 'Jackie Robinson.'" One of his friends nodded. Both friends were black. "What's that?" I said. "A way to survive," he replied. Then he explained: "You start by learning more about your enemies than they know about you. You then ignore their snippy-nips, and start dealing with their big noises. If they now and then get the best of you in public, you never let them beat you inside the head. In other words, you learn how to do your dance better than they do theirs. And always keep your mitt coiled 'cause sometimes nothing else works. If you have to go that far, be sure you have only friendly witnesses. The originator, the real Jackie, makes his slides with the baseman between him and the ump. None of those umps belong to the NAACP. When he's got to spike someone, he makes sure they aren't in a position to see. You understand?" I told him that I thought I did. Then and there I gave his advice a try. Glancing around, I caught Perkins's judging eyes. I stared back, then shook my head. I later smiled at Gilley and Crawford. Ball didn't give me a chance. Eventually the others stopped looking. After a while Vernor turned and spoke by tilting his head and shrugging: it takes practice.

"How many bad rounds did you find?" he said, coming back.

"None, so far."

He nodded, then led me back to the shack, where he turned and said, "I think he's using you. He's not only got you working for him, he's got you on display. This ammo inspection. He's playing you like a pawn in the middle of the board. I don't know why."

I didn't want to violate Shea's confidence by talking about the red-handkerchief tactic. I said only, "I'm sure, in a way, he's using me. But he's also given me a good opportunity."

For a few seconds Vernor didn't respond. I tried to read a response in his eyes but, because of the bright bulb behind him, couldn't. He made no effort to get me to keep what he'd said from Shea.

"To some extent he uses everybody, doesn't he?" I went on. "Isn't that part of being a good leader?"

He didn't answer. Finally he glided into the darkness beyond the shack and was gone.

The bulb shone harshly down. I had to put my hand up to shade my eyes. I looked nervously about, trying to remember where I'd parked the jeep.

That night I slept uneasily. Twice I woke and found I'd kicked the blankets onto the floor. Shivering each time, I picked them up and the last time tucked them tightly in at the sides. When I woke up in the morning the blankets were on me, but I was grinding my teeth. By the time I ate breakfast I was fighting off a biting headache.

Thirty

L ate the next day I finished my report on the ammunition and brought it to the colonel's office. He signaled
me to wait. After signing some papers for the first
sergeant, he read what I'd handed him. "Good, very exact," he
said, looking up. "But you're not finished." He slid it across his
desk. "First, write in the name of every gun chief whose pits had
damaged ammunition. I'm going to give you a follow-up task
that involves each of them."

"Punishment?"

"That's right."

"Isn't . . . finding the bad rounds enough?"

"Finding them doesn't make a point. We need to make a point.
The fact is, your work has just started." He pulled his chair
toward the cabinet farthest from him, opened the bottom
drawer, removed a handful of files, held them above his head.
"My records on everyone in the battalion are in here," he said
without turning around. "My scorecard on each of you. These
are just a few." He slapped them back into the drawer, wheeled
the chair back to his desk. "Sooner or later someone's going to
make a complaint. Or maybe I'm going to have to get rid of
someone. Or maybe there's going to be some sort of challenge to
the way I run this outfit. I keep records on everyone's screw-ups.
Yours included. The last report on you had something to do with

a remark you made about the swagger sticks. It's all there. I've got back-information on those who let bad ammo get into their gun pits."

"They were just unlucky, weren't they? I mean, that's what was given to them."

He shook his head. "A round of ammo enters your pit, and you're responsible."

"What about those who sent us the ammo?"

"Not in my command. But you do remind me of something. Give me a copy of the report for Gilley's file. He should have noticed the bad stuff by now and reported it."

"Maybe he did notice but said nothing because he knew I was doing a report."

"No excuse."

I'd taken a lot of time from my studies during my junior year in college to watch the televised Army-McCarthy hearings. Shea's secret list reminded me of the papers Senator McCarthy raised out of his jacket pocket now and then, saying in his grave villainous baritone, "I have here a list of known traitors . . ."

He was tapping the eraser end of his long unsharpened wooden pencil against his desk blotter. "I appreciate good officers and men. I don't spend a lot of time harassing Vernor or Pryzbyskowski even though I can't stand either of them and know neither would cross a street to give me water. But they do their jobs." He nodded. "Now, there's more to your job than just naming the sergeants with the faulty ammo. Who, by the way, are they?"

"Bird, Curry and Rivera."

"I want you to investigate. Find out exactly who supervised the loading of the ammo at each pit."

"Why, sir?"

He stopped tapping and looked across. "Because I'm probably going to court-martial one or more of them."

"God!" I slid forward. "Just for dented ammunition?"

"Dented means damaged, and damaged ammunition can produce dead gun crews."

"But . . . not if it's not used." I reminded him that we'd gone to the firing range without bringing the ammunition from Greenham because seventy-five rounds were available at the range. "According to what you told me, we'll never use what's here at Greenham, against the Russians or anyone. It won't *ever* be fired."

"What's that got to do with the price of anything?"

The remark was a sharp reminder that what he was up to had nothing to do with defending anything. It was part of his game. He had to conceal the painful absurdities from those in his command. There'd be no war, but he had to maintain the illusion that sooner or later the Russians were going to come. He had to pretend the failure to check ammunition mattered vitally. Maybe I could at least persuade him to lighten the punishment. "Is Article 15 a possibility?" This was a nonjudicial punishment that could be administered by the battery COs. The degree of punishment was limited.

"It's a possibility, but I'm not interested in it."

"Why?"

"Figure it out." He was tapping the pencil again.

"You need to wave another red handkerchief?"

"And why do I?"

I recalled that a few noncoms had gotten into trouble in recent weeks. One had spent three days in the guardhouse for trying to fight half a dozen Air Force people at the NCO club. Another had dented the sentry box at the front gate returning from Reading. A third had impregnated a sixteen-year-old Newbury girl he'd met in a pub and claimed to believe was twenty-one. Only one of the sergeants in trouble was a gun sergeant, however. Why was he picking on them? "I guess you want to shake up all NCOs and intend to, well, use the gun sergeants as examples."

"Close enough." The tapping was fast now, like my heartbeat after a long run. "I want you to find out all the circumstances. Did the gun sergeant himself check the ammo? If someone else did, did he report the dented rounds to the sergeant? Did the sergeant then report anything to his battery commander? To anyone? And so on. Make it thorough."

"Suppose I find that one or more of the sergeants aren't directly responsible?"

"I doubt if you will, but if you do the penalty will be less severe."

"What would the penalty be if, say, the sergeant is directly responsible?"

"Depends. If your report shows they might have violated standing Army and brigade regulations regarding live ammo, I'll recommend a special court-martial, and it could be a dishonorable discharge and two years at hard labor."

"Jesus!" I said. "How could . . . how could it possibly be so severe?"

He gave me a troubled frown. "I didn't make the damned Punitive Articles, Thomas. Sit down."

Only after he told me to sit did I realize I'd stood. I sank back into the chair.

"If they're found guilty of dereliction of duty, a lesser offense," he went on, "it could be up to three months at hard labor and forfeiture of pay for the same period."

All the possibilities shocked me. I didn't know Curry, but Bird and Rivera were conscientious crew chiefs and had by now become friends. "Is there a chance you'll issue or recommend a lesser punishment?"

"Of course not! They'd laugh. Putting letters of reprimand in their files or letting their battery COs do an Article 15 or doing a summary court-martial would be just the signal not only the NCOs but the officers and enlisted men would be looking for, a sign of weakness. Generally speaking, I never go for the mildest charges but the harshest. It saves me from having to mete out more punishment later."

Our battalion led the brigade with fewest arrests, confinements and court-martials. I supposed that was because Shea had brought his heels down hard after arriving. But there had been a general loosening-up since the firing.

"What you come up with is going to determine what kind of punishment I lay out," he said. "Everyone's going to know there's a connection. They're all waiting to see how tough you can be, how far you can go along with me. That's why the officers are giving you trouble. Wait'll you see what the NCOs do if they sense any weakness." He must have noticed my uneasiness. "You sure you can stomach this assignment, Thomas?"

I hesitated, then said reluctantly but honestly, "I don't know, sir."

He let the pencil fall on the blotter, watching it, not me. "I said you could opt out of the assistant's job in two weeks. The time's nearly up. If you want to avoid this assignment, and others to come, I'll have orders cut to send you to whatever battery you want. No penalties."

I said nothing.

"If you end up choosing to do the investigation, do it carefully. I don't want you tipping off anyone accidentally. You don't need to say why you're asking questions. Just ask them. Find out what needs to be found out."

I thought about requesting time to consider getting out of both the assignment and my increasingly troubled job as his assistant. But all fears, apprehensions and other arguments for escape were overcome by my desire to adapt to a philosophy, or whatever Shea's approach to the world was, which seemed more applicable to the military life I was actually living than anyone else's, including my risky own.

"It's Friday," he added before I could reply. "You can take the weekend. Let me know by noon on Monday."

"No," I told him, not yet sure I'd hold up. "I'd like to start the investigation right away, if you don't mind."

His smile let me know he didn't mind at all.

Thirty-one

.r.r.r.r.r.r

Sergeant Bird approached my jeep, penguin-walking
faster than usual. When he came close, I saw that he
was holding up a handful of photos. "Got to show you
the kid, lieutenant. The wife took some pictures at the play-
ground in Bayonne. Have a look." He extended the photos, then
began dealing them from the front of the pack to the back.
"Hyarr! Looks like me, no?"

She did, just like him, more like him than she had in the last
photos I'd seen: short arms, no neck, and now his prankster's
smile. He'd said her name was Maggie. "She and Momma are
coming over to be with me for my last year. We just decided."

"When?"

"They leave by plane on the second."

I wanted to grab his lapels and say, "Tell me you weren't on
duty when the new ammo was brought to your pit. Tell me it
was Sergeant Waxman or Corporals Hoskins or Canfield. Otherwise your child might get her first look at her father from the
visitor's side of steel bars. Speak!" I just stood there, nodding
and cooing at the photos.

"So what you doing out here?"

"Got to ask some questions about that bad ammo," I replied,
falsely casual.

"Two rounds only came to me. Not bad. Rivera told me four of his were bad. Somebody else—"

"Curry."

"Right. He had one."

I didn't want *anyone* to be punished, but Waxman and Hoskins and Canfield were younger, not married, and Shea would give the corporals mild punishments because they weren't NCOs. He might also go easy on Waxman because he'd only recently been promoted from corporal.

Bird began flipping through his photos for a second time.

I phrased my next question carefully, hoping it would stir some cautious thought. "You weren't the one who checked the new ammo the night it was delivered, were you?"

"Huh?" he said, looking up.

"You weren't the one in charge when the bad ammo came in." I paused. "Were you?"

"I was right here," he said, sounding accused. He removed folded waxed paper from the pocket of his fatigue jacket, placed his dozen or so photos in it, folded the paper carefully and tucked it back into his pocket.

"But you weren't, were you . . . the one who checked, actually looked at and discovered the faulty ammo?"

"Hey, lieutenant, you know me better than that." He carefully buttoned the flap of the pocket with the photos. "I'm the one in charge here. Ask anyone in this crew. No ammo gets in my gun pit without me seeing it."

"I thought there might be an exception."

"Why you asking me this stuff?"

"I have to," I said. "Orders." Was that enough of a clue? I didn't know. It was the most I could give. I'd be sure to give the same to Rivera and Curry.

"You can tell the boss, if that's who you're asking for, I spotted both of the bad rounds before you came and found them. The crates were busted. That's what made me look."

"But," I said tensely, "did you then report the damage to anyone?"

"Nah." I trailed him to the gun shack. He took a pack of Lucky Strikes out of the jacket pocket above the one with the photos of Maggie. After lighting up, he said, "I carried them myself over there where they sit now." He pointed to the storage spaces, where I'd found them, carefully separated from the undamaged ammo. "I got it on a note to tell Pryzbo. But he hasn't stopped here since a couple of weeks ago, before it came in."

"Do you have the note you wrote yourself to remind you to tell . . ."

"What's going on?" he said, suddenly suspicious.

"I can't tell you, but . . . well, you can figure it out if you . . . if you think about it for a few minutes."

"Shit," he whispered, backing up. "Shit, shit, shit." He gave me a desperate look. "He's headhunting?"

Bird would question me for hours if I said anything more about my presence. "Get me that note. It'll . . . maybe it'll help."

"Son of a bitch," he said desperately, turning, pulling open the gun-shack door. His eyes were wild with fear. "Son! Of! A! Bitch!" In a few moments he came back with the note.

I grabbed it and fled.

Thirty-two

·/·/·/·/·/·/·

I felt a tap on the shoulder and turned.

A tired-looking man about forty was withdrawing the pair of shears with which he'd apparently touched me. "Are you all right, sir?" He wore the dark green war-surplus coveralls all the groundskeepers at Greenham wore.

I'd been leaning against my jeep with my head resting on my arms, which were crossed over each other on the vehicle's canvas top. I hadn't been asleep but, I quickly realized, in something like a trance.

"What time is it?"

"I don't carry a watch, sir, but I'd say about a quarter past two."

I tried to patch events together. I'd left Bird's gun site at about 1220, had gone . . . where? Directly to the club, into the nearly empty dining room, where I'd eaten lunch. No. Had ordered lunch but then began to think about Bird, the possible consequences of his failure to report his damaged ammo. Suddenly not hungry, I left the dining room, went out and sat down in one of the soft dark leather sofas at the corner of the ballroom and grabbed the day's *Stars & Stripes*, hoping to distract myself. Little good it did. I'd remembered Bird's photos, Maggie's face smiling up at the camera, at him. The child and wife wouldn't be coming to England at all; he would be going to the States in handcuffs, under guard, to serve his time at Fort Leavenworth, or wherever. His wife wasn't in the photos, and I therefore imagined her: a short round woman with auburn hair and a very white face with pale green, sad-looking eyes. "Lieutenant Hanlon found a few dented rounds in my gun pit," he'd tell her. "I was court-martialed and must spend years in here—without pay." In my mind the years passed, and I saw him afterward, dragging the remnants of himself up a stone path toward a tiny brown bungalow surrounded by weeds where his wife wearily stood at the door with the girl, five or six now, peeking from behind her skirts. They rushed him, and he picked up Maggie and all held each other, hugging and kissing and finally weeping together, and he said, "Don't worry, darlings! There must be some kind of a job for a man with a bad-conduct discharge and time in prison. . . ." I saw much more: the endless job hunting, the cruel taunts Maggie had to take at school, the wife Molly's futile efforts to help by cleaning houses and taking in sewing. I tossed the paper aside, got up, went to the dining room and ordered a sandwich, which I forced myself to eat, looking at no one because I was caught in yet other post-conviction miseries of Bird and family. I'll lie, I thought. *Yes*! I'd persuade one of Bird's gunners to accept responsibility for finding and not reporting the bad ammo. *No*! Shea would see right through that. What should I do?

I next remembered that I was or had been leaving the club, not arriving, had been about to go to the gun site of Sergeant Curry. After that I'd planned to go to Rivera's site. Yes. Today was Saturday, and while other officers were headed for London and Stratford and Brighton, I was going to begin *and* complete my ammo investigation. I got into the jeep, started it, wheeled about and headed for the base.

My hands shook on the steering wheel. You're overworking yourself, I told myself, at the same time realizing that *not* to work now, this weekend, not to try to solve the mystery of the unreported ammo, would assure me of a couple of sleepless nights. And then what sort of condition would I be in? I approached the base with the hope that I'd find some marvelous accident that would stop Shea from having to bring Bird and the others to court-martial.

I next saw myself at a distance, as if I were someone else. I was wearing my Ike uniform and was moving slowly, not aimlessly, but with deliberation, toward the tall rushes that surrounded most of the lily pond below the manor house. I wasn't trying to avoid them but going right on, into them, sinking, sinking as they parted for me. And then the pond itself opened darkly. Calmly I watched myself go peacefully down, jacket bubbling out with air, arms spreading, darkening and disappearing, then, more slowly, the head going in, inch by inch, cap floating off, hair being pulled to one side by water, darkening as it entered, all of it, until not a strand, not a trace of me remained. This was the vision I'd had standing beside the jeep. No wonder I'd blotted it out!

I was now approaching the back gate to the base.

The Air Force sentinel saluted.

To free myself from the memory of my morbid vision, as vivid now as it had been the first time, I made conversation. "You see those Hawker Hunters doing maneuvers over the base the other day?"

He had, thank goodness. The Hunters were specially painted British fighter planes, part of a new RAF aerobatic team. "I like the umbrella maneuver," he said. "You see that?"

"No. What was it like?"

"All four shoot up together and then kind of fan out."

"I looked up a little after they started. It must have been terrific."

"Really nice, lieutenant. You missed the best one."

We talked of trivial matters for a few minutes, long enough for me to get a distance on my suicidal vision. Obviously it was a child of the other, the vision of Bird in his pitiable condition. I talked to the sentinel until the last traces of it had disappeared. Pulling away from the gate, I warned myself: no charges have been brought against Bird or anyone yet. Calm down!

Yet suppose there appeared no marvelous accident?

Thirty-three

.r.r.r.r.r.r.r

*H*erbert Claude Curry was a sergeant first class who'd been in the Army since 1944, one of several blacks in the battalion who'd served before segregated units were dissolved in 1947. Tall, wide and muscular, he reminded me of a pro football tackle. He had a powerful baritone voice and was said to be a spit-and-polish disciplinarian. "Life ain't a barrel of fun under Sergeant Curry," one of his crew members assigned to my convoy had complained.

Curry didn't come out to meet me as Bird had. After glancing at the jeep, he seemed almost indifferent as he turned and stood, back to me, beside his radar, a screwdriver in his fist. He peered over the technician crouching before him. I saw that the side panel under the radar dish had been removed.

"Excuse me, sergeant," I said, stepping softly up beside him. "I wonder if I can ask you a few questions about some dented rounds I found here the other day."

He didn't turn. He spoke not to me but to the technician, Rawlins, who wore beige overalls. "Try tightening the lock nut." He continued watching as the technician did what he'd told him to. Only after Rawlins finished tightening the lock nut did the sergeant speak to me. But not in response to what I'd said. "You went and got me a sick cow, lieutenant."

His was one of the guns I'd brought back in the exchange. "The ones I took out weren't any better," I said.

"Mine was." He turned. "Now what's this about ammo?"

I told him again why I'd come to his site, asked if he'd inspected the new rounds the night they were delivered and then reported any damage.

"No. Maybe Chicken-neck did." Chicken-neck was a skinny six-foot-two white from South Georgia who, for some reason, followed Curry around as though he, Chicken-neck, real name Bobby Lou Roberts, were his cocker spaniel. In fact, he was one of Curry's gun corporals.

"But then did *you* check on Chicken-neck?"

Curry closed his eyes the way sergeants often did when speaking to second lieutenants. "What's the old man doin' now?" he said. "Nigger-huntin'?"

"No. I've just got to question you and two other crew chiefs, Bird and Rivera."

"Sergeant-huntin'."

I admitted nothing.

"Hey, Chicken!" Curry called, turning. When Chicken didn't appear, he began to make chicken sounds, loudly: "Cluck cluck cluck . . . cluck cluck cluck." He watched the gun shack, waiting. Finally he said, "Hang on, lieutenant. That scrawny little cracker must be sleepin'." He moved toward the gun shack.

Would I soon be having waking nightmares about Curry and Chicken-neck? My fantasies were, I decided, the product of sentimentality—"the mawkish and excessive outpouring of useless feelings," according to my favorite college English professor. Sentimentality, I knew, marked not only bad literature but bad philosophy and history. Bad life too.

Hadn't the Army also warned about sentimentality? Captain Sloan, newly back from Korea, startled our senior-level class one day by speaking of his favorite gunner in his forty-millimeter battery, Billy Arnold: "Took a piece of shrapnel in the eye that come out the back of his neck." He'd spoken as calmly as if he'd said Arnold had scratched his finger, then went on: "That little

fucker would bring down two planes with the same round.
That's how good he was. We went fishing together between
battles a couple of times. Stray mortar round came into our area.
He was handing me his watch to hold for him when he became a
statistic." No tears, no regrets. The next thing Sloan said,
matter-of-factly, was, "What page were we on before I told you
about Billy?"

Like Sloan, I had to stay away from sentimentality—in
thoughts, actions, dreams, nightmares, all of it.

There came another reinforcing recollection. Old leathery
Sergeant Elmer Thornwhistle at Bliss listened as one of my
comrades, Lieutenant Gerald Terry, who was leading us on a
march, said, "I think we'd better take a rest, sergeant, or the
other guys are going to get touchy with me." Thornwhistle
winced at the word "guys," and again at the word "touchy," then
said, fiercely and without turning, "This ain't no goddam
poppa-larity contest, loooo-tenant." The memories seemed to
help, because when Curry came out of his shack with sleepy-
looking Chicken-neck dragging behind him like a white Steppin
Fetchit, I was ready to storm him with tough questions.

Before I could do so, Curry said to me, "Here I pull this rag of
a creature out of his cot, lieutenant, and tell him it appears he's
going to be doing thirty-five to eighty years in the penitentiary
'cause of not checking and reporting the bad ammo, and he says
back to me, 'What ammo, sarge?'"

"That so?" I said coldly, turning to Chicken, who'd floated to a
stop at the side of and partly behind the sergeant. "Are you
denying that you detected the faulty ammunition the night it
was delivered?" I raised my clipboard with blank sheet and
pencil, letting him know I would record his answer.

"Ah'm denying I know what in hell you're talking about,
lieutenant."

"Watch your tone!" Curry said.

"Come here," I commanded, putting the clipboard aside. I led
both of them to the end of the stacked ammo, for it was there,

after using a black indelible marker to put an X on the packing box with the bad round, I'd left both box and round.

"You don't mess around with officers," Curry, behind me, was telling Chicken. "They say they saw something, you say, 'What color was it?' Like that. Understand?"

"Well . . . ah guess so."

"Here," I said, then noticed something. "Wait." The crate I was pointing to was in the slot where I'd left the bad round but wasn't marked. "Must be . . ." I checked slots nearby. "No." I looked at the ends of all the crates. None had an X on it. "Did someone turn these crates around?"

"No, *sir*," said Curry, shaking his head. "Noses in, back ends out. See there, on all of 'em, it says 'bottom.'" He looked to the sky, streaked with wispy clouds, seemed to study one of the clouds, then looked back at me.

Chicken and he and I counted the ammunition. We found one hundred and forty-four rounds. Not one was dented or damaged in any way.

Chicken grinned at me. "Ain't that nice to see, lieutenant?"

"Get the rest of the crew out here, Sergeant Curry," I said.

They were soon lined up outside the pit, Chicken-neck among them, Curry beside me looking on. I mentioned the missing round and said, "I know what I saw when I was out here the other day, and it's not here anymore. One seventy-five-millimeter round. Any of you who have any information as to where it might be, you should, for your own sake, step forward this instant."

Chicken-neck, at the right end of the line, turned to the others, none of whom stepped forward, then looked back at me and gave me a shrug.

Curry, in deep and severe tones, chided them, saying, "In case you nobodies have forgot, the person speaking to you is an officer in the U.S. Army which you don't mess with, meaning if you have taken, hidden or in some other way misappropriated a seventy-five-millimeter round or know of or heard of the scum who did any of the above, or even might have, step forward. Otherwise count the minutes until you are locked or strung up."

Though his hyperbolic speech bothered me, I held back my urge to say, "Just let me handle it," hoping he might draw a quick confession out of someone.

After speaking about what it would be like in prison—"And they let your loved ones come and visit once per month only, so it just might be you will end up begging for the noose"—Curry drew nothing more than a few oohs and ahhs. Finally he turned to me and said, "What I am seeing here, sir, is three men, four if you count Chicken a man, who say they don't know anything about what happened to the round that you saw sitting in this gun pit last time you were here."

"What about the others in your section, the ones on the other shifts?"

"Dang," he said, as if to let me know he should have thought of that himself. "We can go check at the barracks, where the ones not on pass are sleeping."

"All right," I said, though I was worried that I'd end up facing dumb stares like the ones now before me. "First, however, I'm going to Sergeant Rivera's site, where I . . ." I turned to the crew, each standing disheveled in some odd form at the at-ease position, all looking to me like escapees from a mental hospital. ". . . hope to get more cooperation than I've gotten here."

Chicken-neck nodded, as if to say, "That's just what I'd do."

"You no good flea-eaten mongrels, you!" I heard Curry say as I moved to my jeep.

Thirty-four

.~.~.~.~.~.~

Sergeant Rivera got up from the rocking chair his crew had given him last birthday and in which he sat in warm weather, usually smoking small Italian cigars. "What brings you out on a nice sunny day like this, Lieutenant Hanlon?" he said, shooting me a near-perfect salute.

"Business, I'm afraid," I told him.

He smiled and said, "Please don't tell me you want to take Granny away. We're just now getting used to her." He and his crew had named the new gun Granny because it was slow and gentle in its responses, unlike the one with the bad tube we'd exchanged.

"Yours to keep," I told him. Two of his skeleton crew were sunbathing with fatigue tops off on top of the sandbags. Both simultaneously sat up and turned to me when I told the sergeant I wanted to look at his damaged rounds.

Rivera took off his cap and massaged his thick, barely graying hair. "What you talking about?" he asked.

I told him impatiently that I was there to look at the four rounds I'd found and marked unusable. "The ones I put in the supplemental ammo slots in your gun pit."

He was frowning.

"Here," I said, bolting past him and into the pit. He hadn't been at the gun site when I found the damaged rounds. I led him to the place where I'd left the rounds in their marked crates. "Look," I said, but when I myself looked I found the slots empty. "Where are they?"

"Where are what, lieutenant?"

The sunbathers were leaning over, watching, their expressions blank.

"Let's count your rounds, sergeant . . . just you and me."

We did.

Before I reached one hundred, Rivera said, "One-forty-four, just like when I got out here today."

He'd made me lose count. I started over. I needn't have bothered. He was right: one-forty-four. Without the dented rounds there should have been one-forty.

By now not only the sunbathers but two others, from the shack I suppose, were leaning over the top of the pit, watching only me, as though I were a trained monkey Rivera had ordered in to entertain them. "Please come down here," I said impatiently, moving my eyes from one to another.

When they came down, I had them form two teams, had each team open and show me seventy-two rounds.

Rivera stood beside me. "Looks good to me, no? . . . This one too. . . . Nothing wrong, so far, eh, lieutenant? . . . Hey, look at that. All one-forty-four just like new Cadillacs."

I turned to him fiercely. "Where are the dented rounds?"

He ended as he'd started: "What dented rounds?"

Don't lose your cool, I warned myself, but a second later I shouted, "Shit!" and started toward the jeep.

They'd defeat me only if I let them. Who did I mean? I didn't know. Rivera? Curry? Chicken-neck? I didn't know. No matter. What they couldn't do was erase what I'd seen. Or could they? Wasn't it doubt about my perceptions that was now driving me to Bird's site?

I found him wearing an incredible outfit: chartreuse pants, a white shirt with black bow tie, a garish tweed sport coat with big black and yellow squares. He was standing beside a jeep, just about to get in. "Back again, eh, lieutenant?" He seemed awfully cheerful for a man who'd just a short time ago seemed to know he might be court-martialed. And why, at such a grim time, was he so happily dressed? "Off till Monday morning, sir. Just came out to get my show tickets, which I left in the shack. Some of my men on passes this weekend wanted me to go to Reading to hear some new skiffle group, but I told 'em, no way when Spike Jones and His City Slickers are in London."

I nodded, fine, fine, but said, "Before you go, please take a moment with me to look at that bad ammo."

He nodded, said he had plenty of time, since the first shuttle bus to the train depot didn't leave for half an hour.

Together we looked.

We found no damaged ammunition. None!

"Bless my feet!" he said, turning. "Where in the hell did they go?"

"Let's check all the crates."

He put his whole crew to work.

We counted and checked every round, found one hundred and forty-four, none dented.

I raised my foot, sent the toe of my boot violently into a sandbag and shouted, "Where in the hell are they?"

Bird looked searchingly up, as though the answer or maybe the bad rounds themselves would momentarily fall from the heavens.

"Goddammit!"

I then went to every one of our remaining gun sites and searched, then over to the concrete-enclosed ammo storage area at the far end of the base, then to the battery supply rooms, then to battalion supply, finally to the Air Force bomb and ammo area. At each place I personally looked at every round of ammunition. I spoke to all the gun sergeants and gun corporals not on pass. I spoke to every Air Force person having anything to do with ammo. I learned nothing. I was going to keep Bird from going on pass but didn't because I didn't know whether or not he had anything to do with the damaged ammo missing from his site.

I silently invoked the names of philosophers, some of whom I'd never read, pleading for guidance. None arrived, and I soon began digging for the courage to call Shea and make my report. Fortunately he'd be at home. This was one message I didn't want to deliver face to face.

Thirty-five

.r.r.r.r.r.r

<big>B</big>efore I finished delivering my report, the breathing sounds that had been punctuating it through the earpiece of my office phone stopped.

"Sir?"

I heard a crunching sound, somewhat distant. A wooden box being stepped on? I pictured the colonel's record player. But a moment later there came a thump that sounded like a small body being thrown against a wall. His fist hitting something? Next came a roaring curse followed by another thump, louder, bringing to mind a larger body. Possibly he'd flipped his overloaded sofa onto its back. Clippety-clapping footsteps approached the phone. Again came the sound of breathing in the earpiece.

"Colonel?"

"These gun sergeants have sharked us, lieutenant."

"Sharked?"

"Hoodwinked, bamboozled, snookered, flimflammed, slickered, slugged. Got the picture, Thomas?"

"Are you saying the investigation is finished?"

"Yep."

He, of all people? "Sir, before I called, I prepared some suggestions as to . . . well, what I might do next, and I wanted your opinion." I'd anticipated an angry reaction, had imagined even more noise than there'd been. But, now, suddenly . . .

"Why do you say we're finished?"

"Because we don't have the damaged ammo, that's why."

"I was going to suggest we check at the other bases. It might
be hidden there."

"And it might be in the English Channel."

I shook my head, as though he could see me. "It couldn't be
far away," I said anxiously. "I saw Bird's this very morning."

"Hah. It could be in Germany." He paused for a few seconds.
"My fault, Thomas. I should have told you at the start to pick it
all up and bring it back to battalion headquarters. Should have
had you put it in the safe in intelligence."

I gave another suggestion: "Can't we figure out from the lot
numbers of the remaining ammo what the lot numbers of the
missing rounds are and . . . well, have them make a search at the
other bases?"

"Why? They'll already have many of the same lot numbers
as us."

"Do you think they went to those bases for the clean
undamaged ammo to replace the bad stuff?"

"They probably contacted one base, where someone had a
connection."

"Crews there took damaged ammo for good and put themselves at risk?"

"Risk shit. Within a week that bad stuff will be at brigade's
arsenal and new stuff will be in its place. Good NCOs can make
deals for damn near anything. For all I know, our three sergeants
sent someone to brigade today and traded direct."

"And we can't trace it?"

"Ah, Thomas, you're still green."

"There's no way?"

"No way. Bird sang you a happy bird song about that kid of
his. Good NCO bullshit. But when he found out you were
investigating, he made a plan. The minute you were gone he
contacted Rivera and Curry and God knows who else and the sly
work began. My guess—while you ate your lunch and fretted

and did whatever else you did, they cleaned out their nests." He paused, then said, "Why can't half my officers be just half as smart as those half-assed NCOs?"

"What do we do now?"

"I'll think of something. It sure as hell won't involve the NCOs. Them I'll get back to some other time. Right now I'm going to go outside and finish training my rambler roses to stay on their trellises."

"Sir, you said it was important to establish, more or less, my authority among the officers and men, including NCOs. I'm wondering if what just happened didn't serve to . . ."

"We've taken a defeat, Thomas, but one battle doesn't make a war. I'll cook up a bleeder for the NCOs later. In the meantime, after I trim my ramblers, I'll think up a new project for you, a good one. The next battle's got to be ours."

Thirty-six

.r.r.r.r.r.r

*T*he first shot, fired on Monday morning, was aimed at the officers, with one I barely knew, Captain Buckles, playing bull's-eye:

Promotion review of Captain Homer R. Buckles, USAR, will be completed ten (10) days following date of this order. Second Lieutenant Thomas V. Hanlon, Special Asst., CO, will collect and coordinate data pertinent to this review. All officers in this command are expected to cooperate with him fully.

Shea
CO

The captain's upcoming review had been high-level scuttlebutt in club conversations since before I'd left with the convoy. Preoccupied, I'd paid little attention but did know it would be critical. Buckles, before joining the 46th, had been passed over once for the rank of major. If he was passed over again, he'd have to leave the Army within a year, a few months short of the date when he'd qualify for retirement. "After nearly twenty years he could end up with nothing," Perkins had said.

"Your ears must be burning," Paul Kinsella, one of the colonel's clerks, remarked as he dropped off schedules the morning after Shea had assigned me to collect Buckles's records.

"Why do you say that?"

"Been listening to them gossip over at the snack bar."

"Who?"

"The staff officers."

"And what are they saying?"

"Not nice, sir." He started to leave.

"Wait. Were they . . . talking about the ammo inspection?"

"Well, sir . . ." He hesitated, then said, "One of them called you 'the colonel's first mistake.' "

I didn't ask who, hoping the pain from the remark would dissolve sooner if it had no one on whom to blame it. "Anything else?"

"One of them claimed he heard the NCOs had started a pool where each puts up five bucks and picks a date when you'll be dumped."

"Was that the worst you heard?"

"Well . . . no, sir."

"What else?"

He started to leave.

"Wait," I said. "You started. Now finish."

He hesitated, then told me only that it had to do with favors I might be performing for the colonel.

"Favors?"

"Look, sir, I shouldn't have said anything."

"But you did. Please go on."

He turned away, thinking, turned back. "Most I'd like to say is someone called you 'the colonel's concubine.' "

I now wished he'd never mentioned my burning ears. "Thanks," I said weakly.

His news depressed but didn't surprise me.

I felt its impact an hour later, when I went into personnel to get Buckles's records. Perkins watched me search through five file cabinets. I found the records in the sixth. He could have saved me an hour by simply pointing to the last cabinet on the left. As I was leaving his office, he said, "Don't lose those." Irritated, I stopped, told him I'd be glad to do my record-making in his office. "I don't *want* you in here," he said.

In the next few days others displayed their feelings more openly than ever: Gilley did an abrupt and exaggerated about-face when I approached in the headquarters hallway, Ewald slammed a door, Matzusaki whistled songs like "Paper Doll," full of innuendo. The worst was Buckles himself. Thin and sullen, he seemed to be leaning against the wall outside supply every time I entered the hallway, eyes stalking me as he sucked on a toothpick. He didn't speak or even nod.

Shea stopped in my office and said, "Summarize everything that seems pertinent to you, the pluses and minuses. If you're not sure about something, list it. I'm nearly sure about what I'm going to do about him, but I want the info I'm going to need to argue both ways." He didn't tell me how he was leaning or why he wanted both pluses and minuses.

I shared a worry: "If I, somehow, get tripped on this assignment or . . . trip myself up, I doubt I'll have much credibility on whatever you give me next."

"You won't need it."

"I won't?"

"There wouldn't be another assignment, Thomas. I'd have to send you to a battery."

And even in Vernor's battery life would be difficult, made so not only by the other officers and by the NCOs but by enlisted men too. I would become a Minelli or, worse, "the blond kid." There'd be little I could do to change any of this, little Shea could do.

Inspired by fear, I worked hard.

The material I put together during the next few days left little doubt. Buckles's record was truly undistinguished. He'd enlisted as a private in 1937 and, between then and the U.S. entry into World War II, spent much time in the guardhouse, once for gambling, four times for disorderly conduct and once for being AWOL. Four-plus years after he'd enlisted, the Japanese bombed Pearl Harbor. He'd by then reached no higher than the rank of private first class. World War II saved him. Promotion to corporal and then sergeant took place within a year, because there was a desperate need for experienced personnel to train the large number of troops being drafted. In March 1942, Buckles, now a sergeant, was assigned to an antiaircraft artillery training battalion at Fort Bliss. Though he didn't distinguish himself, he was offered a rare opportunity. With the rapid buildup of men and supplies prior to the North African campaign of late 1942, noncommissioned officers were allowed to apply for an abbreviated officers' training course. Buckles applied, was accepted and squeaked through. Afterward, in March 1943, he was attached to corps headquarters in Tebessa, North Africa. His services there and later, on Luzon in the Philippines, weren't notable except for a single event: while retreating from a Japanese counterattack, First Lieutenant Buckles failed to read a map correctly and lost himself and three forty-millimeter guns and crews. He and the others were discovered several days later, when the counterattack was repelled. He was reprimanded. Following the war he served almost exclusively as a supply officer for several units in the United States, then was assigned to England. His efficiency reports were consistently unenthusiastic and frequently contained terms like "average" and (more frequently) "below average," "slipshod," "plodding," "lethargic," and "uninspired." There was one area of exception, represented by the following remark: "Buckles, despite his faults, can find nearly any kind of equipment a CO needs. I never ask him how." Several comments like that appeared in his file. He'd been in the 46th for nearly a year and had done nothing to change his reputation. During the last two major inspections, one by officers from U.S. Army, Europe, and one by officers from brigade headquarters, his supply operation was rated "low average."

After completing my summary I called the colonel and told him it was ready. He soon came into my office and surprised me by saying, "Well, do we recommend him or not?"

"I'd say you don't have much choice." In fact, there were matters I hadn't mentioned, like his frequent duty-time trips to

Reading to stay with his girlfriend, Darlene. "Even if I've left something good out, like a decoration or commendation, I don't see that it would help." I hesitated. "Am I supposed to be giving this opinion?"

"If I say you are, you are."

"Well then, I'll tell you just what I think. When I started I was bothered by having to deal with another person's career, even indirectly, still am, but I was rooting for him, wanting him to be promoted so that he won't be put out before he qualifies for retirement. But now my only question is how he made it to captain. Aside from the promotions that came from lucky breaks and accidents, there doesn't seem to be an explanation. No wonder he's been passed over for major."

"Textbook analysis," he said. He picked up my report—three pages in all—flipped through it, put it down, looked across. "Do you like Indian food?"

"I've never had Indian food."

"Lots of curry powder, a bit hot, like Mexican food."

"I like Mexican food. What are you going to do?"

"Take you to an Indian restaurant in London."

"No. I mean about Buckles."

"You tell me."

"I already know . . . I think."

"What?"

"Not recommend him for promotion."

He'd picked up my ball-point pen, was punching the silver button top, making the tip go in and out, watching it, not me. He smiled, stuck my pen in his shirt pocket, stood and said, "I'll pick you up in front of the club at eighteen hundred tomorrow."

"What about Captain Buckles?"

"I'm going to promote him."

"Why?"

"If you're going to stay on the team, Thomas—and the team really isn't the battalion, it's you and me—then you're going to have to learn to think like a team member. Try, between now and tomorrow, to figure out why I'm promoting Buckles. I'll ask you about it about the time I'm sprinkling curry powder on my rice."

The Buckles promotion had something to do with his red-handkerchief game.

But what?

Thirty-seven

W^e didn't get to London.

Just as we were pulling out of the officers' club parking lot, Shea brought his car to a skidding stop and pointed past me to the sky over the Newbury racecourse.

I turned and saw what appeared to be purple orchids falling from a thin layer of clouds about a quarter-mile beyond the track.

He bent low to look through the side window behind me. "Damn," he said, straightening.

"What's going on?"

He swung the car around, toward the club entrance. "They're parachutes. A couple of months ago, at a meeting of battalion COs up at brigade, we were told that the British would make a surprise mock attack on one of our bases sometime in the near future. It's a test of Army ground defenses called Operation Night Watch." He stopped at the main doors. "Those are parachutes and ours is the base. I didn't think it would happen so soon and didn't think it would happen to us." He looked out at the track again.

My eyes followed.

The first chutists were already landing on the infield. The track was less than a mile away.

"They'll regroup and try to take the base after dark."

"Can't *we* go after *them?*"

"Just what they want. It's the beginning of a weekend. We've got only a small contingent. Getting us off base would suit them just fine." Blinking with a nervousness I hadn't seen in him, he hurriedly gave me instructions, let me out, then spun his Karmann Ghia around and squealed off toward the base.

The officer of the day was Vernor. He'd looked through the dining-room window and seen the parachutes. He'd already carried out the instructions I was about to relay: alert all the officers who happen to be at the club and tell them to get to their posts as soon as possible. When I told Vernor about Night Watch, he shook his head and said, "He should have warned us right after that meeting at brigade."

As officers scrambled to the front of the club from the bar, snack bar and dining room, I hurried to my room and quickly changed into military fatigues.

When I returned to the doors, Vernor assigned four officers to me and the headquarters jeep I'd been keeping at the club. He took the remaining five in his OD jeep.

After delivering the others to their batteries, I found Shea alone in his office, bent over a map spread open on his desk. Moving toward him, I saw the Newbury area, including the base. At the top of the map was the back entrance and at the bottom the main gate. There were two wooded areas, one about forty-five degrees to the left of the back entrance, beyond the officers' club, another about forty-five degrees to the right.

"Where do you think they're going to come in, Thomas?"

"Don't you know, sir?"

"I've got a good idea. I want to see what you think . . . "

I looked more closely at the map. The base had a nine-mile perimeter. How was I supposed to know where they'd come in? I took a guess:

"At one of the far ends."

He shook his head.

"Where?"

"Just a minute."

Maybe he *didn't* know.

And why were there only a few officers at battalion headquarters? After he finished moving his pencil from one point to another on the map, I asked, "Where's the rest of the staff, sir?"

"Those who didn't leave for the weekend are coming in from their houses. Sergeant major's making calls now. Some of them may get caught."

"You mean the enemy force can stop them out there?"

He turned, said stiffly, "Would a real enemy let someone return to a base it was about to take? Of course not. Combat exercises are the same. It's a battle without bullets. All else is the same. There's no saying 'We're ready to start now,' or 'Time out. I have to take a crap.' Understand?"

I nodded.

"Good. I'm going to need you. Why are you staring at the map?"

"You were going to show me where they're going to come at us."

"Near the back gate. Here." He signaled me to move closer to the map. With his pencil he pointed to the top. "I'm going to deploy Batteries B and C behind the back fence, not far from the gate, B facing one of the wooded areas, C facing the second. The enemy is probably going to reconnoiter at the racetrack, come up to the base through one of those woods, maybe both. They'll look for vulnerable points, where they'll try to cut the fence and go under. My guess is that they'll come in to the left of the gate, since that would put them closest to base headquarters and the control tower." He spoke firmly, untrippingly, as if he himself had written the enemy's attack plan. "They're figuring we're thinking of someplace less obvious. They'll therefore try a feinting move at one of the far ends, maybe even at the front gate. Since it's nearly five miles around the fence going around left or right and since they'd have to go through heavy woods on one side or through fenced properties on the other, I doubt they'll make a false attack at the front gate."

I heard others stumbling into the building. The phone rang. Shea answered and began taking notes.

When he hung up, he told me, "That was Colonel Cavellini from brigade operations. He's just arrived with the referee team and, among other things, told me to assign an officer to act as official recorder, to make a report for him."

My confidence in myself rested much on his in me. "Me?" I said, hopeful.

"Right. You're also liaison for me. I'll send you around to the sites as soon as everyone's dug in." He picked up the phone, told the base operator to connect him on a conference call to all the batteries, then told me to tell all staff officers to come to his office.

Within fifteen minutes he'd shared with all of us his plan for the defense of Greenham Common. Not once did he backtrack or hesitate. Despite the nervousness apparent now in the quick movements of his hands, he showed no impatience with anyone's questions. After outlining the general plan, he gave specific instructions:

"First thing the British are going to do if they get through the fence is cut wires," he told Chief Matzusaki, communications officer. "Have the battery COs communicate with us here by ANGR-5 radios. Bring one in here and get one over to the base commander's office."

He told First Lieutenant Orren Lee Gamble, assistant S-2 officer, "Take all Top Secret and Secret documents out of the battalion safe and carry them to Hangar Number One, where there's an underground bomb shelter with a safe. Keep them there and stay with them, along with your sergeant and clerk."

And to Gilley he said, "Check for periscope firing on all guns and make sure the battery COs have the seventy-fives near the possible breakthrough points, ready for use against ground targets."

When he was finished he asked everyone in the room and on the other ends of the phone lines, "Do you have any questions or suggestions?"

There wasn't a peep from those in the room, and there were no sounds from the phone.

"Let's take it to them then," he said like a football coach moments before a kickoff.

The officers moved out quickly, some actually clapping their hands.

Thirty-eight

~·~·~·~·~·~·~·

*I*n lingering twilight I watched first Vernor and then Pryzbyskowski complete impressive defenses near the back gate. Taking sandbags from nearby seventy-five gun pits, they'd made a small fortification around the sentry post, added extra protection around foxholes (even as the holes were being dug) and built barriers to protect their command posts, each of which they'd located in a covered area well back from the gate. Removal of the sandbags also made it easier for crews to aim the guns against ground targets, including crawling commandos.

After checking the solid but less impressive defenses at the far ends of the base and relaying to Captain Carroll at one end and Lieutenant Baker at the other what the two captains had done, I drove to the main gate and looked for Captain Ball, who'd been put in charge of the defense of the front gate.

He was nowhere in sight.

What I found was unorganized clusters of enlisted men strolling about and swinging their loosely strung rifles like the batons of high school cheerleaders. Shea had assigned Ball only twenty troops plus Crawford and available noncoms. But where was Crawford and where were the noncoms? None of the men seemed to be aware they were supposed to be defending anything. The sentry box and other structures lay exposed. I moved on, toward the main gate.

"Where's Captain Ball?" I asked a private first class and a private who were squatting at the side of the road, picking at the grass as though they'd been assigned to find four-leaf clovers.

"I don't know," said the PFC, as both men slowly rose.

"Over there, sir," said the private, sending his hand laconically toward the nearby base information booth.

The building was an oversized box, certainly the most exposed and vulnerable structure around. I pulled up, saw the captain, a puzzled mannequin, gazing out of the single large window. Puzzlement turned to disappointment after he saw me. And when I entered the booth, he snapped, "What's he sending you around here for, to snoop?"

"No, sir," I said back quickly. "I've brought you a copy of the defense plan to look over, plus code names and some information on what the other perimeter commanders are doing. I'm supposed to get your proposed defense plan in return. I'm also supposed to find out if you need extra equipment. Flashlights. Entrenching tools. Things like that."

Things like that, his mouth repeated silently.

He was wearing an oversized GI overcoat and reminded me of the grim and weary Josef Goebbels I'd seen in documentaries about the last days of the Third Reich. He shook his head, then turned and peered through the window, toward the runway.

"Sir?"

He grunted.

"Where's Mike?"

"Lvvrrpll," he said from behind clenched teeth.

"Sergeant Grey?"

"Lnndnn."

"And . . . Sergeant Bronowski?"

"Shit!" he shouted, making a circle of breath on the window. He turned. "I don't *have* any goddam officers!" The coat quivered. His hands were in his pockets. He began to flap his elbows against his sides like an ostrich who's decided it can fly. "I don't *have* any noncoms!" He turned toward me, eyes frantic. His elbows snapped to his side and stayed. "Which is why it's *not* what I'm doing not on my own that matters."

The remark made little sense, but I didn't try to unravel it, said only, "What's not, sir?"

"*That's* what's not."

I gave up.

When he was under pressure, his replies were paper airplanes flying into meaningless curlicues. Without Crawford and Grey and, to a lesser extent, Sergeants Berry and Bronowski, the captain couldn't think straight. His assistants kept his mind going more or less in one direction, prevented him from embarrassing himself. They'd developed numerous tricks to keep him calm. I'd learned none of the tricks, which is probably one reason he had no use for me.

"Minutes," he said, spinning toward me.

"Yes, sir." By responding to everything he said I might at least prevent him from uttering complete babble, which I had a feeling he'd been doing before I entered. Had he even noticed the men under his command wandering about?

He now began bouncing up and down on his toes.

"Captain?"

He didn't give any sign he'd heard. Eventually he stopped bouncing and pressed his face to the window like a child anticipating Santa Claus.

I heard the rumble of a large truck.

"Sir?"

No answer.

The sound grew louder, and soon a five-ton loomed hugely outside the window.

The captain waltzed to the door, turned, said, "Did I say you have to call?"

"Call, sir?"

"I think I did," he said cheerfully. "And . . . oh, how many minutes?"

"Minutes?"

"Minutes. Did I say?"

"No, sir."

"Ten. Repeat."

"Ten?"

He nodded, went out, pranced to the passenger side of the truck, climbed in. The driver, Miller, shrugged at me. I shrugged back. We both looked at Ball, who flicked his hand, which meant he wanted Miller to get moving.

The vehicle slowly pulled away, headed toward, of all places, the front gate.

Before I'd left battalion headquarters the base commander had issued an order: no vehicles on or off the base after dark. Surely Ball would be turned back.

But, watching, I saw the Air Police sentinel wave him through.

The five-ton, growling loudly, pulled away from the sentry station and moved toward the highway.

I threw open the door and hurried toward the gate.

The sentry, wearing a flak jacket and blue steel helmet with JONES painted in white across the front, told me that the captain had gone into Newbury to pick up troops.

"Troops!"

"Yes, sir, lieutenant."

"I thought, because an attack is imminent, you were told to keep everyone here after dark."

"That's true, sir, but . . ." He looked to the west, where a strip of pastel green held at the horizon. ". . . the dark isn't here yet."

"It will be by the time he gets back, if he does."

"Well, now, that's true. I just guess I better let him back in, though, no matter."

"What troops was he talking about?"

The sentry shook his head. "Real hard to say." His forehead wrinkled. "I didn't understand him. He said there was twelve or fifteen. He didn't say twelve or thirteen but twelve or fifteen, like that, then he pounded his hands on his knees and said, 'Oh God damn!' Like that. I didn't know what he meant."

"Did he say which noncom?"

"Well, he did mention a name. Barry?"

"Berry?"

"Berry. Yes, sir. This Sergeant Berry had phoned me at the gate here and said him and some others were down at the Goat and Whistle. He said he heard about the base being attacked and wanted to come back and help. I'd been watching this Captain Bell—"

"Ball."

"He was sort of hopping around, and I called him over to the phone. He listened to Berry for a couple of minutes and then hung up and called someone. I was standing outside the box but could hear him asking about a truck to come pick him up at his command post. Whoever it was must have asked what command post, because he put the phone down and came out and said to me, 'What would be a good command post?' Hell, I didn't know. He said, 'Oh, shit, never mind,' then looked around and went back and said, 'The base information booth.' After that he hung up and went over there to wait."

"He didn't try to put the troops here into defensive positions?"

"He didn't pay no more attention to them than I would to someone else's kids at the PX."

"Thanks." I turned and hurried back to the information booth.

I took the radio out of its case. The captain should have done this. I'd take no pleasure in telling Shea what Ball had done. I got the antenna up and began to hear static. I found the right frequency, but the static remained. Was it the right frequency? I checked the three-by-five card on which I'd written it, turned on the "mike" button:

"Discount One to Poppa. Discount One to Poppa."

No answer.

I wondered if I should forget the call and try to set up the defense around the gate and surrounding fence.

No. That was the captain's job. He could do it when he returned.

Would he return?

If he did, would he have time to set up a defense?

Was he capable?

Shea would have to instruct me.

"Discount One to Poppa."

"Poppa to Discount One."

"Discount One to Poppa. Need instructions from Poppa One."

Shea listened to my report, first about the status of the batteries, then about Ball.

When I concluded, he said nothing.

The static cleared.

At least another minute passed.

Then came Shea's voice, booming: "Poppa One to Discount One. Tell Able One report to Hilltop on return. Over."

I asked about the troops that might be on the truck. He said he wanted truck, Ball, troops and all to report to headquarters as soon as possible. He concluded by saying, "Take command for Able One, Discount One." Then, in lowered voice, he added, "Here's an opportunity for you. Over and out."

For the next few minutes I paced about in the tiny information booth, grateful for the confidence Shea had shown by giving me command of the front gate. He wanted Ball to report to him when the captain returned, which probably meant I'd stay in command throughout the mock battle. The opportunity he'd spoken about was, I guessed, the chance for an early promotion. As I swelled with ambitious thoughts I looked through the window and saw enlisted men throwing pebbles at each other. "Damn!" I said, making toward the door.

Thirty-nine

·,·'·,·'·,·'·,·'

I ordered the pebble throwers to follow me and soon found the rest of A's leaderless mob playing a game with bayonets on the long grassy mound twenty yards inside the front gate. The mound was bordered by skull-size stones painted white. At its center tiny blue flowers spelled out a message:

RAF BASE GREENHAM COMMON
WELCOME

I watched someone flip his bayonet into the grass among other bayonets. The game held their attention so completely they didn't notice that I and three others had joined them.

"Who's in charge here?"

Several turned, a few tossing lazy salutes.

I didn't bother to return the salutes, only repeated my question more loudly.

The rest of the men turned around. I counted three corporals. One of them said, "Either one of them or me, sir," pointing to the other two. I knew them all from my time in Ball's battery. The speaker was Earl Detwiler. His eyes moved nervously about.

"Figure it out and tell me," I said.

The three talked among themselves, and finally Detwiler said he'd been in rank longest.

I said, "That's a shame, Detwiler."

"Why, sir?"

"Because your ass has just been dipped in trouble."

"Why are you saying that?"

"I found this detachment in disarray, and you're the senior noncom."

His eyes fluttered as if I'd spit in them. "What are you talking about? I'm just a stinking corporal."

"The *senior* stinking corporal. It was your job to find out why you were sent out here, then to take charge."

"The captain's in charge, sir."

"Captain? I don't see a captain."

I'd hated officers at Bliss who'd talked to me in the domineering tone I was using on Detwiler. I was using it because I didn't have time to be nice. I wanted attentive responses, not only from him but from the others.

"He *was* here."

"But he's not now, and you were in charge when he left."

"He didn't say—"

"Doesn't matter. As next in command, you should have taken charge." I pointed out that he'd also allowed his men to misuse equipment. "There are probably other offenses. It looks like we might have an Article 15 here."

"Wheeooo," said one of the privates.

"Unless maybe you can get these clowns together."

"I *can*," said Detwiler. He turned. He took a deep breath, said, "Some of you pick up those bayonets." It may have been the first command he'd ever given. He seemed surprised when they started to pick them up.

"We're involved in a combatlike situation," I told them. "You'd better treat it like the real thing or you'll be spending time in the jug. Right now, you're the only ones in the battalion not melting your asses to get ready." I raised my voice. "Are you going to change that?"

I saw nods, including Detwiler's.

I counted heads. Twenty. A mile of fence, maybe a little more. Nearly impossible to defend with twenty. I reminded myself of what Shea had said: the British would make a move at the front of the base only to divert attention from the back. That comforted me until I realized that if Ball was captured, he just might go into a panic and tell the British the way our defenses were laid out. That might cause them to send their main force against the front of the base.

Detwiler and the others stood around me, waiting.

"Headquarters and some of A Battery are covering the fence on the far end"—I stuck out my left arm—"up to a mile from here. A combination of troops from B and C are covering the fence on the other side up to about a quarter of a mile away. You're a small part of A and are going to have to spread out thinly, I'm afraid. I'll keep Corporal Detwiler and a runner with me near the gate. Corporal Kelly, take twelve men and spread them out equidistant, to the far end. Corporal Franks, take five and spread them out equidistant at the near end."

All three corporals were nodding, a good sign. But then one, Franks, asked, "How do we let you know if we see something suspicious?"

If Ball had stayed, given a list of needs, this group might now have walkie-talkies. Or flares. Whistles. Something.

"Bark," I said.

"Bark?" repeated Franks.

"B-a-r-k, bark." It had popped to mind and seemed workable. "When we were kids we imitated barking dogs. We all know how. Try, Cervelli," I said, pointing to the tallest. He was at the back of the group, a former high school basketball star from Pittsburgh. His grin shone like a lamp over the heads of the others.

"Go ahead."

"Whu-ufff! Whu-uhhfff!"

It reminded me of an Irish setter we'd had in our neighborhood when I was growing up. "Do it again, louder."

He did. It was very authentic.

I called on others. Most made credible dog sounds. I noticed that each had a distinctive bark. The differences would let me know who was signaling. I told them to use the signal only if they were sure they'd seen the enemy. It was too late for fox-holes. I said they'd have to lie in the deepest grass, with a clear view of the other side. "If you signal, I'll call battalion for reinforcements. Remain where you are. You may end up being captured. It won't be a disgrace. Your main job is to signal me here at the mound if there's an attempted breakthrough. If you do that, you've done all you can."

Franks and Kelly put their groups together and were soon gone.

I told Cervelli to stay at the far side of the mound and kept Detwiler beside me. We curled down behind the mound. I peered around, being sure I could see the main gate and the approach to it. All the base lights had been turned off, and the moon, behind the thin sheet of clouds, delivered a purple glow that made objects visible for about fifty yards, somehow more visible than they were when the base lights were on. I relaxed, believing that, if the enemy appeared, I'd have time to signal battalion headquarters.

I lay back.

I'd created a defense. It wasn't a very good one, but it was as good as I could make it. I regretted that Shea hadn't seen me handle Detwiler, who was now beside me, as tame as the pup he'd imitated. I closed my eyes, more or less satisfied. Then, remembering something, I popped up.

"What?" said the corporal anxiously.

"Get the radio in the information booth."

Within a few minutes I'd called Shea and told him where I was located and how I'd deployed my troops.

He didn't order any changes.

I myself was confident that those I'd spread out so thinly along our line of defense could pick up unusual movements beyond the fence in time for me to call for reinforcements, if necessary.

I lay back again and closed my eyes.

Ball's screw-ups—failing to organize his troops and abandoning his post to go to Newbury—were, I soon decided, a symptom of a general military malaise that had been manifesting itself in numerous ways. I recalled Flu's strange attachment to his swagger stick, Gilley's incompetence around the weapon he was supposed to understand, Buckles's countless manipulations. Hadn't I become the world's leading expert on Buckles? He'd spent years malingering, cheating, lying, in general using the Army for his own purposes. He and others like him seemed to undermine the country more effectively than the Japanese or Germans or North Koreans or Chinese had, surely more than the Soviet Union ever would. I didn't understand why Shea was going to recommend he be promoted to the rank of major. The acronym from World War II, SNAFU (Situation Normal, All Fouled Up), wasn't a joke at all but a description of the way things really were.

Yes, there were officers like Vernor as well as those like Buckles, but it seemed that for every twelve Buckleses—or, say, three Buckleses, six Balls, two Flus and a Gilley—there might be one Vernor. Yet would the odds be any better in civilian life? Why should they be?

I knew something about one field, education. Though I was in the honors class at St. Ignatius High School, only two of my teachers, Father Sterrett in freshman Latin and Mr. Black, who soon afterward left both the Jesuits and teaching, had provided me with anything I'd found it necessary to recall even once since.

College had provided few illuminations, those coming from three or maybe four professors. There were a couple of philosophy seminars, a large lecture class on the classics, a literature course. I'd blamed the Jesuits and myself, for not doing more to teach myself, but at Bliss I'd met a Harvard graduate who said that he thought only five of his professors had taught well. Were these the ratios one might expect in law or commerce or any other field I might enter if I left the Army? Probably.

And in which of them would I find a mentor like Shea? If he'd been right about us not fighting the Russians, I'd spend a relatively peaceful, if at times trying, twenty years and retire at age forty-one, not an old man.

Forty

I turned my attention to Detwiler. After using his bayonet to make a place for the radio, he searched the sky beyond a break in the thin cloud layer, intensely, as if he were expecting the British to send strafing planes.

The silence around us was pure, broken only once, by Cervelli's feet shuffling at the far side of the mound.

Detwiler's eyes remained on the opening in the clouds.

Mine stayed below.

Everything around us lay frozen in the rare grayish-blue light, touched only on its edges by the orange glow reflected from the lamps of Newbury. Suppose we stay this way, I thought—Detwiler, the sentry, Cervelli, the clouds, the bushes, even the scrap of paper once fluttering, and now still before us, the cloud-light itself, even my eyes holding it. Every being and thing would be transported this way into eternity.

Finally Detwiler said, "Do you hear something?"

I didn't, then did, the growl of an old grumbly dog. It grew louder.

"Look," said Detwiler, pointing.

Moving slowly up toward the main gate from the Newbury highway came a greenish elephant.

"The five-ton," he said.

The sentry, Jones, who'd been crouched behind his concrete station, leaned out and rested his carbine on his knee.

The truck slowed, and now I could see a slope-shouldered figure in the passenger seat and a tilted hat on the driver: Ball and Miller, all right.

I heard the crackling of gunfire from behind us, at the other side of the base.

The sentry didn't let it bother him. He walked to the back of the vehicle, stayed there for a couple of minutes, then came around to Ball's side and waved the captain on.

I stood, moved to the front and center of the oval and raised my hand, indicating that I wanted the truck to stop.

There was the sound of more gunfire, much more. Now it was coming from several places behind us.

The truck didn't slow.

I waved my hand.

Miller's eyes were on the road, not me, as he turned to go around the oval. The captain's nose was haughtily in the air. He brought to mind a duke out in his carriage for a Sunday ride.

"Captain!" I called.

They went around the turn.

The gunfire was steady now. I could also hear shouting. Everything was coming from the back side of the base. I crouched, expecting to hear barks. There were none. I turned, told Detwiler to contact battalion headquarters, report that Ball and the five-ton had come onto the base but wouldn't stop. I was curious about how many men Ball had picked up, if any. Jones would know. "Be right back," I told Detwiler.

The sentry was lying down behind his little station, feet spread. I saw now what a fine view he had of the approach road. I stopped a few feet behind him and called out. Apparently he didn't hear. I moved closer. "Jones?"

He swung around, pointing his carbine at my stomach. His face was blackened with cork. "Lie down with your hands spread toward me, lieutenant." It wasn't Jones.

I went forward onto my hands.

He got up and searched me. "Stand, sir. If you please." English. "Kindly have your men leave their weapons on the ground and lead me to your command post."

Where was Jones?

I and all the men in my detachment were soon marching to battalion headquarters with hands clasped behind our heads in front of three Englishmen, two of whom were dressed in camouflage suits and one of whom, the false sentry, was dressed in Jones's Air Force uniform. We reached the battalion headquarters parking lot. There had been guards there when I left. The guards were gone.

"March right in, sir," said the black-faced one from behind as if this were his headquarters, not mine. And then, moving ahead, he pulled open the main door, held it for me, went past me to Shea's office, where a British soldier was standing, and pointed. "You, sir. The others I shall take into your personnel office."

He seemed to know where everything was located.

I stopped through the office doorway, stunned by what I saw: Shea and his staff ignobly stripped to their T-shirts—all olive-drab but for Gilley's, which was white, old-fashioned and sleeveless—their open hands pressed against the wall.

More stunning yet was the sight I encountered a couple of minutes later, when, following Shea's icy stare to the side wall, I saw Captain Ball. His hands were raised like the others, but he was sinking. I watched as he went all the way to the floor.

My vision of him was broken when a British officer wearing a black face and dark camouflage suit, a colonel, I guessed from his insignia, appeared in front of me. He had heavy brows and a jaw like a plow blade. "Remove your shirt and all the objects in your pockets and join your fellow officers, young man." He turned to Shea's round back and said, "We'll be finished in a few minutes, colonel."

Shea didn't seem to hear. His head was still turned to Ball, who lay groaning as one of the British soldiers, a sergeant, bent over him. The sergeant said something I couldn't hear and then Ball, as if in reply, let out a shrill cry and began to retch.

"Sir?" the sergeant said, touching his shoulder.

The captain began to weep.

Chilled by his sounds, I quickly turned my gaze back to Shea.

Forty-one

.//*/*/*/*/

A week passed, a remarkably calm week, during which I gathered information for my report on the mock battle. From first shot to surrender, it had lasted only seventeen minutes. Some in the battalion were already calling it The Redcoats' Revenge.

"I'm surprised he hasn't had a meeting," Vernor said at week's end when he and I were having lunch together at the club.

I'd seen the colonel only a few times. He hadn't even hinted at a meeting. He'd seemed anxious and distracted, which didn't surprise me, but had shown no anger, which did. An hour or so before I left for lunch that day he'd gone to the base infirmary to check on Ball. I'd seen the first of two medical reports: peptic ulcers with hemorrhaging. A second report had arrived that morning, but the colonel had left for the infirmary without showing it to me. "I suppose he's waiting for Ball to come back."

Vernor nodded. "He likes to have his scapegoats sitting in front of him, doesn't he?"

Lately remarks critical of the colonel seemed also to be aimed at me. I replied crisply, "When you put the blame on someone who actually *is* responsible, you're not making him a scapegoat, are you?"

The captain shrugged and signaled for a waiter.

The more I'd gathered material, the more certain I was that

Ball had been key to what Colonel Cavellini had told me was the
quickest British takeover of a U.S. installation since exercises
between the two forces had begun after World War II. Yes,
others had made mistakes. Shea had failed to brief his officers
about Operation Night Watch and had overloaded defenses at
the back of the base at the expense of those at the front. Vernor
and Pryzbyskowski, for all their good work on fortifications, had
made the serious error of not establishing communications
between each other's command posts. There had been a number
of other mistakes. But the blue-ribbon foul-up had been Ball's.

About a half-mile from the front gate, he and Miller had been
stopped by someone Miller described as "an old man in a long
dark coat carrying a crutch." Ball said, "What's that fool doing
out on a highway at night? Pull over and we'll take him into
town." When they stopped, the "old man" slipped off not an
overcoat but a gray military blanket, raised a pistol from the
camouflage suit underneath, pointed the weapon at the captain
and introduced himself as Lance Corporal Fred Pennington of
the British 16th Parachute Battalion. "I'm sorry, sir," he said
politely, "but we must take your lorry." Ball, gasping, said, "You
can't *do* that! We're in the middle of war exercises." "Just so, sir,"
said Pennington. By then British troops had begun coming out
of the woods along the highway and stuffing themselves into the
canopied bed of the five-ton. A Lieutenant Graham Sally arrived
at the cab and introduced himself as commander of the detachment. "Please instruct your driver to return to your base, captain," he said. "I'll be just behind you with my pistol to your
head. Do, therefore, follow the instructions I give you." Miller
said Ball sat stiff and wordless for a few seconds, then ordered
Miller to turn the five-ton around. Sally, the last one to get into
the truck bed, pulled the canvas flap closed behind him. The flap
was next opened at the front gate by Jones, when he went back to
check the bed. He was yanked inside and stripped of his uniform, which was then given to British Sergeant Edward Kraft,
his look-alike. Kraft, soon afterward, would arrest me. My failure to be cautious when I approached the main gate was yet

another error. Miller, under instructions from Sally, drove past me and parked in a secluded place between base headquarters and battalion headquarters. The invaders had been divided into two groups. One group stormed and quickly took battalion headquarters and the other did the same at base headquarters. A diversionary skirmish had begun at the far side of the base. It didn't last long. Within minutes both headquarters fell, and the base commander and Shea were issuing orders that all U.S. personnel drop their weapons and surrender. The captors then gathered all of the 46th's officers in Shea's office, where Ball eventually collapsed.

"Have you finished getting all your information?" Vernor now wanted to know.

I looked across, saw him holding a small British version of a hamburger. I glanced down. Before me sat a chicken sandwich. I'd been lost in thought, didn't remember it arriving. "No. I've got a couple of more stops to make." One of the stops was the infirmary. I'd postponed Ball as long as possible, not wanting the sight of me, let alone my questions, to stir up his ulcer. But I was near the end and couldn't postpone much longer.

"You want some advice?"

I looked across and smiled. "I'd probably be willing to pay for some."

"Keep the report outside yourself."

"What does that mean?"

"Gather the information. Don't start shaping it. That's not your job."

He must have seen a downcast look or some other sign that I was letting what I'd found affect me. I thanked him but then, almost instantly, started thinking about Ball once more. He'd lost the battle before the rest of us had had a chance to get into it. What he'd done would, once reported, surely ruin any thin chance he might have had for promotion to major and could lead to charges of incompetence.

I saw again the surrender scene. It had come back to me several times, each time more vividly than the last: the captain crying out, then going down, curling up, finally weeping. I stayed with it longer this time and noticed a detail I'd missed the other times. Once more I played it out. The new detail was still there. Was I adding it in, like the stroke an artist makes on a picture that, in retrospect, seems unfinished?

"I have something you ought to check into," Vernor said. "Yesterday I went to the infirmary to visit Ball. They wouldn't let me in."

"Who wouldn't?"

"The head nurse. Said the doctor wouldn't allow anyone but line-of-duty people to visit."

"Is he *that* bad?"

"I knew an officer at Fort Hood who had a bleeding ulcer. It took them weeks to get it to settle, but a bleeding ulcer shouldn't mean you can't talk. Have you seen him yet?"

"I was going in today, after I check something at the motor pool."

"You'll have no problem. You're line-of-duty." He attacked a large triangle of apple pie and ordered a third cup of coffee.

I picked at my sandwich but had no interest and gave up. Again I saw the detail that had caught my attention moments earlier. I closed my eyes, hoping it would go away.

It didn't.

Forty-two

،ی،ی،ی،ی،ی

Captain Cogwell's beet-colored face rose like an insult. His tiny nearly browless eyes caught and held me as he shot tobacco juice into a spittoon a few feet from his desk. "What you think you're gonna do, interrogate me?"

I explained that I had to check his file for information but said I didn't think there'd be a need to question him.

He raised his hand and used his thumb to wipe brown juice from the side of his mouth. "Who's this so-called information for, the limeys?"

"Brigade. But I guess they'll send a copy to . . . the limeys."

"Came at us with our backs turned. Half the goddam battalion was on pass. A Boy Scout troop could have taken this base last Friday."

Or, I thought, done a better job defending it. "All I need to do is find out about the times of vehicle movements during the battle."

He used his tongue to swing a lump of tobacco from one cheek to the other. "No fuckin' battle, lieutenant. They walked in and took us. Don't call what wasn't a battle a battle."

"Well, sir, whatever it was."

The door behind him opened, and one of the mechanics, Corporal P. D. Decker, came in holding out a piece of radiator hose. "Found it on B's number-one jeep. Then went and looked at some other jeeps. Same in all."

"Same what?" Cogswell said loudly.

"Cracks. Ever' damn one could liable to spout a leak!"

While Cogswell checked the hose, I moved to the filing cabinet just inside the main door and opened the ledger on top, labeled "Daily Vehicle Log." On each page there were four columns—"Vehicle Identification," "Time Out," "Time In" and "Comments." I flipped the pages backward until I found Friday's page. I moved my finger down the entries. Then something that looked like a large ham landed on the sheet. I felt a soft, warm belly press against my side, smelled pungent tobacco breath. The ham moved sideways, taking the log sheet with it.

I turned to see Cogswell backing away.

"This ain't a public li-berry," he said. "And I ain't giving you permission to look at what's here."

He hadn't removed the sheet quickly enough. I'd seen an entry that stung me with surprise. I turned, said, "Sorry, but, if you don't mind, I'd like to have that, sir."

He'd gone behind his desk, was holding the sheet against his stomach. "You don't come in a man's office and start nosin' through his papers. I'll have my sergeant copy what's here when he gets back from his coffee. I'll send it." He slid it into a pile on the desk, reached to the side and picked up the cracked piece of hose Decker had left.

"Sir?"

He grunted, not looking up.

"My instructions say I should collect appropriate documents." I didn't add Colonel Cavellini's qualifier: "whenever feasible." "I guess copying it wouldn't be good." My hope was that he'd give in out of fear I'd report him for not cooperating.

He mumbled something I couldn't make out, took the sheet out of the pile and tore it in half lengthwise. He then spit between the two sides, not even aiming at his spittoon. The brown goo landed on the floor a couple of feet in front of me. It would soon dry and be one among the other dark stains on the wooden floor, which I'd taken for oil droppings from the mechanics' shoes. He turned the two halves sideways and tore again. His wad of tobacco moved from one cheek to the other. He kept tearing. Soon tiny flakes of paper were falling all around him. He tore until there was no more paper in his hands.

What I'd seen in the log sheet had surprised me. What he'd done with the sheet frightened me.

"Know what you're thinkin'." His eyes were no longer visible. "You're thinkin' you're gonna come back here after I go home and find all those tiny pieces in the wastebasket and stick 'em back together."

"Not true, sir." It wasn't.

"Don't believe you, 'cause you're a snoop. The colonel trusts you, but I don't. No way." He grinned. "Nothin' there worth anything, but you might try and make somethin' of it. Yep. I should prob'ly eat those little specks of paper. But I ain't goin' to. Goin' to have Decker pick 'em up and burn 'em in my ashtray. Got it?"

I nodded.

"Anything you want to know now you got to ask me," he said tensely. "What you want to know?"

"Well . . ." I looked at the flakes, the stains, at him. "Nothing, I guess."

"Then there ain't nothin' to stay for."

He was right.

I backed away, opened the door, turned and hurried to the jeep. Something big had happened, something ominous. I wasn't sure what. As a result, my body, not my mind, reacted. My heart had begun pounding as Cogswell tore up the log sheet, was thumping so loudly by the time I reached the jeep I could hear it. My mind soon tried to match my body's panic. When I crossed the runway, it presented me with a vision of a B-47 plummeting silently down onto the jeep. I leaned forward,

looked into the sky, left, then right. There was no B-47. I shook
my head. I'd help no one by losing control.

There were several tasks I'd intended to perform before regular infirmary visiting hours, 1400 to 1600, but I now decided the
information I needed from the captain couldn't wait, and made a
turn toward the infirmary. Already going five miles an hour over
the twenty-five-mile-an-hour base speed limit, I pressed the
accelerator until I was doing forty. Eventually I skidded to a stop
in a space marked EMERGENCY ONLY, rushed across a grassy
strip, slid past someone who'd just opened the door, stopped
before the first desk I reached. "Lieutenant Hanlon . . . from the
46th. I must . . . would like to speak to Captain Ball."

A nurse about thirty was writing something. My voice stilled
her pen. She looked up slowly with a frown that told me she
didn't welcome distractions. "He isn't here anymore," she said.
The badge on her uniform identified her as A. Kelly. "He's been
sent to Wimpole Park."

Wimpole Park, near Cambridge, was the site of a U.S. Air
Force Hospital. "Why?" Her frown tightened, which caused
me to add, "It's line-of-duty. I'm preparing a report on the
recent war exercise. There are a few questions I'd like to ask
him."

She was ash-blond and had a youthful look despite faint lines
around her eyes and mouth. She blinked, looked away, then
back. "I doubt you'll be allowed to see him."

"May I see Dr. Michaels?" He was Ball's doctor.

"He's no longer in charge of the captain's case."

"He's not?"

"Not since he's been transferred."

"You mean some doctor at Wimpole Park is?"

She nodded.

"How do I get there?"

Her eyes narrowed on my forehead as though an exotic bug
had landed there. She didn't reply. She blinked and looked away.
Maybe she was thinking about calling an orderly or an Air
Policeman to have me removed. Finally she opened her middle

drawer and took out a small map, mimeographed. She slid it across the desk toward me.

I picked it up, saw that it showed the way from Greenham Common to Wimpole Park, guessed it was a map used by ambulance drivers. "Thanks," I said, looking across.

She'd gone back to what she'd been writing.

Forty-three

....

The assistant administrator at U.S. Air Force Hospital, Wimpole Park, Chief Warrant Officer Edwin P. Carey, a pale and dapper man about thirty-five, said in reply to my request to speak to Captain Ball, "Absolutely not! He's in no condition to see anyone."

"Because of his ulcer?"

"I'm sorry. I can't discuss his condition." A nod followed the statement. Was he giving me a standard answer, or was the hospital making a special effort to keep the captain secluded?

"I only want to see him for . . . well, a short time, less than an hour."

"I'm sorry, sir, but our administrator, Colonel Feathers, has a policy on matters like this."

"May I have permission to speak to the administrator?"

He looked at his watch then let out a noisy sigh. "I'm afraid he's gone to conference and will be there all afternoon."

"Couldn't he . . . come to the door of the conference room?"

He evened out a stack of papers on the shelf below the counter over which we were speaking, then handed the stack to a nurse who was seated beside him. He opened a drawer, removed a mechanical pencil and hooked it into the pocket of his blue shirt. Finally he looked up and said impatiently, "Tell me what you'd like to say to the colonel. I'll pass it on."

He already knew what I wanted to say. I guessed he was stalling, trying to wear me down. One delay might lead to another, then another, and finally I'd drag myself back to the jeep, defeated. "I want two things," I said. "I want to spend enough time with Captain Ball to have my questions to him answered, at least a half-hour. And I want to let you and Colonel Feathers know that if I'm prevented from interviewing him, which is part of a duty assigned by my brigade commander, Colonel Ernest F. Stark, through his S-3 officer, Lieutenant Colonel Aldo R. Cavellini"—I didn't know their middle initials, was making them up so that my statement would sound more official—"I will have no choice but to file a report saying, in effect, that I was prevented from following orders."

"Medical priorities," he said in a robot voice, "take precedence over all others." He paused, I suppose to give me time to catch the momentousness of his statement, then said, "But I shall speak to the colonel. Excuse me." He did a snappy about-face and went tip-tapping down a hall beyond the counter.

I resolved that I wouldn't let Colonel Feathers or anyone else stop me from interviewing Ball. If necessary, I'd find Ball's window and get to him by climbing through it.

The nurse was playing an unfriendly peek-a-boo game with me.

I felt my back muscles tighten and fixed my eyes on her until she turned away.

She issued a grateful sigh when Carey reappeared.

"You will be permitted to question Captain Ball for three minutes."

"Three minutes?" I replied, startled. "I don't understand. I'll need at least fifteen."

"The colonel is, under the circumstances, being quite generous. Please follow me." He came from behind the counter and led me down a long corridor.

"What circumstances?"

He didn't reply.

"Is it possible for me to speak to the captain's doctor?"

He didn't reply.

The three minutes would permit them to claim, if necessary, that I hadn't been prevented from interviewing Ball. Was that it?

We reached the end of the hallway. Carey used two keys to unlock a sturdy steel door. We were in another, shorter, hallway. He pointed to the two men who stood at the other end, a large and muscular Air Policeman and a small frail-looking man with persecuted eyes who wore a white frock and was wringing his hands.

"Dr. Bumpus," said Carey, "this is Lieutenant Hanlon."

Bumpus raised his eyes as far as my throat. His thin mouse-colored hair seemed to be pasted to his elongated head. He pointed to a small rectangular box on the wall. The box had two light bulbs, one green and one red, with a button beneath. Bumpus made a hissing sound, and the Air Policeman pressed the button. The green light came on. "Observer," said a voice from the box.

"Thirteen," said the Air Policeman.

Hissing again, the doctor pointed past the Air Policeman's stomach to a steel door like the door at the end of the corridors except that it was wider and had a peephole, not a window. It also had two locks.

Carey opened one, then the other.

"Tss," said Bumpus, who'd somehow gotten behind me. I didn't know what the sound meant but soon felt a finger in my back, heard another hiss, and realized he wanted me to move.

I stepped forward, past Carey, into a warm humid room with sheet-white walls. A very bright light, almost blinding, shone not from the ceiling but from the far wall, causing me to shut my eyes tightly. The floor felt soft against my shoes. I smelled a medicinal smell but another too, a familiar musky smell. Opening my eyes, turning, squinting against the light, I saw that the walls had a cream-colored cushiony surface. Looking further, I saw that the only window was at the center of the ceiling. It was dark, and nothing behind it was visible. I turned back to the source of all the room's near-blinding light and saw that the bulb was covered by a huge cage. I turned again. Bumpus stood with his back against the closed door, hands flat against it, watching me. I sensed movement and turned more. There, squatting in the corner, was Ball, his thin hairy legs sticking out from a prisoner-gray robe. The robe, I noticed, had no arms. He raised his head. His hair had fallen wildly over his eyes, which now reached toward me. His mouth shaped but didn't speak my name: *Hanlon.*

Why was he in this situation? Bumpus could best tell me that. I wouldn't ask now. How much time had passed? I'd failed to look at my watch coming in. "Captain . . . the night the British attacked the base, who, if anyone, authorized you to take the five-ton truck to Newbury?"

He stared at me, mouth jaggedly open. It closed. It opened again.

"Inky."

"What?"

"Dinkey."

"Dinkey?"

He drew in air, closed his eyes, blew out a whisper: "Par-*lay*-voo." His head fell to one side, and he laughed. He was staring at his right foot, its big toe disproportionately large. He wiggled it. "Do . . . you remember . . . a song called 'Daddy.' "

I might have. What the hell did it matter? "Captain, did you call the motor pool and tell Captain Cogswell you wanted a truck. Is that it? Or did he . . . or someone else . . . first have to give permission?"

"Oh, Daddy," he sang, or tried to sing, "you're gonna get the best for me."

I heard Bumpus's fingers dancing uneasily on the door's padding.

"Is that how it went or was it, 'Oh, Daddy, I want to get the best of you'?"

"Sir?"

"Is that how it went, Hanlon?"

"Yes, sir."

"No, it's not. You . . . you never could get anything straight. Come here!" He wiggled his index finger at me.

I guessed two minutes had passed. Why wasn't I wearing my watch? I'd gotten nothing but gibberish. "Sir," I said complainingly.

"Come here!"

Damn him! I stepped forward, bent down.

"Closer," he whispered.

I went closer. His breath smelled like an animal several days dead. I turned my head, my eyes landing on Bumpus, whose mouth was twitching.

When my ear was close to Ball's mouth, he whispered, "Daddy gave me the snake. Put *that* in your fry pan and cook it."

The snake?

Bumpus was now tugging at my jacket.

I turned.

"Tssss," he said, shaking his head disapprovingly.

In the hallway a bell sounded.

The door began to make clicking sounds. Bumpus pushed it open, held it and turned, his eyes telling me to go through it.

I glanced back at the captain.

His head had fallen to one side.

I moved past Bumpus into the hallway. "Sir?" I was looking at the side of his head, which was turned toward the box on the wall. "May I speak to you for a few minutes about the captain's condition?"

He watched the box until the red light came on, then turned and moved in precise little steps toward the far end of the hallway.

Only after the door had closed behind Bumpus did Carey put out his hand and usher me in the same direction. He said, "In answer to your question to the doctor: no."

Forty-four

T he base's streetlights began popping on as, heavy in my bones, I approached the parking lot in front of battalion headquarters, where I'd planned to organize my notes and do an outline of my report before heading for the officers' club. The following morning, after meeting with Shea, I'd write the final version of the report.

As I swung the jeep into the lot, however, I noticed that Shea's light was on. *Bad luck.* I quickly switched off the headlights, then engine, and glided into a parking space. It was 2140. Why was he there? I didn't know but decided I'd better go carefully over my notes before chancing an encounter.

From the snack bar behind me came the relentless beat of newly popular rock-and-roll music. The snack bar wasn't the place for me to review anything.

I thought of going to the club, reviewing my notes there, coming back in the morning.

Finally I decided I was being unnecessarily fearful. I'd have to deal with Shea sooner or later. Why not now? I knew what was in my notes. I'd made them, after all.

Taking my clipboard, I got out and headed for the front entrance, the one that led past the colonel's office. At his doorway I made myself stop and look in.

His feet, in combat boots, rested, ankles crossed, on the desk's pull-out tray, where his small black portable Smith-Corona usually sat. Sometimes he sensed my presence. This time he didn't look across or say anything.

"Good evening, sir."

He tilted his head slightly toward me. "You finding the world the way you'd like it to be, Thomas?" he said when his eyes found me.

It was one of those oblique questions of his that only a few weeks ago would have caused me to stammer or retreat into silence. "Not quite, sir," I replied cautiously.

Within his reach sat a fifth of Smirnoff and, beside it, two shot glasses, one empty, the other full. From the look of the vodka in the bottle, the shot was all that had been poured. He reached out and twisted off the cap.

"Not for me, I hope."

He hesitated, an eyebrow flickering.

"I've got more work to do on my report."

"Tonight?"

"Yes, sir."

He shrugged and lowered the bottle.

"How'd he look?"

"Look?"

"Ball, Thomas. You know who I mean."

Coming back, I'd warned myself not to be surprised if he'd learned, before I told him, where I'd been. Still my heart gave an extra kick. "Pretty bad, I'd say."

"You get the diagnosis?"

"No, sir." I'd tried to squeeze it out of Carey before leaving Wimpole Park but had gotten nothing.

He tilted his head, examined his full shot glass, pinched it between thumb and forefinger and raised it so delicately the vodka didn't seem to ripple. "Gone more than seven hours." He brought the glass over his head, leaned back, opened his mouth, then turned the glass upside down. The vodka fell like a wad of paper into a wastebasket. Lowering the glass, he exhaled loudly, then, turning, whispered, "Must have found out something."

"I did, sir." I watched for the signs of anger I'd learned to recognize—rumbling voice, tightening shoulders, sparks coming off the eyes—but didn't detect any.

"The diagnosis, for your information, is manic depression." He reached for the bottle. "Complicated by sieges of paranoia. Michaels made it yesterday. Bumpus confirmed it."

I'd taken only an introductory course in psychology. I didn't remember what manic depression involved but I knew it was serious.

"Seems you wasted a lot of the government's gasoline, Thomas."

"Sir?"

"If you'd bothered to speak to me or Michaels with my permission, you wouldn't have had to drive through much of England."

"If you or Michaels had wanted me to know what Captain Ball's condition was, sir, you could have told me. I went there thinking he had an ulcer only."

He was staring at his shot glass. "When are you going to finish your report?"

"In the morning, I hope."

"Your enthusiasm for this assignment's impressive." He pushed the shot glass toward me. "One before you go?"

I wanted a drink badly. But I also wanted to do my outline and official report with an uncluttered head. "I've got just one more interview," I said. "Maybe I could do that, outline my report, *then* have that drink."

He'd picked up the bottle. My remark stalled it in midair. "What do you mean, one more interview? I thought you were finished with the interviews."

"No, sir."

"Well, then, go do it, do your outline, and come back."

"But . . . I don't need to go anywhere. It's with you, sir."

"What are you talking about?" The bottle slowly descended. "I talked to you for at least an hour after the fiasco. Analyzed the whole thing! There's no need to interview me."

I recalled him pacing my small office the Saturday before, sorting out the events of the previous night, examining each, identifying the mistakes—his own as well as others—showing anger only when he came to the actions of Ball. ("How in Jesus's name could he be so stupid as to stop that truck?") By the time he'd finished, the events had begun to connect like links on a chain. Indeed, my subsequent searching had verified nearly everything he'd told me. Nearly. "I just don't think I've yet gotten the complete truth."

He laughed. "Thomas," he said, his eyes suddenly playful, "you should have been born in the Middle Ages. You'd have been comfortable in that simple world. They believed in *the* truth. There is no *the* truth, Thomas," he went on patiently. "Only truths. If you get that straight, you might have a chance in the modern world. You have to adapt yourself."

"I try to believe that, sir. I've been working at it."

"Glad to hear it."

"But, regarding my reports . . . as much as I've found out, I'm not sure I've yet gotten to . . . I guess I'll have to say 'truths' about Operation Night Watch. I believe some things may not have happened . . . quite the way they seemed to have."

"That so?"

"Yes, sir."

"Nothing ever does, does it?"

"Sir?"

"Happen quite the way we think it has."

"I guess not. That's, sort of, why I have to ask more questions."

"You going to change what happened, lieutenant?"

"I don't think I'm going to change anything."

"Neither do I. Listen. Captain Ball took a truck into Newbury to pick up a sergeant and some men but instead let himself be captured by the enemy, who turned the truck into a Trojan horse and moved surreptitiously onto the base . . . and then *took* the fucking thing. Despite all the boo-boos the rest of us—including *you*, Thomas—made, it was Captain Ball's actions that caused our quick and inglorious defeat. Any doubt about any of that?"

"None, sir."

"Good."

"I just don't be—rather, I have reason to doubt that . . . that his stopping is the whole story."

"Of course it's not the *whole* story." He emphasized the statement by shaking his head.

"I mean what's missing may be, well, I'd say *is*, even more important."

He came forward, making his chair squeal. "That so? And what's missing?"

"I don't think facts. I think I have all or most of the facts. I think what's missing is, more or less, how the facts came to be what they are."

He flicked his hand above his shot glass to chase away a fly. "You aren't a goddam reporter for Associated Press," he said in a heavy tone. "You're my assistant, who was designated by me to be the one who carries out the simple assignment of writing a report of a—it turns out—brief war exercise, to be given to Colonel Cavellini at brigade. You're supposed to present, chronologically, all the events that took place, from the time of the alert to the time of our surrender. Briefly. Parachutes observed by Colonel Shea and Lieutenant Hanlon at such and such a time. Like that. Chronologically and briefly. This happened and that happened. Period."

After flicking at the fly, he placed his cupped hand over his shot glass, concealing it like a ball under a magician's cup. I fancied the glass disappearing and actually felt disappointment when he finally lifted his hand and the glass was still there.

"Am I wrong?"

"No, sir."

"Of course not." He leaned toward the deep drawer on his right, began pushing things aside, searching for something.

His movement cleared my view to the wall behind him, the

one against which he and some others had stood during the surrender. Again I saw all the hands open against it, sticking to it as if glued there. Again I watched the captain fall, again heard his mournful groans, again heard him retch. Again I watched the colonel's eyes go down and again saw the captain curl like the closing petals of a flower. Again I heard him weep.

I now abruptly turned my eyes from the wall, wanting to break the vision before it was completed. I'd broken it several times since the surrender. This time, however, it seemed to insist on playing itself out:

Shea had smiled. He's grimacing, I'd told myself the night of the surrender, grimacing because of the captain's weakness. But he hadn't been; I was able to accept that only today. And now again I saw his hands, both of them, close into fists, one subsequently rising and then coming softly back down onto the wall in what I only now realized had been a gesture of conquest. Out of the remembrance came a responsibility I didn't want. He *had* smiled.

He now reached into the deep drawer to his right and removed a lemon, took an Army pocket knife from his wide center drawer, pulled out the long blade, picked up the fruit and, cradling it, delicately cut off a sliver of peel and dropped it into the glass, which he filled almost to the top with vodka. He raised the glass and moved it from side to side, watching the sliver of lemon wiggle about. "Any questions about how you're supposed to do the report, Thomas?"

"None, sir."

"Good." He found and removed a bottle of tonic water, then two glasses, tumblers so darkly green I couldn't, at least from where I sat, see through them. He set everything on his desk, opened his pocket knife and began to slice the lemon. "I bought this stuff at the PX. After I found out where you were, I came here, waiting for you so we could celebrate."

"Celebrate what, sir?"

"There." He aimed the tip of his knife at his in-basket.

"A memo saying that I'm going to be assigned to Munich as a special adviser in Operations, Headquarters, Europe."

"Congratulations."

"Not just to me, Thomas." He'd cut two slices of lemon peel, was rubbing the edge of a tumbler with one. "To you too."

"Why?"

He dropped the peel into the tumbler that had been rubbed, picked up the second peel and began to rub the other glass. "Because the memo also says . . ." He stopped rubbing, leaned across his desk, pulled a paper part way out of the out-basket and read: " '. . . may recommend one junior officer as Special Assistant.' And . . ." He raised his eyes to mine. ". . . they rarely turn down the assignee's recommendation." He pushed the paper back. "The assistant's position allows for a rank as high as captain. Can't get you that, but I'm sure I can get you into the rank of first lieutenant before we leave here."

I desired, still desired, to go with him. But I didn't want to linger in the possibility until I'd written a report, an uncontaminated report. When that was completed, the way it had to be completed, then filed, I'd go with him if he still wanted me. No question.

"Wipe away the pensive look, Thomas. There's no need to decide tonight. Hell, my assignment isn't official yet." He dropped the second peel into the second tumbler. "Buckles has a little refrigerator he swiped somewhere at the back of his office if you want ice."

"Sir?" I closed my eyes. "I can't, rather don't want to have a drink until I have finished my interview with you . . . and then written my report and, well, shown it to you."

I heard a timbal's boom. I opened my eyes to see his fist on his desk. "Goddammit!" he shouted.

"I'm sorry, sir."

"Stop being sorry! Get on with it! Ask me the fucking questions!" His eyes shot blue fire.

I took a couple of deep breaths, said, "There are only two . . .

or three." I managed to pull a pencil from my pants pocket. I looked across.

His first two fingers formed a V beginning at the top of his nose. He was looking at me around the base of the V.

"Did you order or authorize Captain Ball to take the five-ton to Newbury during the combat exercise Friday night?"

"No," he said back flatly.

My hand moved stiffly yet shook as I copied his words. "Captain Cogswell, this afternoon, took the log sheet for Friday away from me, then tore it up. But before he did, I saw in the 'Comments' column opposite the five-ton Miller signed out the phrase 'Auth. by FPS.' Your initials in Cogswell's handwriting."

He lowered the hand which had shaped the V to the top of his other, which rested on the desk. "What's the question?"

"I . . . I'm not sure there is one. It's only that Captain Cogswell wrote that phrase for some reason. I think you should know that, because I'm going to have to report what I saw in the log book."

He stood, slowly shook his head and moved to his window, where he stuffed his hands into his back pockets and looked toward a cluster of lights on a distant hill. "You imagined seeing my initials."

No answer could have troubled me more.

"What's your next question?"

"Well . . . did you persuade . . . er, somehow influence, er, indicate to Major Michaels there was a reason to . . . have Captain Ball, well, committed?"

His hands rose slowly out of his pockets, which he then calmly buttoned. He turned, glanced toward his desk, where the bottles, glasses and lemon sat, took a step toward them, hesitated, then stepped toward me. "This isn't an interview but the goddam Inquisition," he said after stopping only inches away. His eyes seared mine. I turned away. He moved past me to the doorway behind me, stopped, said, "Put a copy of the report on my desk when it's finished." He didn't close his office door. But the main door he slammed.

Forty-five

A light from the parking lot projected the shadows of a crab-apple tree onto the far wall of my office. The trees, I'd recently learned, were a Japanese variety purchased by Colonel Smathers to beautify the space around the battalion headquarters building. I'd made a couple of attempts to start the report but had each time been drawn to the shadows doing mirthful dances on the wall. They were hypnotic, and I soon worried that they might cause me to fall asleep. After watching a lengthy *pas de deux*, I forced myself back to the notes.

Once more I tried. I didn't get past the introductory paragraph.

I opened the desk's middle drawer, where I put things I collected, saving them until I figured out what to do with them. I felt around, touched an old dried half-eaten Snickers bar, removed it and tossed it into my wastebasket. I found a Parker 51 fountain pen I'd gotten from an uncle as a graduation present. It had never worked properly. I slid my hand away, reminding myself to take the pen to the repair shop near the PX. I felt the scabbard of my bayonet and pulled it out. After laying it on the desk, I removed the bayonet itself.

Fingering the blade brought to mind a scene from a film, prewar, in which a Japanese man in a formal dark Western suit kneels on a silky cushion before a small altar with an icon of

Buddha and, with great dignity, presses a dagger into himself and commits hara-kiri. I placed the sharp point against myself just beneath my breastbone. I remembered the Japanese man's upward thrust, apparently intended to get the blade quickly behind the bone and into the heart. I pressed slightly, feeling the tip like a beesting. I expected my thoughts to rise to metaphysical altitudes. They didn't, and I soon slid scabbard and blade back into the drawer and felt around for other distractions. My hand touched the edge of the box of battalion stationery I'd purchased to use for letters to my mother and friends. I'd yet to send any of them more than postcards. ("Mother—Just took some big guns across England, brought others back. Some adventurous moments. More later. Love, T.") Finally my little finger touched something soft. I had no idea what it was until, using the finger, I pulled it toward me, then held it up to the parking lot light: a silver-wrapped condom, purchased at the PX as a precaution. Against what? I now wondered. None of the females I'd seen had shown an interest in me. I'd been stirred by only one, Norma, and nearly by another, A. Kelly. What had I supposed when I made the purchase? That there'd be camp followers grabbing at coat sleeves and pants legs whenever we stepped off the base the way, in movies, European women offered themselves to GI's when their towns were liberated? Embarrassed, I slid the condom aside and felt again, this time finding the spine of a book I'd brought from the States, the only book in my office. It was *The Life of Christ* by Riggietti Zizzamia, a factual study I'd purchased at the university bookstore after my junior year in the hope I'd find something in it that would buttress my rapidly crumbling religious faith.

My fingers bumped a familiar object I'd left in the drawer before going to the club for lunch that day, my swagger stick. Today was the first time I'd failed to carry it since it had been issued. I hadn't realized it wasn't with me until I touched it. As I began to remove the stick, my hand again touched the scabbard. I reached in, clasped both and raised them to my desk, then removed the bayonet from the scabbard. I watched myself begin to slice the swagger stick. I spoke words I might have spoken if I'd walked into the orderly room at A Battery and found Crawford doing what I was doing:

Are you crazy?

Your ass is going to burn.

Put the knife down and try to stick the pieces back together!

I kept cutting. But the stick's leather resisted like muscled flesh. The pieces were turning out to be about the size of Vienna sausages. By the time I was through I had a neat little pile. Now, hurriedly, I used the edge of the bayonet blade to scrape them back into the drawer. I wasn't hurrying to conceal them. The ritual of mutilation had somehow freed me to do my report. I returned the knife to scabbard and scabbard to drawer and closed the drawer.

For a few moments I watched one leaf chase another in circles. I effectively fought off a desire to go to Shea's office and pour a reinforcing shot of vodka. I got up, turned on the light, the glaring light that seemed to permit nothing beneath it to hide, went back to my desk, rolled a sheet of paper into my typewriter and pecked out my report.

Forty-six

.·´·´·´·´·´·

Waking with an aching bladder, I untangled myself from my sheet and blankets, got shakily to my feet and noticed that, though light was coming through the latticed glass, I couldn't see objects beyond. The reason, I soon figured out, was a thick gloomy fog that clung so tightly to the glass it blinded me even from the ancient oak that sometimes pressed its branches against the windows.

As I made my way to the bathroom, I remembered Reggie, the bartender, telling me that during World War II he and his family in London prayed for heavy fogs after the German air raids had begun so that enemy pilots would become confused and lost. Approaching the urinal, I heard a distant engine and pictured not its probable source, a car, but a wounded Heinkel bomber, a straggler limping away from London in the wrong direction, a couple of bombs still tucked under its belly. The sound of the engine grew louder, then stopped abruptly. I realized it had come from below. When I finished at the urinal, I stepped over to one of the narrow bathroom windows and glanced down.

The fog on this side, blocked by the manor house itself, wasn't nearly as thick as it was on the other, and I was able to make out the outline of a dark military sedan. It had pulled up near the club entrance. I saw the driver's door open. Recognizing the hunching back of Shea, I pulled myself back from the window. I heard the car door slam. I guessed the hour was early, because I heard no sounds in the building. Why was he here *now?* I heard another slam, supposed he'd gone back for something.

After returning to my room, I put on my fatigue pants and shirt, slipped my bare feet into my combat boots, pushed aside sheet and blanket and sat down on my bed. I expected the phone to ring, expected the airman at the desk to tell me the colonel was downstairs wanting to see me.

The phone didn't ring.

Soon I heard unmistakable footsteps on the main staircase. They reminded me of footsteps from a recurring childhood nightmare in which a creature who looked like the Wolf Man came thumping up the front steps of our house night after night and swept me away from my parents. I waited, stiffening. As the footsteps neared my door, I took a deep breath and, for some reason, stood.

The door, already half open, came completely open and Shea stepped in, smiling. "Thought I'd have to put a toe in your ass," he said, "but there you are, up and ready to take on another day."

"I . . . uh, was going to sleep longer. I got up and went to the bathroom, then saw you getting out of the sedan."

He flipped his field cap onto the room's other bed, unassigned, moved past me to the phone on the stand between the two beds, picked up the receiver, turned and said, "I'm having them send me up a cup of coffee. You want one?"

"No, thanks."

After giving his order he turned, looked about, I think for a chair. Both in the room had been borrowed a few days earlier for a poker game. "First thing I did after reading your report this morning was toss it into the wastebasket." He stepped past me and went to the window, where he stuffed his hands into his pockets and looked out at the fog, brightening as the sun began to reach through from behind.

The statement came like an unexpected slap across the face. "I just don't know what to say to that, sir."

"I then went across the road to the snack bar for some breakfast. Sitting there eating, I thought, Thomas has been feeling a lot of pressure lately, more than a second lieutenant ought to have to put up with . . . no matter how bright and capable he might be. I made up my mind not to give you any more demanding assignments, for a while anyway." He walked around me, lowered himself to the unassigned bed, where he lay back, resting on his elbows in such a way that his Ike jacket crept up a few inches over his shirt. He looked at the top of my wall locker across from the foot of the bed. "I went back to the office and pulled your report out of the trash basket. By then I'd dropped my plan to call you in, tell you you'd done an unsatisfactory report and suggest you write another."

"Suggest" *was* the appropriate word. The instructions given to me just after Operation Night Watch made it clear that I was preparing the report for submission to Colonel Cavellini at brigade. No approval by the battalion commander was required.

"After rereading the report, I found only one thing that must be changed, one item and a couple of related details. I'm not saying I like all the other things. The report certainly isn't flattering to me or the battalion. But there's really only one item and those related details that need to be removed. It's the phrase you claim to have seen on the log sheet, authorized by FPS, and the statements about my denial and the one about Cogswell destroying the sheet. They have to go. That's all. The rest of the report is just fine."

"Sir," I said, sinking at the end of my bed, "I don't know how your initials and your indication of approval got there, but I did see what I saw. I told you that last night."

He nodded. "I don't for one second doubt you believe that. But . . ." He shrugged an apologetic shrug. "No one else saw the entry. Leave it out."

"But I saw what I saw and have to report it."

Could I find other witnesses, besides Cogswell? Certainly several had opened and closed the log book on the night of the attack, after the entry that included Shea's initials had been made. Had Miller himself looked at the log? And was it possible that some of the many who'd used the book between Night Watch and the time Cogswell destroyed the sheet had noticed it? If I'd been more thorough, I might now have answers to some or all of these questions.

"It's your choice, Thomas."

Even if there were witnesses, could I get them to speak up? I looked across.

"Make those changes, and you and I can get back to where we were yesterday."

Yesterday? Yesterday the one person who might have been able to verify what I'd seen had been delivered to a mental ward. Yesterday I'd heard from that person in a coded way that Shea ("Daddy . . .") was somehow responsible for having him declared insane (". . . gave me the snake," meaning the hissing Bumpus). Would I, continuing to resist, find myself in a mental ward too?

He slid his hand into his breast pocket and pulled out a sheet of paper, folded lengthwise, then reached across and handed it to me. "This is the log sheet from the motor pool for a week ago yesterday."

"Captain Cogswell destroyed the log sheet for that day."

He pointed to the sheet.

I pulled it open and examined it, item by item. It was identical to the sheet I'd seen at the motor pool except for the blank space in the "Comments" section across from the entry for Ball's five-ton, the space in which I'd seen "auth. by FPS." I stood and shakily made my way over to the window.

After leaving Wimpole Park, I'd begun to patch together what had happened during Operation Night Watch, continued doing so during the drive back to Greenham, and later, when I sat in the colonel's office. In fact, I didn't have all the pieces put together until I'd finished the report. I had no reason now to doubt my analysis.

Sometime early during the night of the mock attack, certainly before my arrival at the front gate, Shea became aware that Ball was making a mess of his assignment. The captain's call to headquarters with the request that he be allowed to go to Newbury gave Shea an opportunity he may have been waiting for in the first place, to replace Ball with me. Me doing well in a command situation during a mock battle would surely strengthen the colonel's case for me being given an early promotion to first lieutenant and allowed to go as his assistant to Germany. He therefore ordered Ball to return to his command post and wait there until I arrived, adding that he, meanwhile, would call Cogswell at the motor pool and have him release a truck to take Ball to town. He may have guessed Ball would be captured. Hadn't he earlier told me that those driving in from their homes might be taken? He hadn't, of course, foreseen that the five-ton would be not only taken but used to transport enemy troops onto the base. His initials on the log sheet directly linked him, not Ball, to the crucial event in the battalion's defeat. No wonder he'd shown relief when Ball collapsed in his office!

"Remove the reference to the signature, attach this sheet, and we can put the report in the mail to brigade tomorrow," he said from behind me. "We never did get to London because of the raid. If you're free tonight, we'll go."

Free. What an odd use of the word, I thought.

There sat Ball like a baboon on the floor of the hospital room at Wimpole Park. No, not like a baboon. A baboon wouldn't have been put in a straitjacket. And he was in a straitjacket because he'd been declared insane. But was he? The diagnosis had been made almost overnight—ulcer to manic depression with complications. Shea had been observing the captain for months, had kept notes on him, had stored up plenty of material he could use to urge an "insane" diagnosis on Michaels. Ball had always said and done odd things. But was he insane? Maybe. But if so, it was a brilliant insanity, for it had enabled him to deliver to me, past his psychiatrist, a coded and fairly complicated message. And the gist of the message was, of course, that he'd been made a scapegoat.

"Well, Thomas?"

Yet I hadn't included Shea's signature to save Ball. When I'd made out my report I'd considered the evidence, not its implications, not Ball or what they might do to him next. Only after the report was finished did I ponder its effects. Maybe it would result in a reevaluation of Ball's condition. Maybe it wouldn't. If the diagnosis wasn't changed, he'd probably be given a medical discharge and full disability pay. I pictured him at the back of a rowboat, feet up on the side, straw hat pulled over his eyes, fishing. Peace at last!

"Thomas?"

I wanted to go to London with the colonel tonight, to Germany with him later. Was I resisting because I somehow wanted to punish him? In an instant the thought seemed ridiculous. I'd been witness to his manipulative and at times anarchic ways, had come to accept them—the firing, the tests, the swagger sticks, the Buckles review, the ammo inspection, all—accept and even understand. In any case, he was a combat hero and well-respected commander, a survivor who'd easily survive the simple mistake of sending Ball to Newbury. Didn't *he* realize that?

"What do you say?"

Here I stood, free to choose, responsible for the consequences. I was aware of that by the time I turned and said, "I can't, sir."

"Can't?" He rose and came toward me.

I backed up, felt the warm steam radiator against my legs, then the edge of the window ledge against my butt.

He stopped inches away. I saw tiny red whiskers, large pores, a small tan mole I hadn't noticed near his temple. "Thomas, don't be a stubborn asshole and go down over this." His tone was plaintive. "You *will* be the one, not me." He tightened his mouth in an intense expression I'd never before seen, the lips bloodless. Through them he whispered, "There's no one else in this goddam outfit I care about."

I nodded, choking back my own wish to say, "You're really the only one I care about too." Saying it would have complicated and maybe killed my decision. I forced out something else:

"I appreciate that, sir, but . . . but I'm not going to change my report."

He grabbed the lapels of my fatigue jacket. I felt his fingers biting painfully into my skin between neck and collarbone, on both sides. He pushed me half onto the ledge. "They'll call me up to brigade, and I'll tell them you lied. Cogswell will back me up. Anyone I ask will back me up. Face it. It'll finish you in the Army and damage you long afterward. That's the truth of it. I want you to be my assistant. Don't be a fool! Change the god-damm report."

"I can't change it, sir."

"Why not?" His fingers found my collarbone.

I closed my eyes against the pain. "I don't know, sir." Opened them, sent them clutching at his. "I don't fucking *know.*"

My arm muscles had tensed and were shaking as though I had palsy. I let out a sustained groan. I heard it clearly. It was like the groan of an Asian woman I'd seen in a World War II documentary who sat cross-legged over her dead bloody child, groaning and rocking, groaning and rocking, as if she might continue to do so for the rest of her life.

He pulled back, leaving me to slide off the ledge and onto my feet, watching my eyes as though coins were about to pour out of them.

There was a space to his right, between him and my wall locker, about the size of the spaces I'd once had to get through between blockers while making my way downfield after receiving a pass. I lunged for it, but he'd anticipated and, raising his knee, caught me at the top of the chest and dumped me into the corner to the side of the locker.

I scrambled up.

"Change your mind."

There was no space.

He was bent over, obstructing me.

I pushed him.

He barely moved. He grabbed for me.

I raised both hands to his chest and pushed.

He'd been almost immovable when I first pushed him, but now he fell back onto my bed, then, twisting, attempting to get up, hit the floor, elbows first.

"Oh, shit!" I said. "Sorry."

He started to get up. He didn't seem to be hurt. Determining that, I hurried toward the hall, still in search of space.

The round body of Major Perkins filled the doorway.

In a moment Shea appeared from behind, stopped beside me and said, "You're confined to your quarters until further notice." He turned to Perkins and straightened his coat. "You see it?"

Perkins nodded.

Shea turned back, looking as composed as he had when I left his office the day we'd met. "You've made quite a mistake," he said. Then he turned and left with Perkins at his heels.

I backed shakily up to my bed and sat down.

"Coffee?"

I looked up.

An airman stood in the doorway holding a tray with a large mug emanating steam.

It seemed that about ten minutes had passed.

"Right here." I pointed to the space beside me on the bed. I watched the airman set the tray carefully down. I'd become swollen with anger and frustration and vented some by saying, "Put it on Colonel Shea's bill."

I was still sipping when an Air Police lieutenant and two assistants arrived to arrest me.

Forty-seven

..*.*.*.*.*

Colonel C. L. "Andy" Kerrigan looked like my Irish grandfather on my father's side, or rather like his image in the only photograph I'd seen, mainly because of his thick sweeping mustache and the beaver-smile that shone beneath. He signaled Vernor and me toward the table to the right of the one where he sat with the two other board members, who, I soon learned, were Major Anthony Fosby, brigade intelligence officer, and Major Richard Hollingsworth, a psychiatrist stationed at U.S. Air Force Hospital, Mildenhall.

"Why the psychiatrist?" I asked Vernor.

"It's standard procedure whenever one of the options is discharge on grounds of mental disability."

Hollingsworth had smiled when Vernor and I entered the high-ceilinged hearing room at Brigade Headquarters. Unlike Fosby, whose eyes slipped away whenever mine found them, Hollingsworth's were staying with me. Now he smiled again.

At the table across from Vernor and me sat Shea and Perkins, along with the court counsel, a bald swarthy lieutenant colonel named Frankovich, whose hostile dark brown eyes began to drill holes in me. I noticed black hair sticking out over his collar and from beneath his shirt sleeves. Looking at him and being looked at by him added to my discomfort.

Perkins fidgeted, but Shea was as calm as a sightseer on a bus to Albuquerque. After I'd forced my eyes to his, I found him gazing through one of the room's large windows as if at cacti beyond the bus's window.

Kerrigan told us in his introduction that the two charges under Article 90 brought by my accuser, Colonel Shea, had, at Shea's request, been reduced to one, assaulting a superior officer. What had been dropped was disobeying a superior officer. He wanted it understood that the court's duty wasn't to make a judgment but to produce a finding on the charge and make an appropriate recommendation as to whether or not the case should proceed. Finally he advised me that though we were not involved in a court-martial proceeding, I could request representation by a lawyer, even at this late time. Then he pointedly asked me whether or not I wished to have such representation.

"No, sir."

I heard Vernor stir uneasily.

The captain had been trying to persuade me that I ought to request a lawyer. I knew exactly what had happened and trusted him to help me communicate that to the court.

Within a few minutes Shea, whose eyes had been avoiding me like car thieves, gave a version of the pushing incident that bore as much resemblance to what really had happened as a game of cricket would to a game of baseball. When he finished I whispered this thought to Vernor, and he whispered back: "He has Perkins as a witness. He feels safe in mangling the facts."

I had my first self-doubt about not requesting a lawyer, but I didn't act on it because my faith in Vernor remained in place like a deeply imbedded boulder.

"You still have time."

I shook my head.

Perkins testified. So far I'd twice caught him looking at me, but each time he'd turned quickly away. His eyes were now planted on the far edge of his table. He said he'd witnessed the incident as he was about to enter my room to join Shea. He called the blow I'd struck "very forceful." He said I'd tried to knock Shea down moments before I'd actually succeeded in doing so.

"Did you see the colonel grab the lieutenant by the lapels before you saw the actions you've described?" Vernor asked.

"No, I didn't."

"And you just happened to be standing in the doorway when the striking or pushing occurred?"

"It was a coincidence."

Vernor questioned Shea for the first time:

"You used the word 'struck' when describing Lieutenant Hanlon's action against you. Might there be a more accurate term?"

"Such as?"

" 'Pushed' . . . or 'shoved.' "

Shea shook his head. "He struck me with his forearm under the chin."

The lie brought an icy feeling.

"Could you have been off balance?" Vernor asked.

"No. I was stepping toward him."

"Why were you stepping toward him?"

Shea hesitated, glanced at Kerrigan as if the board president would give him the answer, then looked at Vernor and said, "I was reaching out to take back the log sheet I'd shown him."

Another lie.

"Which log sheet?"

"The one he mistakenly thought Captain Cogswell had torn up."

"The one with your initials on it?"

Shea didn't let himself be caught. "The one the lieutenant *said* my initials were on."

After he finished questioning Shea, Vernor told the court he found it hard to believe that a man who weighed about two hundred pounds, while stepping toward another, who weighed about one-seventy, could be knocked several feet through the air with a single forearm blow, especially when the accused, moments earlier, hadn't been able to move his accuser. "A blow such as Colonel Shea and Major Perkins describe would surely have left a bruise or cut or done some damage. Yet the colonel declares no injury and, according to my records, sought no medical attention."

When Vernor finished, Frankovich rose, turned to Shea and asked him if I'd ever made threatening gestures toward him prior to the incident in question.

"No," said the colonel.

"Did the accused ever behave in a way you would call unusual?"

Vernor requested that the question be withdrawn on the grounds that it led the witness and was too general.

Kerrigan smiled as if he were going to agree but said, "Captain, this is a court of inquiry, not a court-martial. We are seeking information and can be a little freer with our questions and answers." He turned to Shea. "Please respond."

"Yes," said the colonel. "I'd say so. From the time he arrived at Greenham he seemed moody and uncommunicative. Suspicious, too. He believed Captain South and I had arranged to have planes brought down without legitimate hits. Later, I was told, he secretly tried to stir up trouble over the wearing of swagger sticks. In neither case, I want to emphasize, did he make his feelings known to me at the time. He did do a good job with the convoy overall, and for a while afterward seemed to act normally—until he imagined I was involved in some plot to 'get' Captain Ball. Emotionally he was up and down, from the time he arrived in the battalion up to and including the moment he struck me."

Maybe what he said shouldn't by then have surprised me, but it did, as did the calm, controlled and, worst of all, persuasive way he'd made his delivery. I leaned over to Vernor. "Why did he mention the conversation at the range and the Ball situation, since both might make him look suspicious in the board's eyes?"

"Because he figures you might bring them up as part of your defense, and it's useful now for him to appear to be completely open. They'll hear his version first and measure everything you say against it. That's why I tried to stop that . . . bowling ball over there from going on." He paused, glaring at Frankovich. "Witnesses," he went on. "He has them. You don't."

I was sworn in and, in answer to Frankovich, described the pushing incident exactly as I'd experienced it.

"Do you realize what a contrast you've offered to the versions given by your accuser and his witness?"

"Sir," I responded, "I would tell you the same thing if there were many witnesses saying something else. I've described accurately what happened, to the best of my ability."

"Are you saying your accuser and his witness are lying?"

"I'm saying I'm giving—just gave—an accurate account of what happened."

Frankovich twisted his head toward Shea and smiled, or seemed to.

The smile ignited me. "Think what you want," I snapped. "Colonel Shea did come at me, and he did so out of frustration." I felt Vernor's nudging elbow. I didn't stop but slowed the pace of my speech. "Sorry, but what happened in my room occurred in a context, sir. I hadn't done what the colonel wanted. He didn't just want me not to report his signature. What he really wanted was—I know this is going to sound strange—to shape the world for me. It maddened him that I wouldn't let him."

"Shape the world?"

Vernor tugged at my shirt sleeve.

I ignored him. "My ideas, opinions and such about it. He'd already begun to—"

"Please!" said Vernor, rising and waving his hands in an erasing motion. He was, I saw, addressing Kerrigan. "Counsel is taking advantage of this tense situation to lead the accused into saying things that don't belong in this inquiry."

"No," Frankovich protested. "I'm trying to establish the atmosphere surrounding the incident. He himself just said that the incident has a context."

Kerrigan intervened. "I don't like putting restrictions on anyone's statements. I think the question of 'atmosphere' might be pertinent. Continue, Colonel Frankovich."

"Thank you," said Frankovich, stepping toward me. "What do you mean, he tried to shape your world?"

"It's an expression. What I mean is, he pretty much wanted me to see everything as he did. The battalion. Foreign policy. Everything."

"Be specific."

"Specific. He . . . he wanted me to accept that Captain Ball . . . not that Captain Ball was insane, which he isn't, I believe and would say the colonel believes, but . . . but that it was necessary, acceptable, that Captain Ball be diagnosed as insane."

"Someone mistakenly diagnosed Captain Ball's condition?"

"I don't know that for sure. I think so. I suspect—"

"What do you *know*, lieutenant? Do you know that Colonel Shea had Captain Ball sent to the mental ward?"

"He's not a doctor. But . . ."

". . . he controlled the doctor? Dr. what-is-it? Michaels? Yes. Michaels. Did he control Dr. Michaels?"

"He didn't *control* Dr. Michaels. He . . . I believe he probably influenced him."

"To have Ball put away."

"Yes."

"It's a serious charge, not only against your commanding officer but against Dr. Michaels. Can you prove it?"

"No, sir. I . . . I can't. But that surely doesn't mean it's not true."

"In here it does," said Frankovich sharply, backing toward his table.

Was the truth, because unwitnessed by another, therefore false? I didn't speak the question. It would have fallen to the floor like a dropped watch. Before I could patch more thoughts together—should I be cautious and back away from all truths, actions, whatever, no one else had witnessed? If so, how far?

And when would the substituted realities, the lies, seem to be truths themselves? —Hollingsworth was questioning me:

"Please describe your feelings just before you pushed the colonel."

"I just . . . wanted more space."

"Why?"

"He was trying to trap me in the corner."

"Did you feel at other times the colonel was trying to trap or keep or confine you?"

"Not physically."

"What do you mean, not physically?"

"Well, from the time I came to the battalion I felt sort of mentally trapped or captured by him . . . as did others, I think. I mean, from the beginning I spent a lot of time wondering what he was thinking."

"For example?"

"Well . . . there was the first inspection. Afterward I was sure he thought I was strange because of a couple of things he said. But a better example was the firing. I *did* hear him and Captain South make some sort of deal, and —"

"Please," Kerrigan said, shaking his head, "we aren't here to judge the actions of Colonel Shea or Captain South. We're not even here to judge yours. We're here to determine whether an alleged event took place and to make a recommendation regarding it. Please continue."

His remarks were a letdown. What happened in my room at the club was bound up with what had happened before. I went on, "It wasn't just one feeling. I was at first sort of stunned by what . . . what I mentioned, but then I was angry, then frightened."

"Frightened?" said Hollingsworth.

"I thought Colonel Shea might have suspected I, well, knew something about the firing I wasn't supposed to. The truth is, I did. I missed the celebration party. It was when I woke up during the night that I began to feel the fear."

"For a few minutes? Hours?"

"No. I'd have to say longer. It lasted until a few weeks later, until I returned to the base following a convoy assignment. Even after that."

"Had there been other feelings in between?"

"Quite a few."

"Such as?"

"Anger, frustration and, when he introduced the swagger sticks, disgust. More. I spoke a lot about my feelings in the deposition. But I also admired him for the way he controlled his battalion."

"And afterward? After the convoy?"

"I was very positive. It was because he, when he took me to his house, clarified a lot of what he was, had been, doing and how he saw things in general." I nodded. "Yes, my attitude changed quite a bit."

"Would you say you found him at any time to be like a father?"

The question was too personal, too intimidating somehow. I didn't answer. The silence around me told me everyone was waiting. I felt "yes" but didn't want to say it because to do so would have been somehow to dishonor my father.

I glanced at Shea.

His shoulders were tucked in and his eyes were locked on his hands, clasped before him.

"Lieutenant Hanlon?" said Hollingsworth finally.

"My father," I told him, "wouldn't have done what he did, what I believe he did, to Captain Ball. I know I can't go into that here, but when I found out about that I started to lose faith in him. I knew the power he had over me, all of us, wasn't after all being used for our good or the Army's good or the country's good. It was being used for his own purposes. That's my opinion."

Shea was shaking his head in a familiar gesture of disapproval.

Frankovich stood. "I object to the characterization of Colonel Shea as—"

"Please, colonel," said Hollingsworth, his hand out in an impatient gesture. He turned and whispered to Kerrigan, who began nodding. Fosby was by now leaning toward the other two. When, after about a minute, they all spread apart, Kerrigan said, "Under the circumstances, counsel, I believe we should let the accused complete his statement."

"Be careful," Vernor whispered.

"Go on," said Hollingsworth.

"I guess I don't have much more to say except that I'm sure it bothered and maybe even hurt the colonel that I wouldn't back off on the report. We'd . . . become close. Maybe it *was* like a father-and-son relationship. Maybe that's why he grabbed me by the lapels before I tried to get out of the room and why he tried to grab me before I pushed him."

The three board members went into another huddle, and after it broke, Kerrigan announced there would be a fifteen-minute recess.

Forty-eight

␣␣␣␣␣␣

I sat on a bench in the spacious hallway watching Vernor pace and tried not to wonder what he was thinking or why the recess had been called. Moving fast at first, he finally slowed and, after about three minutes, came over and sat down.

"They're going to come back with a finding and recommendation," he said.

"Already?" He'd earlier told me to expect the inquiry to last two or three days.

"It's the sudden way they broke off. Do you want to go over the possibilities?"

"We don't need to." He'd reviewed those after the charges had been filed. The court would determine whether or not there was sufficient substance to the charge, then announce one of three recommendations. I looked down the hallway, one way, then the other.

Frankovich stood with one foot on a bench, smoking a cigarette and talking to one of the Air Policemen who'd escorted me to brigade headquarters.

Neither Shea nor Perkins was in the hallway. I chose to think of this as evidence of their shame. I pictured them at a small table in the corner of a basement coffee shop, crouching like rats, letting out hideous screeching noises as their eyes darted guiltily about.

My escapist thoughts were broken when, less than ten minutes after we'd left the hearing room, we were called back.

Kerrigan announced that the court had made a finding. He read from a sheet on the table before him:

"No evidence has been brought forward either by the counsel for the accused or the accused's sole witness, himself, that refutes the charge that the accused did, in some manner, strike the accuser on the date and at the time specified. One of the instructions given to the court has been to determine under guidelines set forth in Article 90, Section One, Uniform Code of Military Justice, whether or not there is sufficient substance to warrant further action in this case. The court has decided that there is.

"The court will conclude by recommending one of two actions: trial by court-martial or dismissal from the service on grounds of mental disability. Before doing so, however, it will permit final statements from trial counsel and counsel for the accused and from the accused himself, if he so desires."

The somber tone in which Kerrigan had read the statement caused me to wonder why I felt no chill in my back, no hollowness in my stomach, no throat gagging with tears. Was my calm, almost numb response the result of the long periods I'd spent with Vernor going over not only the possible recommendations but their implications as well? I don't think so. From the very first, even before Vernor came to my quarters to offer his help, I'd wanted the issue to be resolved and had decided that between discharge and trial, I preferred trial. Nothing he'd said, nothing I'd read, had steered me from my resolution, and that soon became a point of friction between us.

Frankovich, after conferring with Shea briefly, said he would have no final statement.

Vernor asked Kerrigan how much time we would have to prepare.

Kerrigan, tilting his head apologetically, replied, "We'd hoped to hear the statements now, if possible."

Vernor shook his head. "We hadn't expected closing statements for a couple of days. We'll need . . ." He turned to me. I had no idea. He turned back. ". . . at least a couple of hours," he said.

While Kerrigan conferred with Fosby and Hollingsworth, Vernor turned again and whispered, "They're letting us, if we want to, bring forward reasons why you shouldn't go to trial. Frankovich isn't interested in pushing for a trial, which is why he turned down the chance to say something."

Finally Kerrigan said, "Captain Vernor, you and the accused can have one hour. You may remain here and prepare the statement. The rest of us will leave."

My eyes found Shea. He'd been exchanging back-of-the-hand whispers with Perkins. They were like a couple of kids planning a prank. Shea had become animated the moment Kerrigan had announced the court's finding. The rest—whether they discharged me or put me on trial—apparently didn't matter to him. I did wonder what they were whispering about. Was he going to make Perkins his executive officer? Surely the major had earned such a favor.

Forty-nine

.r.r.r.r.r

*A*fter the others had left, Vernor got up and walked over to the room's double doors, glancing left and then right through the small window of one. Satisfied, he came back to the table and said, "I want you to change your mind."

"About what?"

"Your preference for a trial. I want to work up an argument for the discharge. I'll emphasize the mental strain you've been under, your age and experience in relation to the responsibilities you've been given lately, the nature of some of those—"

"Wait," I said, stiffening. "We've known all along that it might come to a choice between discharge and court-martial, and you agreed—"

"Keep your voice down," he said, twisting toward the door. "Be just like Shea or Perkins to stand near those doors and eavesdrop."

I had no idea I'd raised my voice. I'd done it because he'd surprised me.

We'd hammered at each other for days over what to do if it came down to the choice now before us. He of course had wanted discharge. "I'm confident I can bargain to keep any reference to mental disability off your records. If I succeed there'll be no more stigma than there would be if you left because you'd developed asthma or arthritis." But before he'd shown up at my room and offered to help me, my resolution had been planted. "I didn't assault him, captain." He pointed out that what a court ended up believing, not what had really happened, made the difference.

"Why are you so definite in your recommendation?" I wanted to know.

He'd moved to the accuser's table, was standing behind it with his hands resting on the back of the chair Perkins had been using, looking at the table's face, not mine. "A trial just isn't worth the risk."

"You knew Shea had the only witness. You knew the senior officer has the advantage. You knew the court's questions would be tough."

He shook his head, clearly disappointed that I wasn't giving in. He looked through one of the high windows behind the table the board had used, seemed to fix on a slender oak stiffening against a breeze.

Earlier he'd admitted that, with the help of a good lawyer from the Judge Advocate General's office, I might come out of a court-martial without even a reprimand. Suddenly he'd changed. Was it because of my accuser's arguments? Had Shea caused him to think I was crazy? I was afraid to ask.

He turned. "You don't stand a chance, Thomas."

"Why?" I said finally.

He shook his head. "I guess I'm pretty good at playing lawyer but pretty lousy as a psychologist. I was prepared for him to have the only witness but didn't anticipate both him *and* the witness lying from here to Christmas. And convincingly. He'll do whatever it takes to punish you—if, that is, you choose to take him to trial. It's clear to me Perkins'll back Shea up. You could end up with a maximum sentence. Too many years out of a man's life."

"What about requesting a lawyer from JAG?"

"You'd *have* to get one for a trial. It's required. Anyway, I couldn't do it all alone. The point is, we mustn't go to trial."

"Whatever lies they throw at us, they can't change what happened in that room. Can they?"

"Thomas." His eyes closed painfully. "Please." He was straining to be patient.

"I'd know when either one was lying. I'd tell the JAG lawyer. He'd trip them up, captain. I'm sure of it. If he questioned them carefully, they'd contradict each other."

"No." He moved around the table like a stalking cat, eyes glistening. "Do you want to punish him the way he wants to punish you? Is that it?"

"No, sir." I stepped back. "I don't care if he's punished or not. I want to be able to show that what happened . . . well, happened."

"That's foolish pride."

"No, sir. It's . . ."

"You're ignorant when it comes to knowing how the world really works. You can't do it." He moved closer. "I've seen what I've seen. I know that even a lawyer from JAG isn't going to break down what those two deal out as testimony. I'm sure they're huddled somewhere, agreeing on what's to be said and what's not, correcting what needs to be corrected. To contend with them any longer amounts to . . . to martyrdom." He stopped inches away. "I hope you don't want to be a martyr, Thomas."

I didn't want martyrdom. Dying for any cause seemed to me as stupid as war itself. I wasn't Hamlet, carrying a kingdom on my shoulders. I was only Thomas V-for-Valentine Hanlon, Second Lieutenant, U.S. Army Reserves, serial number 04027773, seeking . . . what?

"Time is getting away from us."

Where was my report to Brigade now? Perkins! I guessed he'd been appointed to complete it. He'd make the change Shea wanted. I knew where Perkins was. Where was Ball? He was on the floor at Wimpole Park. Shea was—would again be in minutes—at the accuser's table.

"Please answer my question."

"Sir?"

"What are we going to do?"

"I want to request a court-martial."

He turned. His open hand came down on our table like a thunderbolt and bounced up, nearly to his nose. He moved past me, bumping me so that I half-turned. He now showed no concern for who might be at the doors. He stooped over and opened his briefcase, searching until he found a couple of freshly sharpened pencils. He rose. "Here," he said coldly, handing me one. "Sit down. We're going to work on a statement."

I stood there holding the pencil until he sat.

Only then did it seem all right for me to sit, too.

Fifty

Vernor's hand moved rapidly over his yellow tablet. Now and then his pencil would rise and go still and he'd groan or look to the wall or ask me a question. But soon again he'd be writing. I began to read over his shoulder. Some thoughts were those I myself would have put down. Others were new to me, particularly those concerning my rights. The trembling doubts I'd been having about my position (*Maybe you're crazy*) began to dissolve. He was more than a pretty good lawyer, I decided as our hour neared an end. A lawyer who could write so effectively in support of a position he himself didn't believe in seemed to me, at that desperate time, another Clarence Darrow.

Barely three minutes after he, with only a little help from me, finished making corrections, the others returned.

My eyes found Shea as soon as he entered and followed him to his table.

When he sat down he raised his own eyes, giving me a pestered look. He was a man caught in traffic and I was the stoplight. *Let's get this crap over with*, the eyes seemed to be saying.

I forced myself to keep watching, trying to show none of the new fear I was feeling, did so until Kerrigan said Vernor could read his statement.

The captain stood, turning slightly so that he faced neither the accuser's table nor the board's, but the space in between. He raised the tablet nearly eye level and read:

"Lieutenant Hanlon requests that this body recommend he be court-martialed on the charge before him and not recommend that he be given an administrative or medical discharge. Not to grant him this opportunity would not only deny him constitutional rights he did not sacrifice when he joined the Army but would also leave him officially in a limbo between guilt and no guilt, possibly for the rest of his life."

Shea watched with a deepening frown, and when Vernor mentioned constitutional rights, his mouth silently pronounced the word, *Bullshit*. He looked at me and shook his head. It was a warning gesture.

Vernor continued, "He acted under a legal order from brigade which required that he include all pertinent data on Operation Night Watch, and that is exactly, to the letter, what he did in his report. His commanding officer tried to get him to change his report, first by persuasion, then by the offer of reward, finally by physical coercion. Hanlon refused and then resisted. He was arrested, charged with assaulting a superior officer, and now, apparently, faces the stigmatization—real and psychological—of a discharge on the grounds of mental disability.

"A full-fledged court-martial would or might permit him to show that his accuser was, has been and is being allowed to function not under the Constitution or any federal or military law or regulation but on the quicksand of his own law, exercised under the protective concealment and in the name of military regulations. Should a colonel or a general or, for that matter, even the President be allowed such protection that he can dispatch those who don't please him with the ease of a signature or whispered innuendo? Not to allow him the give-and-take of cross-examination would amount to an abridgment of his right to freedom of speech under Amendment One of the U.S. Constitution and his right to due process under Amendment Five. Those are two pillars of American law on which other laws, including military regulations, depend.

"These, then, are the reasons he should be given the chance to defend what he has done."

When Vernor finished I was tense and breathless, as though I had made the speech myself. I looked across at Shea. His eyes rose past me to something on the wall behind me, perhaps a face in one of the photographs of former brigade commanders that hung there. *Well*, the eyes seemed to ask, *has the stoplight finally changed?*

Kerrigan and his court were in another huddle.

I leaned over to Vernor and said, "Nicely done."

Kerrigan made notes on one of the two handwritten sheets he'd placed on the table after the hour-long break. Fosby and Hollingsworth watched him finish the first sheet and go to the second. When he completed his corrections, he handed the sheets to Hollingsworth, who read, nodding. He then offered them to Fosby, who shook his head. Kerrigan took them, cleared his throat and read.

"After hearing Captain Vernor's statement, I've altered a few of the remarks I intend to make before announcing our recommendation.

"Before I read what we've prepared, captain, I think I should tell you—admit, I suppose—that your statement caught us by surprise. We expected the lieutenant to request discharge, not court-martial." He gave me a quick and, I thought, sympathetic smile. I turned toward Vernor. The captain was gazing at Hollingsworth and showing no more expression than he might have had the colonel just announced the time.

"Finally," Kerrigan went on, "I guess I should remind all of you"—he looked at us, then at those at the accuser's table— "that this is a court of inquiry, less formal than a court-martial. We welcome questions and comments." He paused, waiting, as if now there might be some. There weren't.

I felt my stomach tightening. I knew my feelings—fear and pessimism mainly—were now advertising themselves on my face, and I didn't dare look across at Shea. Instead, crossing my arms over my chest, I fixed my gaze on the edge of the table.

Glancing frequently at his notes, Kerrigan began: "It's clear that, from the time he arrived in the 46th Antiaircraft Artillery Battalion, Lieutenant Hanlon has been deeply affected by the words and actions of his commanding officer, Colonel—formerly Major—Francis P. Shea. To borrow from his own words, spoken here and in pre-inquiry deposition, he was at one time 'troubled,' at another 'frightened,' at another 'admiring,' at another 'disgusted,' and so on. Sometimes he experienced a simultaneous complex of reactions. He has said, 'After we returned from the range I was full of feelings that puzzled and confused me.' We know that later he felt the commanding officer might be lurking somewhere in the officers' club watching him. The sense that he was being watched by his commander, he says, came over him more than once. He spent a good deal of time hiding from the major. Why? Because, he says, he believed Shea had been involved in a conspiracy with Captain South to destroy target planes in an unauthorized way. Was he being realistic? He has no witnesses to support his suspicions. Isn't the reality that a number of experienced gunnery men, including the brigade commander, witnessed the firing and detected no ill-doing? The lieutenant's main evidence seems to be the high scores his battalion produced. Yet Colonel Potts and the 4th Battalion recently scored only fifteen percent lower than the 46th. Could it be that the brigade's officers and gun crews, with increasing experience, are simply becoming more efficient?"

"You see where they're going?" whispered Vernor, leaning toward me.

My heart had begun to miss beats. I took a couple of deep breaths, waited until the heart seemed to beat normally again, finally whispered back, "They're trying to make me look crazy."

He didn't acknowledge that, said only, "They're building the argument for the discharge on the grounds of mental impairment."

To me it amounted to the same thing.

Kerrigan had paused, was looking at Vernor. "Is it something you wish to share, captain?"

"No, sir. I'm sorry. I just wanted to interpret—"

"Perfectly all right," said the colonel. "But ask me to delay my remarks next time, so that you hear all that I'm saying." He'd lowered his sheet and now raised it again.

Whether consultation was "all right" or not, his comments seemed to me a way of saying he *didn't* want to be interrupted. I picked up the pencil Vernor had provided, in case I wanted to write down something.

"And what of other matters?" said Kerrigan. "Lieutenant Hanlon alone, the newest officer in the battalion, decided that the introduction of swagger sticks was some kind of sinister game his commander had introduced to mock his officers. The wearing of them disgusted him, so much so that later, at a time of emotional crisis, he chopped his up with his bayonet. Yet, oddly, for a period, he had managed not simply to adjust to the swagger sticks but to vigorously participate in a contest regarding their proper use. In short, with the swagger sticks alone, he experienced not only a variety of feelings but a variety of extremely different feelings.

"In the brief period during which the accused led a convoy to several Strategic Air Command bases in an exchange of guns, he seems not only to have mastered his feelings but to have shown initiative in leading his group back from a mistaken route, guiding them past a group of protesters and repairing, apparently single-handedly, a faulty gun delivered to the base at Upper Heyford. Appearances, however, sometimes deceive. The lieutenant confesses to have been asleep in his jeep just prior to his convoy getting lost. Would the mistaken route have been taken had he been more alert? And, if he was able to get his convoy past the protesters eventually, could he have done so without stopping to engage them, which clearly invited an incident? As for delivery of the faulty gun, records supplied by the accuser show that it was known by Hanlon to be malfunctioning for several days prior to delivery. Why, then, did he not repair the weapon until he arrived at Upper Heyford and was told by Colonel Potts that it would not be accepted in the condition delivered? These questions may on the surface seem only questions of judgment, but they aren't. They reflect fluctuating mental states. The accused was one moment awake, the next asleep; one minute intimidated by protesters, the next willing to drive through them; one day unable to fix a weapon, the next a master repairman. Again there is evidence of rapid shifts."

I'd written on my pad, "They're distorting everything, even what I did well." I slid it across to Vernor.

Beneath my remark he wrote, "Hard as it might be to believe, they probably think they're doing you a favor. More 'impaired' you are, better chance of not having to go to court-martial."

I snatched the pad and wrote, "I *want* court-martial!"

He leaned across and wrote on the side of the tablet, "What *they* think is best for you."

And you, too, I thought.

"On his return to the base the accused, in a single evening—covering, according to pre-inquiry testimony from both the accused and accuser, only a few hours—underwent what amounted to a conversion, literally overnight becoming a believer in the philosophy and actions of a man he'd feared and possibly despised. 'When I understood the premises from which the colonel operated,' he stated, 'what he had been doing—even the swagger sticks—made sense.' Seeing that the commander brought order where there had been none, to paraphrase the accused, he accepted the position as assistant to his CO. Colonel Shea has confessed to having been impressed with his young officer's accomplishments with the convoy, his intelligence and potential for leadership. In fact, during Operation Night Watch, Colonel Shea replaced Captain Ball with Lieutenant Hanlon at the front gate.

"But Lieutenant Hanlon began to undergo yet another change following a visit to the motor-pool office of Captain Cogswell following the mock attack. He began to believe that Colonel Shea somehow arranged for Captain Ball to take a five-ton troop carrier to Newbury to bring several troops back to the base. Captain Cogswell and Colonel Shea have denied this. In any case, the lieutenant, once again in conflict with his commanding officer, eventually set out on an odyssey that was intended to prove not only that Ball had been sacrificed during the mock battle but that Colonel Shea influenced the base surgeon to have him committed to the mental ward at U.S. Air Force Hospital, Wimpole Park. Based on remarks reportedly made by the captain that Hanlon believes were coded, he confirmed, for himself at least, his new theory that the colonel had, in effect, had the captain committed. From the affidavit of Greenham Common Air Force base surgeon, Dr. Walter Michaels, I now read: 'Within forty-eight hours after Captain Ball was admitted with a bleeding ulcer, I noted erratic speech and made a decision to send him for a psychiatric examination to Wimpole Park.' Here also is Michaels's answer to the question 'How much were you influenced by Colonel Shea in that decision?' The answer: 'Colonel Shea had informed me of earlier erratic acts and remarks by the captain. This was welcome information and caused me to observe Ball more closely than I might have otherwise.' Yet Lieutenant Hanlon apparently continues to believe that Ball is in a mental ward because Colonel Shea decided to have him sent there."

Kerrigan had already silenced me, and now stilled me. I made no effort to pick up the pencil and scribble my desperate protests on the pad. Worse, I was beginning to believe what he was saying. The person they were talking about *did* seem erratic.

"We must conclude that the lieutenant's emotions have been consistently unstable, particularly with respect to his dealings with his commanding officer, Colonel Shea. Major Hollingsworth believes that Hanlon has a 'fixation' about Shea and sees the remarkable display of a variety of reactions as a possible working out of a deeply imbedded father-conflict. As the major points out, 'The accused would be likely under other commanders to create other father figures, along with conflicts similar to those developed under Colonel Shea.' Whatever its causes, a serious problem exists, and, as a result, we are recommending discharge for reasons of mental disability. Recommendations made by boards of inquiries such as this, it should be noted, are normally upheld."

Fifty-one

ᵛᵛᵛᵛᵛᵛ

I turned, saw Vernor sitting slumped in his chair, head tilted to one side, hands limp on the table. Seeking hope, I found defeat. My throat tightened, and I knew that if I swallowed tears would come. I raised my hand to shield my eyes from Shea and Perkins.

The captain's voice soon sounded from someplace in front of me. "Is it allowable for me to speak again?" I looked over the top of my hand, saw that he'd gotten up, moved silently around our table and was standing in front of Kerrigan, his left hand tenuously extended. "I'd like to say something in response to your remarks."

"This isn't, as I said, a court-martial," Kerrigan replied uncertainly. He glanced at Hollingsworth, then turned to Fosby. Neither seemed to give him any help. Looking back at Vernor, he said, "I suppose that if there's something you've left out . . ."

His hand descended. "As you were speaking I became aware of something I should have recognized sooner."

"What do you mean by that?"

"Since Major Shea arrived in the battalion, we've all had contradictory feelings about him. Admiration. Anger. Fear. Frustration. And sometimes we've acted on them. If the accused's behavior is unstable, then every officer who's served under Shea in the 46th is a candidate for an administrative discharge."

I heard a groan, Shea's I was sure.

"Be specific, Captain."

"Yes, sir. I'll use myself as an example. After I learned which of my guns the CO had chosen to transfer, I became so angry I gave my battery clerk a shove as I crossed the orderly room, pushed him right onto the first sergeant's desk. And my clerk hadn't, beforehand, pressed me against a window ledge or trapped me in a corner. Other officers have reacted in similar ways."

Shea's eyes were fixed on Vernor with an angry threatening stare.

Frankovich's voice sounded harshly. "The behavior of counsel for the accused and that of officers other than Hanlon aren't under review here."

"The court needs to see the accused in the context of the rest of us," Vernor said quickly. "In my opinion it hasn't."

Kerrigan nodded but said, "State specifically the point you're trying to make."

"I'm trying to say that unstable behavior hasn't been unusual in the 46th under the command of Shea."

"Who is *not* on trial here!" Frankovich snapped.

"As long as counsel is seeking to establish atmosphere," Kerrigan said, "which in this case I believe he is, such remarks are proper. He may continue."

"Thank you, sir." Vernor turned and pointed toward me. "Consider. Into a battalion full of uneasy officers comes a new, maybe brighter than average, second lieutenant. Right away he's given a lot of mixed signals. The guns don't work, but they're the reason we're the best outfit in the U.K. You must follow regulations in this battalion but how about having a drink on duty. You're smart and show a lot of promise but there's something untrustworthy about you. Was the inconsistency, the instability, in Hanlon? Or . . ."

"I object!" Frankovich was rising as Shea's insulted eyes found him. "There's no need for this sort of innuendo. Everyone knows who counsel is referring to. Besides, the court's recommendation has already been made."

Fosby seemed to be nodding.

But Kerrigan said, "This has got to be a thorough inquiry. As long as counsel does not characterize . . ."

"He *is* characterizing," Frankovich insisted.

"Sir," Vernor interrupted, "I can finish without using or even paraphrasing anyone's words or referring to specific actions. My purpose is to persuade you to change the recommendation and to permit the accused to have an opportunity to call witnesses and cross-examine them and exercise all the rights a court-martial would permit. It's not to attack someone else."

"Go on."

"Within hours after arriving the lieutenant heard something that struck him as unusual. More than unusual. He then saw, thought he saw, something fraudulent, possibly criminal. Whether he was right or wrong, he believed he'd witnessed these things."

"So you're not asserting that he did hear or see them?" said Kerrigan, leaning forward.

"I can't *say* whether he heard or saw them. But I do know that Hanlon isn't the only one who thought he saw something unusual at the firing range. There were other doubters. Gun sergeants. Officers. I'm one of them. We were closer to what was happening than the brigade commander or anyone else. But we'd all been around long enough to know about the dangers of questioning what happened. And none of us had heard what the lieutenant heard or thinks he heard. It stayed with him. He believed it was his duty to report it. He tried to tell his battery commander. He was cut off. He tried to tell me. I cut him off. He eventually, at the time of the convoy assignment, risked bringing it to the attention of the CO himself. Again he was cut off. Only with a trial can we know what really happened."

Shea knew, yet now wore a look of cool surprise that should have won him an acting award.

"The firing has nothing to do with what recently went on in the accused's quarters," Frankovich interjected.

"It has much to do with it," Vernor snapped back. "This frightened and discouraged him. He soon learned that no one, in effect, cared about what he'd heard and seen. And, soon he also learned that the atmosphere in the battalion was in general a fearful one where officers were mocked and insulted and even punished if they didn't pass a make-or-break sort of personal test. More than that, he was led to believe that, because he was reacting to life in the battalion differently than most, his test would be one of the toughest. As it turns out, it was."

Frankovich had come to his feet again. "However he tries to disguise it, counsel is attempting to turn the accuser into the accused. I see no reason you should allow him to go on, sir." He began to sit down, but Shea whispered something to him and he added, "Testing the strength of a new officer in one area or another is a common practice."

"Testing in an authorized way," Vernor replied.

"Don't refer to these tests again," said Kerrigan firmly.

Vernor nodded. " I was going to mention the effect they had on the accused, but I'll skip that and state why I'm making this request."

I'd hoped Kerrigan would allow the captain to go over the tests, particularly Williston's. His story *had* influenced me. Even in my best moments with the colonel, such as at his cottage, I'd remembered it and felt threatened.

"In putting Lieutenant Hanlon on trial, you wouldn't exactly be putting Colonel Shea on trial but might test the system that seems to have protected him and his methods."

"It amounts to the same thing!" said Frankovich.

"State your request," said Kerrigan, now frowning at Vernor.

"I ask that you reconsider your finding and recommend a court-martial."

Kerrigan looked across at me, than addressed Vernor. "Does the accused know the risks of a court-martial, the full range of possible penalties?"

"He does, sir."

Shea's pencil was tense in the air, being pressed forward by his lower or left thumb, against the bottom of his right hand. If he'd pulled back his right hand, the pencil would have boomeranged against, perhaps into, Vernor's back.

With new hope rising, I watched Kerrigan and the others go into a huddle.

" I could have said more," Vernor told me after returning to his seat. "Didn't have time to put it all together . . ."

"You did fine," I said.

The huddle broke apart quickly, too quickly I sensed.

"We want to compliment Captain Vernor on his eloquent appeal," Kerrigan said, "but we believe that the ideas, facts and circumstances he's presented do not warrant a change in our recommendation. It therefore stands."

I felt an icy sting in my groin.

Shea's pencil glided back to the table like a B-47 doing a perfect three-pointer. He whispered something to Perkins, smiled, than sat there patiently, looking at the landed pencil, until Kerrigan concluded the proceedings.

It was Shea who led all of us out of the hearing room.

Fifty-two

.r.r.r.r.r.r

A lawyer assigned from the Judge Advocate General's office in London, Captain Doug Phillips, prepared with Vernor an appeal of the court of inquiry's recommendation on the grounds that the brief exchange between Hollingsworth and me didn't provide sufficient evidence of mental instability. Phillips requested that the review board act expeditiously, pointing out that, having been convicted of no crime or misdemeanor, my confinement in a guarded room at Greenham Common's base hospital amounted to "cruelty and mistreatment" under Article 93.

Within a week after Phillips made the appeal, the base commander ordered that I be returned to my quarters. I was to remain unguarded in the three-acre area around the officers' club until such time as the review board made its final decision.

The day the base commander issued his order, Phillips, a slow-talking Minnesotan, came to my room and told Vernor and me that he'd do his best to hurry the appeal process, but added, "It's like soup, the best kind anyway. You can watch it and stir it, but it's going to taste good only when it's ready to."

A couple of hours after Phillips left, Vernor came to my room with a fifth of bourbon and said, "I don't know if 'celebrate' is the right word when someone's been confined to a three-acre area, but I'm going to use it anyway." I washed out a couple of glasses while he called the kitchen and ordered ice and soda (for me) and Coca-Cola (for him). Returning from the bathroom I noticed that the whiskey bottle had a silver label with large black letters that spelled out the name Shale. He saw me looking and said, "Only whiskey in Kentucky made by Negroes. The distillery is in some run-down town near Louisville." He poured us each a generous shot and said, "PX keeps it by popular demand. Us colored folk."

The whiskey had a sting but a distinctive taste as well.

He sat down on the bed opposite. We were using the little table between us as a bar. He reached out, picked up the bottle and handed it to me. "Read what it says under the name."

All the print underneath was small. Just under the name was a slogan, in quotes: "Whiskey is Whisky."

I laughed, said, "I guess they can't be sued for false advertising."

"The Tuskegee Air Force kept a good supply of it in World War Two." He was referring to a segregated fighter plane unit that had compiled an outstanding record fighting the Luftwaffe in Italy. "That bunch avoided the terrible flu that swept through other units, didn't have a single cavity all through the war and had more 'kills' per plane than most other fighter squadrons."

"The whiskey?"

"What else could it have been?"

Neither of us talked about my appeal or anything related to it. For that I was grateful. Since the court of inquiry meeting, I'd awakened two or three times nearly every night, sooner or later each night groping to understand why I couldn't turn away from my decision. Reason and common sense kept urging me to. I sometimes tracked back through a dream I'd remember on waking, seeking in it some sort of illumination. I found none. The night before Vernor arrived with the bottle, I'd awakened from a nightmare in which I stood on an out-jutting part of a high cliff that hung over an enormous white capped sea. But this time, instead of tracing the nightmare back, I stayed, watched myself in my mind's eye. The apprehension I'd felt on awakening faded away. Finally I watched myself jump. I floated toward the sea. I went in not like a rock but like a parachutist. I didn't sink. "See?" I said joyfully. I didn't know what I was supposed to be seeing. Yet that night I was able to get back to sleep, and for the first time in days I slept peacefully until morning.

Vernor was adding Coke to his drink. What a contrast this was to drinking with Shea! Vernor was delivering no messages, and I felt a lessening, not an increase, of tension.

Day by day I'd become increasingly curious about the captain. He wore a gold band on his left ring finger but hadn't once referred to his wife. I asked about her.

"You're gonna make me homesick, Thomas."

"She's not here?"

"Mobile. Teaching school."

"We can talk about something else."

"No. No, no." He smiled. "I like to talk about her. Tell you how I met her. I was on my way home on leave after boot camp right after the war, and saw this pretty young woman from my window in one of the two Negro cars on the train. She was with two young girls, dressed identical. This white railway man was telling her two of the three tickets she had were torn and she'd have to buy two new ones. She was giving him fire. 'One of my sisters pulled them out of her book. They tore by accident. They're all there. You let us on!' He smiled at some of the white people who'd gathered around and become his attentive audience. He was clearly playing to them. I opened the train window to see if I could give her help when she suddenly motioned the train man to come closer. He looked puzzled, but he came closer and listened, his eyes on me. As she spoke softly to him, his eyes started to bulge out. When he stepped back, he looked at the tickets for a few seconds, then handed them to her. 'All right,' he said. 'You get on the train right now.' "

"What did she tell the man?"

"That's about the third thing I asked her after I introduced myself on the train. She said, 'I don't want to think about that marshmallow-head.' And she didn't tell me until after we'd been married three or four months. 'It's a long story,' she said then."

"A brief exchange of words was a long story?"

He put his glass on the table, loosened his tie and opened his collar. "Fact is, there was a tale going around Alabama in those days about a crazy young Negro roaming the countryside killing white men, and his name was supposed to be Whipsnake the Ferocious. Lord knows how many Negroes were lynched on the suspicion that they were Whipsnake the Ferocious. What Doris, my wife, had done was tell the railway man that Whipsnake was her brother. Made it up, of course. Said Whipsnake would do a stuffing-kill on anyone who messed with her or her sisters. She then put out her hand and said, 'I'm going to count to ten.' She told me the railway man had the tickets back before she got to four."

"What's a stuffing-kill?"

"How long ago you eat supper?"

"An hour."

"That's long enough. A stuffing-kill—now, this is according to the white man's tale, the one they'll probably keep telling until God comes or they've killed every possible Whipsnake the Ferocious in the state—is taking off a man's privates and putting them where the words come out."

"Ugh!"

"Anyway, if I hadn't already been married to her before she told me her story, I'd have proposed on the spot. She has what a tactics and strategy manual I read in OCS called 'on-the-spot ingenuity.' "

We drank to Doris and then to the early demise of Whipsnake.

"I call her Doris the Saxophone because of her magical voice. She was with me until the end of last year, when her mother died. Then went back to live with and take care of her two sisters. The father died years ago. She's gonna stay with them until they're out of high school. Two more years." He closed his eyes and made fists.

Music was coming from another room. Glenn Miller. The song was "In the Mood." The captain's head floated from side to side. He was clearly thinking of Doris.

When he looked up I raised my glass. "Thanks."

He nodded, knowing, I think, that I didn't mean only the whiskey or the story. He started talking about staying in the Army. The higher the rank, the more difficult it was for a Negro. "They want us up there," he said, "but not too many."

"How bad is your defense of me going to hurt?"

He shook his head. I guessed he didn't want to answer, or else didn't know.

A lot, I suspected.

He laughed then, said, "If some white officer were representing me, they'd say, 'Look at that crazy representin' that nigger.' Now they're probably saying, 'Look at that nigger representin' that crazy.' Hard to win, isn't it, Thomas?"

We clicked glasses.

He departed, leaving the bottle.

When I wasn't conversing with Vernor, I was reading, taking walks around the club, doing background work on my case or, mostly, trying to write a letter to my mother. Finding words that would communicate what had happened was going to be as difficult with her as it had been with the court of inquiry. Desperate after several failed attempts, I one afternoon tried to put it all on the side of a picture postcard:

Dear Mother,
    I shoved my commanding officer and now they're trying to drum me out as a mental case. More later.

                                        Love,
                                        Tom

She'd either think my message was a joke or believe it and drop dead. So I first thought. Then I realized it would be neither.

She'd call long-distance and assail me with questions she herself was likely to end up answering. I tore up the postcard.

Late one night I saw Gilley from the bathroom window over the main entrance, staggering under the floodlight that pointed down from the tree at the center of the parking area, zigzagging toward the club entrance, possibly coming from a Newbury pub where the spouts had been turned off. If he made it to the bar before it closed, he might be lucky and find he was the highest-ranking officer there—the only one since he was a warrant officer—which meant he could order it to remain open after closing time. He might get even luckier and run into a captain or a major who not only wanted to keep drinking but to keep talking, too—for Gilley a taste of heaven. Neither he nor any battalion officer, except of course Vernor, communicated with me, though nothing prevented them from doing so.

Phillips's briefs, petitions, and letters, when they began to arrive, were like razor slashes in comparison to his wordy phone conversations: "Accused should no longer have to suffer confinement of any sort"; "The Uniform Code requires that there be no unnecessary delays"; "Accused requests at least some preliminary indication as to options the board of review is considering so that he can make contingency plans." He'd had success in his short time as an Army lawyer, as the case results he'd shown Vernor and me seemed to prove. Yet his correspondence fired no hopes. In one note he said, "In a system where they can have a man shot for falling asleep on guard duty, a defendant who, wide awake, shoves his CO, no matter what the reason, can't expect a lot of generosity." The news wasn't pleasing, of course, but it began to prepare me for what finally did happen.

A puffy, oversized business envelope arrived by courier from the JAG office early one afternoon. After signing for it, I placed it softly on the bed beside mine and stepped back as though it contained an explosive. Its arrival brought a need to urinate. After I returned from the bathroom, I only stared at it again. By now a court-martial had come to seem the only tunnel, not only to some sort of justification but also, in some mysterious way, to myself. I couldn't get myself to pick up the envelope. "Damn."

I sat down, started to put on my combat boots, intending to take a walk around the grounds, when Vernor came into the room. He stopped a couple of feet inside the doorway, looked at the envelope, then at me. "Just got a copy at the battery," he said. He then walked over, picked up my envelope and felt the flap on the back. "Didn't read it, huh?"

I shook my head.

"You want me to tell you, or do you want to read?"

I'd stopped lacing the boots. "With you here," I said, "I'm brave enough to read it. Just barely."

He opened the envelope and handed me the thick document inside.

I read those sections of a long official-looking statement that were bordered in red pencil—Phillips's, I supposed:

> . . . and we find that, at the time and place accused struck his accuser he was not, under guidelines set forth in Paragraph 120 b., Uniform Code, "so far free from mental defect, disease or derangement as to be able concerning specific acts charged to distinguish right from wrong."
>
> . . . further, under guidelines set forth in Paragraph 122 c., to wit: "Although the testimony of an expert on mental disorders . . . may be given greater weight than that of a lay witness, a lay witness who has been acquainted with the accused and has observed his behavior may testify as to his observations and may also give such opinion as to the mental condition of the accused as may be within the bounds of common experience and means of observation of men."
>
> . . . board of review therefore denies appeal and orders convening authority to begin processing accused for discharge on the grounds of mental instability.

I read, and understood its meaning. Where, finally, was the disappointment, the fear, the anger? I didn't know. I found only

that increasingly familiar numbness, the kind I'd later experience when reading again and again statistics like, "Five hundred
and seventy people are killed every Memorial Day," or, "One out
of every three alcoholics over the age of forty dies by committing
suicide."

"Where's the Shale?" he said.

"In my wall locker."

He brought it out, got glasses. We had no mix or ice. He
poured and handed me a glass. "What next, Thomas?"

We'd talked about appealing the appeal, early, before Phillips
had had me transferred from the hospital to my quarters. I'd
assumed that my desire—trial at all costs—wouldn't change.
But it had. There was no desire left. "Nothing," I said.

We clicked glasses for the last time.

Thirty-five days after being taken into custody I was discharged at Fort Ord, California, on the grounds of mental disability.

About the Author

PHILIP F. O'CONNOR is the author of several widely praised works of fiction. His first collection of stories, *Old Morals, Small Continents, Darker Times*, won the Iowa School of Letters Award in Short Fiction. His second, *A Season for Unnatural Causes*, helped inaugurate the University of Illinois's Short Fiction Series. *Defending Civilization* is his second novel, following the highly acclaimed *Stealing Home*, which was a Book-of-the-Month Club selection. Mr. O'Connor is currently a professor of English at Bowling Green University, where he also directs the master of fine arts program in creative writing.